# HEARTLAND

'What a book! *Heartland* delivers on the immense promise of *The Afterglow* and then some. The ambition and, more-to-the-point, the achievement shine forth from every sentence of every page. This is what fiction should be and what readers want it to be; passionately engaged'
David Peace

'A resonant tale of love, politics and football, told by a writer with a wonderful ear for dialect and an unblinking sense of Britain as it is today. Anthony Cartwright's patient, attentive storytelling shines a glowing light on areas of our common experience that the English novel usually consigns to darkness'
Jonathan Coe

'*Heartland* is beautiful, moving and important. Victories and defeats on and off the pitch are tenderly rendered in this acute portrait of identity and community'
Catherine O'Flynn

Praise for
## *The Afterglow*

'Anthony Cartwright's first novel shines brightly for British regional fiction'
Zadie Smith

'This is one of those rare novels which gives us the real thing . . . an excellent read'
Alan Sillitoe

'This is a novel you want to let speak for itself, so passionately concerned is it with voice and taboo, with the pressure of the unsaid on the said, with collective and individual utterance. With great tenderness, Cartwright reveals the tentative dreams and aspirations for a better life that underlie the seeming heartlessness of his quiet heroes'
Michèle Roberts, *Independent on Sunday*

'Combining sharp social observation and compassion with the compelling narrative focus of Jon McGregor's *If Nobody Speaks of Remarkable Things*, this is a most impressive debut'
*Guardian*

# HEARTLAND

## Anthony Cartwright

**Tindal
Street
Press**

First published in May 2009
by Tindal Street Press Ltd
217 The Custard Factory, Gibb Street,
Birmingham, B9 4AA
www.tindalstreet.co.uk

Epigraph from 'The Burning Graves at Netherton' by Roy Fisher
in *The Long and the Short of It: Poems 1955–2005* (Bloodaxe)

A CIP catalogue reference for this book is available
from the British Library

ISBN: 978 0 955647 65 9

Typeset by Country Setting, Kingsdown, Kent
Printed and bound in Great Britain by Clays Ltd, St Ives PLC

*For Isabel*

Patchy collapses, unsafe ground.
No cataclysm. Rather
a loss of face, a great
untidiness and shame.

Silence. Absence. Fire.

*Roy Fisher,*
The Burning Graves at Netherton

# FIRST HALF

**God save the Queen.** Rob got up from the table and walked behind the bar. He stood next to Stacey, poured a round of drinks and put the money at the side of the till. A few voices started to sing. He looked up across the room, caught his dad's eye at the table. He couldn't put faces to the voices barking out the anthem at the back of the room. Smoke hung blue in front of the big screen and David Beckham's face. Then Rob's Uncle Jim started bloody singing. Glenn joined in. Send her victorious, happy and glorious.

Andre's reading is coming on, though, Stace.

Rob looked away from the singers, back to Stacey, trying to look down her top as she bent to grab a packet of crisps from one of the boxes under the bar, then glancing back at Glenn to check he hadn't caught him looking at his sister.

Yer keep telling me that, she said. A lot of good iss doin him now.

What dyer mean?

It ay gonna put his face back together, is it?

No, but his reading, iss important for him.

Iss too late. Wait till he's thirteen befower yow teach him to read?

Rob was tempted to tell her she could have had a go herself, but bit his tongue and just said mildly, He's comin on though, honest.

Whatever.

Still OK for later? he asked quietly.

She nodded, didn't look at him. He saw she was smiling though, in spite of herself.

Rob checked again that Glenn wasn't watching. This would just make more complications with him, even though he'd gone years without speaking to Stacey. Rob needn't have worried. Glenn and Jim led the singing to a crescendo. It made perfect sense. They could continue the election here and now. Form some kind of coalition this time. Rob thought he could phone one of the journalists who had come looking for the Tipton Taliban. Long-serving Labour councillor drinks with BNP cronies. What would they make of that? The papers seemed to have lost interest in the place since the election. And since the Wood-house kids had nicked one of those new mobile phones with a camera when they mugged some of the reporters in the Wetherspoon's car park.

That night, his uncle had stood leaning into the bar like he was steering it in a gale. He called a couple of the reporters over, winked at Rob.

A bloke from Tipton goes to New York for his holiday, decides to visit Ground Zero, yer know, pay his respects. He's stondin lookin at the ruins an this chap comes up to him, big ten-gallon hat, typical Yank, from Texas, like Bush, yer know.

Hey, Pardner, this bloke says.

How do, says the bloke from Tipton.

Where the hell you all from?

Me? I'm from Tipton, mate.

Tipton? Tipton? What the hell state's that in?

Our bloke has a look around him an says, Abaht the same bloody state as this.

His uncle had doubled over, banged the bar with glee. The journalists looked nonplussed. Then Jim had said, Stick that in yer bloody papers, suddenly straight-faced, staring hard into them.

The anthem ended to the sound of cheers and the bang-ing of tables. Come on England. Rob felt the hairs on his neck go.

Cinderheath Football Club, Dudley, England, 7th June 2002. England versus Argentina, Sapporo, Japan.

David Beckham's face was in close-up again; more clap-ping and banging tables. Come on England. Rob put the drinks for his uncle's end of the table down heavily, beer sloshing on to the paper tablecloth, edged with Union Jacks, left over in the back cupboard from a royal wedding or jubilee. He sat down next to his dad with their drinks, touched his old man's arm.

They had the top table, of course, all organized by his Uncle Jim. First teamers, committee members, invited guests: an aristocracy of sorts.

**Beckham's face filled the screen, filled the room.** Rob had driven past the giant hoarding over the motorway a few weeks ago. He'd driven for miles, worrying about the game against the mosque and the election, worrying about his dad who'd gone out to do some canvassing for Jim. His old man wasn't meant to be walking too far or getting too worked up since his bypass operation. He wasn't meant to be drinking either, for that matter, but that hadn't stopped him. Though Rob could've offered to drive his dad around, he'd had to get away, anywhere, to find some air, a way of getting the throbbing out of his temples.

The sign underneath Beckham's face said, COMETH THE HOUR. If England won the whole thing they'd leave it up for ever. *If* England won the whole thing. Argentina today, then Nigeria, then on through the knockout rounds.

He'd had the same headache for weeks. It came and went, like the sound of the helicopter on the morning of the game against the mosque, or whatever they were calling themselves now.

Lee came in with the food. They hadn't opened the kitchen, but Charlie the burger man had set up in the car park, pumping out exhaust fumes and the smell of fried onions.

Here we am, five Beckham Double-Cheeseburgers, two Owen Dogs, six chips.

There was a chorus of thanks for Lee as they reached for the food. He dropped the change in a pile on the table.

Why's theer seven things when theer's onny six o we?

Jim reached across the table and took a hot dog and a burger, grinned and shrugged his shoulders.

All these nerves, mekkin me hungry.

Charlie cor cook em fast enough, thought I was gonna miss the kick-off, said Lee.

Yow should've asked for a Butt-Burger, he ay shiftin many o them.

He could goo through the team, couldn't he? Seaman-Shake anybody?

Beckham shook hands with Simeone. Simeone had once said he never knew whether to kick Beckham or kiss him. Veron and Beckham hugged each other. All week the television had been playing Beckham's sending-off four years ago and then the free-kick against Greece, the arc of the ball as it swung into the top corner showing that all things were possible, a little stab of hope every time you saw it. It made a change from looking at X-rays of Beckham's left foot. It was all getting too much.

Rob thought about his dad's voice, irritated by the telly and the papers.

Iss too much on one bloke, too much, I tell yer. He cor win it for yer on his own. He ay fit any road, not match fit, there's no way he can be, look at him. Iss too much for one bloke.

Dyer want some tomater sauce, Jim? Glenn asked.

Just a soupçon, our kid. Jim grinned again, like there'd never been a problem, never a bad word between them.

**The first football match Rob ever went to was up at Dudley Town,** at the old ground, the County Ground. Dudley played Wolves in a friendly to celebrate the new flood-lights. He'd walked it with his dad. It was hard to imagine his old man walking that far now. They'd had a hot dog from a van outside, maybe it had been Charlie's, and then climbed the bank.

Rob remembered the brightness of the new lights, the green of the pitch, white lines and glistening patches of mud through the middle and in the penalty areas, the Wolves players warming up in their tracksuits. His uncle walked across the pitch in his suit, next to the mayor, doing some presentation for the council. In fact, Rob remembered, his dad wasn't even meant to take him. Jim had got tickets in the grandstand but then got caught up in some civic business, so his old man had said, Come on then, I'll tek yer after all.

When the clapping started, people looking at them, he didn't realize it was for them, for his dad, at first. Then the hands started stretching out towards them, the shapes of people looming over Rob, blocking out the floodlights, hands held out for his dad to shake, to ruffle Rob's hair.

Tom Catesby, Tommy Catesby, voices shouted. Rob felt his dad's grip on him get tighter, his arm across Rob's chest, his fingers digging into his shoulder, his other arm held out, shaking hands, fending people off. Then a song: Tommy, Tommy Catesby. Over and over. His dad's arm tighter and tighter across his chest, Rob wriggling around, not breathing properly.

Then the crowd opened up and the singing died down. They'd got to the wrong side of a crush barrier and found a bit of space and Rob could breathe again. His dad bent to check he was OK and his coat was done up properly. They were behind the goal, the newly painted posts gleaming. At the other end of the ground, beyond the glow of the lights, you could see the dark bulk of the hill and part of the castle, the same view from the end of their street but close-up here, dark against the reddish, light-bleached clouds.

His dad signed a few programmes and scraps of paper, didn't say much, didn't have to. Rob had known his dad had been a footballer before then, knew he'd played for the Wolves as a young man, knew he'd been injured and now went to work the same as everyone else's dad. It hadn't seemed very important to him until that night.

They left with a few minutes to go, more ruffled hair and slaps on the back, with the Wolves six-up. On the way out they'd bumped into Adnan and Zubair with their old man, coming out of another turnstile. They'd talked about it the next day at school. It was how they'd become friends.

The ground didn't last that much longer, of course. It slid away into the limestone workings not long after the Wolves game: subsidence, a falling away. The new floodlights rusted along with everything else. The Wolves themselves almost disappeared completely, relegation after relegation, bankruptcy. The Cinderheath works in the same state, finished, a brown chain slung between the iron gates. The gantry raining flakes of rust on the streets around it until they pulled it down.

**There were the flashes of thousands of photographs all being taken at the same time,** diamond patterns across the screen. The flashes illuminated the clubhouse: a hundred or so burgers, cigarettes and pints half to mouths. Rob saw Rodney James, a bloke he'd played with here and at Stourbridge, wearing his postman's uniform. Rodney had been at Crewe, won a Jamaica cap as a kid. Rob tried to motion to him to come and sit down, didn't know if Rodney was ignoring him because of who he was sitting with or if he just hadn't seen him.

The flashes came like explosions through the room. The stadium crowd looked like they were sitting miles from the pitch. It was usually a baseball ground; had seen nothing like this, though.

8

They'm lovin it, ay they, the Japanese.

They'm purrin on a good show.

There were St George's flags everywhere, emblazoned, place names, Harlow, Lincoln, Kidderminster.

Slow seconds before the kick-off. Rob thought about his old man, his silence in the crowd's raucousness, his blue eyes in his drinker's face.

**There were nights when Tom was drinking when the change in him came early.** That transformation into somebody else: a younger, better self. Sometimes it didn't come at night at all, but in the middle of the afternoon if he'd gone for a pint in the Lion's tiled bar or he'd had a couple of early cans with Kathleen gone out or even if he'd walked up the road and got the bus up into Dudley. The car – cars, decent ones too – gone years ago now, which was one of the things he might dwell on as he went over how things had turned out.

It never seemed to last, that feeling, no matter how much he wanted it to, and he did want it to, to be a good husband, father, man, whatever that meant these days. The one sure thing was that it didn't last. Sometimes it didn't come at all. Sometimes, depending on what he'd been drinking, how much, how quickly, it could last all night. Not very often, though. Usually it would be for the length of a swallow or a turn of the head. If Kathleen or Rob or the telly said the wrong thing – and you could never predict what the wrong thing might be – it was gone. His own moods were a mystery even to him, like the weather or a run of form.

When it did come, this feeling, Tom really was someone else. The glow of the television or the streetlights on the estate became the lights of stadiums and furnaces, illuminating the sky, and instead of his slippered feet, cut open these days to ease aching toes, ankles, knees, there were lightweight boots, the sort he'd seen Kocsis, Czibor and Puskas wear on the mud and grass at Molineux, or there were work boots crunching the ice along Cinderheath Lane on the way to work. There was the roar of the crowd, the roar of a furnace. Then the long crunch of a knee disintegrating under the Molineux lights, the way his studs caught in the mud, the weight of his body twisting the wrong way. He knew it was bad straight away. Then the long factory-siren wail of a world disintegrating.

It's bad news, Thomas.

Yome finished, son.

Cinderheath works will close with immediate effect.

They've let me go, Dad. I just ay good enough.

All finished.


**Come on England, Rob muttered into his pint.**

Here we am, his dad said quietly.

England banged it down the middle and Heskey went up and won it easily, murdered Walter Samuel, and for a moment it looked like Owen was on to it.

Goo on! Strangled shouts.

It came to nothing but Heskey would win them all afternoon, especially with Ayala out. They'd be shit-scared of Heskey. Rob thought about the Munich game – Heskey battering German defenders out of the way – and everyone knew how scared of Owen Argentina were.

There was a story Rob wanted to tell. It was about lots of things, he thought, but mainly about how they were all a long way from being finished just yet. He'd start it with something like, I was born on 15th September 1973 at Wordseley Hospital, my dad a professional footballer turned foundry worker, my mom a cleaner. He'd start it with a man sat staring at the canal worrying about his job. He'd start it with the idea of just walking away from your life, just leaving it all behind, of somehow starting anew. He'd go back and forth over things, the way your mind works, he thought, piecing things together, ideas of blood and fire, blood and rust. Silence. Absence.

**Rob sat on an old PE bench he'd dragged outside and looked at the canal,** at a half-loaf of bread floating in the water, the pieces of bread spotted with mould and in a row like dominoes.

Iss too late now, he said into the phone.

It ay. Iss never too late, son, Jim replied. He never gave up, Rob would give him that.

I know what I'm doing.

I doh believe yer do.

Iss ower team.

It ay ower team no more, mate. It ay never bin yower team any road. Sunday football, for Christ's sake. Yome better than that, son.

Cinderheath Sunday Football Club were due to play Cinderheath Muslim Community FC in the last game of the North Dudley & Tipton Football League (Division 1) season. The winners would take the league title. This was hardly something that would usually get national media coverage, but with the terrorist arrests and the local elections, the tabloids had got hold of the story – while they were up here looking for the Taliban – and the next thing was that it was a 'match that could spark a Black Country race war'.

When did the rivalry between the two sides begin, Mr Khan? the Radio 4 interviewer had asked Joey Khan, in that tone of voice reserved for exotic stories about life in the provinces.

Ooh, I should say abaht 1095.

There was a pause.

The first Crusade?

He'd meant it as a joke – a sideswipe at his son who'd stopped playing sport and started growing a beard, learning the Qur'an off by heart, travelling all across Dudley to go to that new ramshackle mosque – but nobody was laughing any more.

It is ower team, whether we like it or not. Any road, iss onny a game, Rob muttered into the phone.

Onny a game! We doh care who pays for we shirts. Now yer really do sahnd like one o them.

Look, I cor talk abaht it now, Uncle Jim. I'll pop rahnd later any road, see if yer want anything doing.

All right, son, I know yome onny tryin to do the right thing but –

Somebody nicked me flag off me car. Con yer believe it?

The front door's gooin. I'll atta move. More bad news, I bet yer. An doh talk to me abaht flags, mate. Wait till yer see em dahn here.

Rob shook his head, continued to worry about his job. The school had a new Head Teacher. She'd started after Christmas and it was becoming clear that she had different ideas to the last Head, Mr Cummings, who'd retired. Rob's position wasn't secure. No contract, just sessional rates, and a vague agreement about what he was meant to be doing. It had been something to tide him over, something he'd drifted into during a difficult time, when Karen had left and he'd stopped playing football. Well, football that paid. He'd written all of his clubs down for one of the kids he worked with the other day: Cinderheath Juniors; the Villa as a trainee; Wrexham (in digs for a season in the rain); Kidder Harriers; Hereford; Aberystwyth (in digs for three months in the rain); Moor Green; a pre-season at the Wolves, somehow; Stourbridge; Gornal; Tipton; Marconi; Cinderheath Firsts and now Cinderheath Sunday.

He'd spent twelve seasons making a long, steady slide into nonentity.

He was packing it all in now, though, he promised; the farce against the mosque team was going to be his last game of football.

He lit a cigarette to confirm his retirement. Rob was timetabled to support a Year 9 boy called Kelvin, which he enjoyed, but Kelvin hadn't been at school for the last two weeks since he was found sniffing paint thinner in the Technology stock cupboard and sent home for a couple of days until his mother came up to school. The problem was, there was no contacting his mother, phone numbers dead, no response to any letter. Rob had banged on their flat door a couple of times, but there was no sign of life. The neighbour had said she hadn't seen them for weeks and wasn't missing them either, with the dog barking and the music and the parade of different men. Rob had written an email about it to the Head of Year and Educational Welfare. Nobody seemed to be moving very swiftly. Kelvin had said his nan lived up Kates Hill. Rob thought he could check somehow.

When he'd been a kid at the school, Rob used to scramble over the fence just here, outside the fire escape next to the Sports Hall, and pull himself up the embankment with great big handfuls of grass to get to the pork sandwich shop or the chippie, exactly the same as the kids did now. They all used to do it – they'd have races up there. Adnan was always the quickest, of course, before he started getting on with his work instead of messing about like that, Rob at his heels, a pack of other kids behind them.

As if on cue, there was a scuffle from behind the fire-exit door and three lads came bursting out, blinking in the sunlight.

Shit! they shouted in unison, almost running straight

into Rob. They turned and ran back in, falling over each other, one of them sprawling across the shiny, just-polished corridor floor. The boy who fell was Rob's cousin, Michael.

Shit, did he see we? Michael giggled.

Course I did, Michael, arr, Rob shouted through the swinging door. He'd been weighing up what to say at home because Michael had been out of lessons too much lately but, after all, his uncle had enough on his plate with the election.

One of the boys dawdled in the corridor and turned back to stand in the doorway. It was Mohammed, cockier than the other two, than Michael certainly, who until recently had been happy to stay in his room tip-tapping on computer games. Michael and Mohammed had become mates lately. Mohammed was wearing a camouflage jacket from Bilston Market with 'US Army' written on a panel on the front. All the kids were wearing them. Rob had heard Michael ask his Aunty Pauline for one. She'd said he had a perfectly good Nike jacket she'd bought for him at the Merry Hill and what did he want one off the market for? Mohammed had customized his with a green star and crescent drawn in permanent marker on the sleeve.

All right, Rob?

All right, Mo. What yow doin aht here?

Doh say nuthin, Rob.

I woh if yow goo back to yer lesson.

Let me goo to the shop?

No.

Giss a fag, Rob.

No.

Why?

Yow ay old enough an cigarettes am bad for yer.

I got me own.

Mohammed took a lighter from his pocket and flicked it on and off.

Yer doh need one o these, then.

Footballers shunt smoke.

I ay a footballer.

Yer was a footballer.

Was is different.

Am yer playin against the mosque?

I am.

Mosque's gonna beat yer, man.

Probly.

They got some sick players.

Good.

They'm gonna beat yer, man. You know Tayub?

Arr.

Yeah, you know him? He's a sick player, man.

He's quick. Me an his brother, Adnan, we used to play in the same team, we went all through school together. And his brother, Zubair. He's me mate. He's a good player. Too old now, though.

Rob grinned, thinking about Zubair. I've still got a season left in me, he'd said every summer for the last three or four years.

Adnan the mujahedin, Mohammed said.

What did yer say?

Nuthin. Yow shunt play for them racists, man.

I cor play for the mosque.

Yow should become a Muslim, Rob, play for Man United.

I'll think abaht it. Goo back to yer lesson.

Rob could've told him that he'd played against Man United once. He'd marked Ryan Giggs, not long after he changed his name from Wilson, not long before he got in the first team. Rob had played well, really well, one of those games, like he knew what was going to happen before it did, so he was always there, tackles, headers, interceptions. Just near the end he'd nicked it off Giggs's toes, hit a

pass out to Froggatt's feet. There'd been a round of applause from the few hundred on the sides. Everyone shook
his hand and slapped him on the back at full-time. He
thought he was making it then.

Adnan the mujahedin. He should've asked him again
what he meant. Of course, he knew full well what he
meant, didn't want to hear it, didn't want to think about it.

**A change was going to come.** Glenn knew that much.
He'd known it before the attacks on New York, before the
arrests down the road and the talk of the supermosque
when all the cards really were on the table. He hadn't
known how it was going to come, of course, no one had,
but things were moving quickly now. Now the enemy had
shown itself, he supposed.

Not that he was interested in what was going on in
Afghanistan or Pakistan or Kashmir or in bloody America,
for that matter. No, the change he wanted was here in
Cinderheath, in Dudley, in England. Mind you, that was
where they all wanted change as well. The arrests and the
house-searches had made that clear, even this government
had woken up to it. They wouldn't go all the way, though.
They'd let the Americans have a few of them, stick them
in Camp X-Ray. Over here they'd keep smoothing things
over – build them a nice new mosque, sort their houses
out for them and the families they'd bring over, push them
to the front of the queue in the schools – keep fussing over
them. What was it that Bailey had said at the meeting the
other day? Keep fuelling the decadent and dangerous fires
of multiculturalism. A change was going to come.

What Glenn knew, though, what he'd found, was that
there were people stronger than that, braver than that,
people prepared to take a stand and defend their own, to
defend England, even against itself. He was one of them.
He was a soldier now.

It would come here after New York, he was certain of that. What he wanted to be sure of was that while they sat dreaming of exploding planes and a rain of blood and their paradise of virgins, there were people dreaming other dreams, dreaming of an England where people looked after their own, were safe to walk the streets, were proud to be English.

He nearly went in the army. He'd been certain when he was a kid that he would. His grandad would tell him stories about Germany at the end of the war, about crossing the Rhine. His grandad looked after him then, while his mum and dad were both away. Even after his mum came out and Stacey moved back with her, he stayed with his grandad. When his grandad saw who Stacey was hanging around with he had a couple of good chats with Glenn about what was right and wrong, told him about the trouble in the sixties up in the town and over in Smethwick, about Enoch and the rivers of blood and the marches to support him. To hear people now you'd think the sixties were all peace and love. History was written by the winners.

Even when Anne was pregnant with Jordan he was still dreaming of the idea. He'd got talking to Dave Wood-house when he was back on leave one February night, telling Glenn about how he'd spent the bells on New Year's Eve with a rifle trained on some Fenians staggering up the Falls Road, his finger itching, how it was more of a thrill than banging back a few in the Lion or getting tickets for Caesar's up in Dudley. After all, you could have your fill of beer when you got back on leave.

Glenn would've done it, but you had to think about your family. It was no life to bring children up in, no life to give Anne. They'd got together at school. Married at eighteen, she'd had Jordan the following year. Toni three years after that, Casey three years later. They might still

have another. Another couple, he thought. He was looking after his family. He wasn't going in the army or in jail.
Work was going OK. It was hard, he'd felt it more in his
knees and back this last winter. Scaffolding was work for
young lads, really. Still, the next couple of years, he could
maybe set something up himself. Let some other bastards
do the donkey work. He'd got a head for it. This political
stuff was helping as well, talking to different people,
getting things organized.

He'd spent the last ten minutes putting some washing
out to dry. Anne would be back from her mother's with
the kids in a minute. She'd do the food when she got in. If
he got this washing out, he'd chop a couple of onions to
start things off. Anne hated the way they made her cry. He
looked out over the low fence, down Dudley Road to the
mosque and the falling-down terraced houses huddled between the canal and the main road. They'd have to move
when the girls got bigger but for now, their own house, in
a row where the old dairy used to be, was great. They kept
their house nice. He looked down the road again – picking
out rubbish in the backyards, roofs that needed doing up,
the mosque in the old school building that still had entrance gates that said Junior Boys and Junior Girls – and
thought about what the area should have been like and
what it was coming to. This was the front line. A change
was going to come. He was sure of that.

**Argentina attacked.** Campbell came across to cover.

Thass it, Sol. Rob wasn't sure where his voice ended
and his dad's began.

He leaned forward in his chair, as if to quicken Campbell's run. Jesus. Batistuta caught him, clattered into him and
it suddenly looked like something from a Sunday morning.

It put Rob in mind of the game the other week. How it
was all suddenly too late to change his mind and how the

18

breath he'd taken as Mark Stanley, the ref, blew the whistle, turned into a sigh. It had been a long time since he'd been nervous for a game and he felt an old tightness in his legs that surprised him. He'd stamped his feet as he glanced at Lee to check he was concentrating and that he was with him.

They'd hit a long, hopeful ball down the middle and it arced through the late April sky and Rob saw it and caught a glimpse of the castle as the ball dropped, taking one, two, three steps as he attacked it and headed it and didn't quite time it, but still sent it away, away, back into their half. He glared at Lee now, urged him towards the halfway line and ran past Tayub, startled how much, in a blur, he moved like Adnan used to. The ball went out for a throw. He heard a couple of half-familiar voices shouting, Well up, son. Someone was clapping. There was the throb of the helicopter overhead.

**Jim looked through the small window as he fiddled with the door chains.** St George's Day: five days to the Cinderheath game, a week and a half to the elections, a month to the World Cup. There were even more flags today, fluttering in the breeze, on cars, draped from upstairs windows, flapping from the balconies of the flats; a plague of monstrous butterflies. It had come to something, he thought, ashamed of your own flag. He wondered for about the hundredth time that week whether he should put one up, join the club. It was their flag as well, after all; he could meet them head-on, like Rob was doing.

All right, Bill.

All right, ower kid. I ay stoppin. Bought yer summat.

Look at that lot.

Jim couldn't keep his eyes off the flags. Bill had wandered off through to the kitchen with a polystyrene tray of baby tomato plants. Jim stood on the front step. He could get one, but specifically a football one, so he could play the patriot card but cover his back. He wouldn't have minded, but years ago he used to wear a rose for St George's day and people used to stop him – even at council meetings – and ask him what it was for. He didn't bother any more.

Am yer theer? Bill called from the kitchen.

Arr, all right, comin. Dyer think I should put a flag up, Bill?

What?

Dyer think it might help if I put a flag up? Yer know, in the front winder.

Mate, I doh think iss gonna mek a blind bit o difference whether yow've got a flag up or not. Yome gooin neurotic, what wi that an this game o football. It ay gonna mek no difference. How many voters dun yer think am gonna traipse past to see whether yow've got a flag up or not? Folks ay that bothered, mate.

They'm bothered enough to put em up in the fust plaece.

Bill messed with the plants, poking his finger into the dark soil around the stalks.

I brought yer that leaflet rahnd an all.

Bill pulled a shiny red, white and blue leaflet from his pocket and put it on the table. Jim picked it up.

Jesus.

Jim looked at the leaflet and then flipped it over to read some of the details. There was a picture of the Cinderheath ward BNP candidate, Philip Bailey, standing in his suit with a Union Flag background. He was youngish, thirties, with gelled blond hair, tanned, good-looking, Jim supposed.

Nice suit.

Says he's a local man in tune with local issues, i.e. the supermosque. These tomaters ull do yer just the job, mate.

I can read, Bill. Local, my backside. He's from bloody Telford.

Talks abaht how his ode mon worked at Cinderheath.

Jesus. The plants ull be lovely. Woss happened to our leaflets?

Still at the printers.

Jim sat at the table and ran his fingers over the embroidery of the tablecloth, then pushed his hand over the top of his head, exasperated.

Can we get em by tomorra?

He kept his voice as calm as he could, thinking about the might of the Labour Party machinery being outflanked by some far-right crackpots, then remembered he wasn't really talking to anybody in his own party any more, apart from Bill. He was on his own.

Arr, I might be able to get em by tonight, but too late to send rahnd. Send em rahnd tomorra night, eh. Doh send em too early, any road. They con look at em over the wikend. They doh read em any road. Cor read, some on em.

Bill tapped the BNP leaflet on the table and patted Jim on the shoulder.

I shudnt a bothered yer wi this. Yow'll atta stop mithering abaht it all. The flags, that game o football, all on it, whatever folks wanna say on the radio or in the paeper, it doh mean nuthin. All as they'm bothered abaht rahnd here is voting for a decent councillor an yome a good councillor. Nobody does more for folks rahnd here than yow so just mek sure yome reminding people, cos iss what I'm doin.

Ta, me old mate.

Jim forced a smile, looked at Bill tapping the edges of the leaflet nervously; his hands were dirty from the allotment. Bill had been branch secretary for as long as Jim had been a councillor. He took it on after his wife Esther died and he'd finished at GKN, rund the bowling an darts and the bowls club. He was a good bloke.

Jim fought back the urge to worry about how bright the BNP leaflet looked and his own monochrome literature. Folks am like magpies rahnd here, he thought.

I just think times am changin a bit, Bill, thass all.

Huh. Come senators, congressmen, please heed the call. Tham allus changin, mate, jus remember tha. Doh worry, any road. I'm off. I'll talk to yer later.

Bill walked back down the hallway. Pauline's done a lovely job wi them flowers, mate, ay er.

In the front-room window was a poster saying VOTE JIM BAYLISS. YOUR LABOUR COUNCILLOR, and a big vase of red and yellow carnations.

Her's a good girl, mate.

Jim pulled himself up from the kitchen chair. It was getting more and more difficult. After the election he was going to try harder with the diet Pauline had put him on and get some of those tobacco patches. To think, I used to be the swiftest bloke dahn that football club, he thought, a long time ago now.

Bill let himself out.

I'll speak to yer later, Bill. Ta-ra. Thanks for the tomaters. He stopped halfway down the hall so he didn't have to look at the flags again and went into the kitchen to enjoy the luxury of smoking indoors while no one was around.

**Owen Hargreaves was injured.** He was limping around outside their penalty area. He'd already had some treatment. You could tell from the way he was shaking his head he was worried.

Shit, that'll be a loss if he has to come off. Hard-working player, he is, just what yer want for this job. Glenn said this loudly to Jim and big Mark Stanley. It was a bit rich, really, coming from Glenn, given that a few months ago, when Rob and Glenn were still speaking to each other, he'd complained about Hargreaves even being picked.

Canadian-German half-breed, he ay even English.

His mother's English.

Have yow heared him spake? Iss barely English. He sahnds like bloody Adolf Eichmann or somebody.

Should be right up yower street then, I'd a thought.

Glenn was a decent player though, Rob would give him that. He'd never got a break. In the game the other week, the mosque had an early corner. The strong lad in midfield, shapes cut into his beard, jogged across to take it. The helicopter turned behind him, came back towards the pitch. A light shone from the helicopter, maybe a news camera. Rob felt a prickling of sweat under his arms. He pulled his shirt away from his body, half out of his shorts, conscious of being watched.

The corner dropped into a space in front of the near post. Rob and the big lad they'd got upfront with Tayub leaned into each other. He wasn't Rob's man, should've been Lee's, but Lee had gone missing. Glenn got back and attacked the ball, hit it on the volley with his left foot, turned with both feet off the floor, and then went straight after it, chasing his own clearance. Rob brought them out quickly, shouting at Lee who had suddenly appeared again.

Come on, halfway line, just leave em in theer. Come on, like he'd shouted every Sunday morning that season.

He slowed to a walk. Two police in hi-vis jackets kept pace in the corner of his vision. He wondered if they were the ones who'd turned up for Andre.

A few hours of Rob's timetable every week involved supporting pupils who needed extra help in their lessons. He hated it. It was like sitting in there as an extra kid on a chair that was too small. If the class caused a problem he was always unsure whether to get involved with telling kids off or helping the teacher – and he always ended up in classes where there was bound to be a problem. There was meant to be training for this sort of thing.

Today, he was in Miss Pale's RE lesson looking after Chelsey. Miss Pale was a young, blonde teacher who looked like Princess Diana. When she'd arrived at Cinderheath a year ago he'd tried to be friendly towards her; partly to chat her up, but partly because Cinderheath was a difficult place to come to if you were a new teacher or you weren't from the area. He'd bought her a vodka and cranberry at the Wetherspoon's. When she'd told him she grew up in the Cotswolds he'd started to tell her something about driving his nan down to Bourton-on-the-Water on a bank holiday and she'd said she didn't understand what he was saying, then gone, Oh, your grandmother, and laughed and said how as a teenager she and her friends spent bank holiday afternoons laughing at townie families come to gawp. She told him that the reality had been loads of cider and spliffs and shagging their way through the fields and river banks and pretty cottages of picture-postcard England. He couldn't tell if she was taking the piss or flirting. He didn't like it, whatever she was doing. He'd felt like asking if she knew who he was. Who he used to be, anyway. Now he'd decided that he didn't like her accent or the way she looked at him or the kids or the neat little registers she kept or those league tables of marks she had that always had the kids he worked with at the bottom. Or the way she looked these days, exhausted, as if she'd just come from a shift at the old Cinderheath works.

Come on, less get this sheet done, he said to Chelsey.

Iss shit.

Come on, less get some work done. First question: What religion are you?

What? I dunno. She put her head down on the table.

Chelsey, come on, sort yerself out. This is easy enough, less just get this done. What religion am yer?

I doh know, do I? She looked vacantly at the sheet in front of her. English.

English ay a religion. Iss yer nationality.

I am English.

No, I know yome English, but that ay a religion. A religion's what yer believe in. Yer know, what God yer believe in.

I doh believe in nuthin.

All right, Chelse, get yer head up, come on, darlin. Remember at yer mom's funeral, what was that?

Cremation.

Yeah, I know, but the service, the things we did, that was Christian. Yer know this. The vicar come to yer house. Dyer remember?

Praise the Lord. Hallelujah.

All right. So what shall we put in this box?

Chelsey looked at the sheet in front of her as if for the first time. English?

Chelsey's religion's shaggin in the canal tunnel. Mohammed turned around from his desk and called down the aisle.

Fuck off. Then, under her breath, Paki.

Mohammed turned again. Thass right, ay it, Michael?

Mohammed, give it a rest and turn round, eh? Rob said.

Is there a problem, sir? Miss Pale came walking towards their side of the room. Rob stood up. He was loath to have a conversation with her while sitting on a child's chair with his knees crammed against a school desk. She called him sir in a way that made it quite clear that she knew he wasn't a teacher and wondered exactly what he was doing in her classroom. He wondered that himself.

Chelsey says her religion's English.

No, that's not right, Miss Pale said slowly. They have to say what religion they are. Christian, Muslim, and then find and draw the symbol for that religion. She can say she's Church of England.

I know that, Rob said, even more slowly. Chelsey doesn't, or just won't do it this morning. Any suggestions?

Miss Pale sighed and then spoke in a louder voice.

I'm sick of trying to deal with her and her rudeness. She can sit and do nothing if you can't get her to do anything and I'll write a referral, again, to Miss Dragovic. Then more quietly: Just get her to write something in the boxes and draw the cross.

Rob sat back down. Chelsey stared at Miss Pale's back.

Bitch, she said quietly, then imitated her voice: I'll write a referral again, to Miss Dragon Witch. Frigid bitch.

Less get on with this, Chelse. Come on, doh get wound up.

She actually did settle down then, and while Miss Pale talked to the rest of the class about different religious festivals Chelsey and Rob did some colouring in.

What yer doin for yer dad's dinner today?

Gooin dahn the chip shop.

I thought yer had no money.

Me uncle gid me some.

Which uncle?

Me Uncle Ted. He come to visit.

Rob frowned. She hadn't got an Uncle Ted. He sighed.

That'll be nice, any road. Yer dad'll enjoy some chips.

If he's up aht o bed. He day get up yesterday till after three.

Maybe he was tired.

Maybe he was pissed.

Rob wanted to say something else to her, but couldn't think what. He'd had a pint with her dad in the Lion a couple of times. He seemed a nice enough bloke. They carried on colouring in together in silence.

Yow like that Paki teacher, doh yer? Rob?

What?

Yow like that Paki teacher, the one in the library.

Doh say Paki, Chelse, come on, yer know that.

OK. Yow like that – I doh know how else to say it – teacher in the library, doh yer?

I doh know what yome on abaht.

Yes yer do. I've sin yer lookin at her in the library.

If you mean Miss Quereishi, I do know her, Chelse. We went to William Perry school together for a bit when we was little. Same primary school you went to, ay it?

I think yer fancy her.

Oh, right.

Yome blushin, look yer.

The bell went. Rob leaned back in his little chair and looked at the kids around him, motioning them to be quiet and settle themselves down to be dismissed.

Enjoy yer chips, Chelse. Hope yer dad's all right.

Yeah, right. Yow havin dinner with yer girlfriend?

Watch yer cheek.

Rob was smiling, though. At this point he caught Miss Pale's eye. She looked at him and then at Chelsey with the same expression. She announced that the class could go. Before Rob could get up Chelsey had pulled herself on to the table top and swung her legs round to bolt for the door, her skirt sliding up over her arse, pulling a packet of Joey Khan's Arabic-squiggled Silk Cut from a little hand-bag that wasn't big enough to accommodate school books.

She's done a bit of colouring, Rob said and handed Miss Pale Chelsey's paper.

Thanks. About all she's good for. That and lying on her back with her legs open.

Miss Pale was already moving fast between the tables, muttering, laying out papers for the afternoon lessons. He thought of grabbing her blond ponytail and smashing her head off one of the tables, the pearls on that necklace bouncing around the room, her body flopping like a caught fish as he pulled her towards the windows. He gritted his teeth.

Look. Her's gooin home now to sort out her dad's dinner. Iss her in charge o the house. Her mom died. I know her's difficult but –

Miss Pale had stopped.

I know, I know, but where does it end? I'm here to teach her and she can't even read.

We could try and teach her, Rob mumbled.

The door flew open and some boys ran in wanting to store their coats and bags. They wrestled with each other in the corner. Miss Pale recovered her composure.

Guys, if you're not sensible you won't be able to leave your stuff.

Rob took some of the papers from her and began putting them out on the empty tables.

Look, thanks for trying with her at least, she said. It's a miracle she stayed in here for the hour.

Thass all right, Rob said at the door.

I won't write the referral on her, she said, back at her desk, looking at her computer screen.

Fantastic. I'm sure that was worrying her.


**Zanetti had a shot; well, a cross that drifted goalwards.** Seaman caught it easily enough but Rob shifted in his seat, put his half-eaten burger back on the table, his mouth drying.

All day, his uncle boomed. They'll have to offer more than that to get anything in this game, eh?

He spoke too loudly and confidently, probably knew it himself, whistling against the dark.

Rob imagined that somewhere, in some run-down football club next to a rusting corned-beef factory in the back end of Argentina, there was a minor local politician proclaiming loudly the inevitability of an Argentinian goal. Sitting next to him, there'd be his nephew, a failed footballer, fidgeting in his seat, barely able to watch, sitting with his old man on the other side, a disabled Malvinas veteran or prisoner of the generals or an old team-mate of Maradona's or something, biting his nails, wondering just quite why and how some men that you didn't even know running around on a field on a different continent, some foot or hand of God, might somehow re-order the world, or at least re-order the world in you.

Dyer want the rest o that, Rob? Jim motioned at the half-eaten burger and reached for it as Rob shook his head.

**The truth was that he wasn't a good councillor.**

This thought was beginning to haunt Jim. He couldn't think of one thing he'd done well in twenty-three years. Not really well. Even things that had been successful, like the vegetable van that came round the estate now or pulling down the Perry Court flats, he'd opposed at first and had to cover his tracks. The things that he could say he'd done well, like getting that Lottery funding for the drainage ditch at the club and organizing all the junior teams, or being on the governors when the school came out of Special Measures, finding this new Head, weren't anything to do with being a councillor, not really. Even little things like helping Stacey with her tax credit forms the other night for instance, that made him feel good, were good things to do, but really, really, what difference did they make in the end? The councillors didn't even run the council anyway, the bloody officers did and they were all Tories.

What was more, for once in his life, he could have done without this game of football on Sunday. It was like some

29

sort of bad joke. The Sunday team used to just be a way of raising the club extra subs towards the pitch and a few quid behind the bar after the game. Nobody took it that seriously. Sometimes a few of the first team squad would turn out, but usually it was a case of sending eleven out from the pub. Sunday football had been a bit of a joke, but something had changed. It became easier to get players out on a Sunday than on Saturday afternoons, even with the promise of a bit of cash and a write-up in the *Sports Argus*. Something had changed. And while Cinderheath FC scraped along on Saturday afternoons at the bottom of the West Midlands League, not knowing if they'd have hot showers or be able to paint the lines that week, these bastards – to add insult to injury – swanned around on Sunday mornings in their new England kits at the top of the league. It wasn't a bad standard these days, as well.

And now they were dead level with Cinderheath Muslim Community FC and playing them on the last day of the season to decide the title, unless some kind of miracle happened – if the game was drawn and the Gurdwara scored a hatful up at Castle Villa then the Sikhs could nick the league. Ordinarily, it would have been quite exciting. As it was, it was like some kind of bus crash.

The newspapers, TV and radio had suddenly begun talking about the 'possibility of new extreme-right West Midland heartlands' emerging in reaction to terrorism, political correctness and multiculturalism – and the Labour government, probably, tame and increasingly disappointing as it was. If they said it often enough it would probably happen. He wished everybody would just shut up.

A phone call earlier that week meant his estrangement from the local Labour Party was almost complete. Trevor Williams urged Jim to give him times when he could send some of the Labour students from the university to come and bang on doors.

We'll do our own door-banging here, Jim had said.

Why won't you just accept some help?

Because it won't be help, just hindrance. Folks doh wanna listen to it, at least, with respect, Trev, from the likes of all that lot.

I'm tryin to help you out.

Yome gonna send em rahnd any road so it doh matter what I suggest.

It might have escaped your attention, but there are other seats, other wards, you know. Why are you so intransigent?

I doh see how folks comin in from outside an tellin people how brilliant it ull be if they vote Labour is gonna work. Crowd of students, outsiders, walkin up and down the streets rahnd here, poking theer noses in is all folks ull think cos they'll soon disappear. All that'll happen is they'll have theer phones nicked an I'll have another mess to deal with.

Even though he'd been working on not blowing his top, he could feel his voice rising and his face reddening. Pauline had come out into the conservatory and mouthed, Calm, calm, calm.

Is that all you think of the people you're meant to represent? Trevor asked.

Doh start with that nonsense.

Why should your cynicism mean we lose a council seat to extremists?

If yer listen to me, I've actually thought it through. I doh wanna stir folks up. Thass what the BNP am dooin. Softly, softly, thass the approach. A bloody twenty per cent turnout ull suit we. Get the Asian vote out and keep it quiet on the estate. Any road, I thought cynicism was what we did these days.

Jim, there's obviously no reasoning with you.

Eh, talking of these students, what happened that time I asked if yow'd get some on em to come dahn an do some reading in the primary school? Lasted abaht a wik, most on em.

With that he'd put the phone down. He was on his own. These days it was how he preferred it.

**Adnan the mujahedin.** Adnan the ghost. He'd been missing now for nearly ten years. One June morning he'd driven off in his taxi and never come back. For a while, as kids, Rob and Adnan had been best mates. They'd been in the same classes at primary school, drifted apart as teenagers. There were a couple of years when they were eight, nine, ten that they'd lived in a kind of state of grace. They'd had the same class teacher, Miss Johnson, for two years running. They'd do projects on space, the sea, knights in shining armour. They'd put on Diwali and Nativity plays. At the end of each day they'd sit on the mat at the front of the classroom – out the window you could see the works' gantry and the castle in the distance behind it – and Miss Johnson would read them stories. *Narnia*, tales from Shakespeare, Roald Dahl. Or they'd read each other's work out. Adnan had written a whole book on his own at the library about journeys to other planets, monsters, ghosts. When school finished they'd play football or cricket on the field, collect frog spawn. A couple of times Rob and Adnan went all the way through the canal tunnel out the other side and over the hill to look for golf balls, showed them off the next day. Rob knew he remembered it how he wanted to remember it, not how it really was, but he didn't care.

This was about the time things had begun to change around there. The works had closed. Their dads lost their jobs. During this time Rob's family had all lived at his grandparents' house on Dudley Road. Then his grandad died, his uncle moved out to live with his Aunty Pauline, Rob and his mum and dad moved into the house they lived in now, further into the estate. His nan went into the old people's flats. Things changed. Miss Johnson left the school, other teachers too. Loads of kids left as well, like Jasmine Quereishi, who Chelsey had seen him talking to. Jasmine's dad had recently saved Rob's dad's life. He was working on how he'd tell her this. It was true. His old man had a heart attack. Her dad was a consultant at Russell's Hall and did his dad's triple bypass.

Adnan saved a girl's life once, at a swimming lesson at Dudley Baths. They were all stood on the edge of the deep end, shivering and shouting in a line, not listening to the teacher's instructions. Suddenly Adnan, standing next to Rob, dived in. Dived properly, God knows how he knew to do it, like someone in the Olympics. Rob remembered his body stretched out like a smooth brown frog's, suspended in the pool's blue light just before the moment of impact. Rob saw him kick his legs under the splashing water and, next thing, he was back out on top with an arm around a tiny, silent girl called Deborah Taylor, dragging her to the side. She was heaving and spluttering, had fallen in with such little splash when they were all making a noise that no one had noticed.

Adnan did everything like that, better than you'd ever seen anyone do it before, then he'd just brush it off like it was nothing. He breezed through school work, read piles of books, back and forth to the library, interested in things, ideas, people. He was fascinated with computers and made tapes with little games on that he'd written himself, things that involved chasing spiky monsters or steering a car around a track. He was good at sport, tall and willowy, and when he'd played football he'd ran and swerved with the ball at his feet like Mark Walters at the Villa, whose sticker they'd plastered up and down the lamppost by the shops. He'd fight if he had to and he had to a lot – he didn't go looking for trouble but never backed down.

33

When they were kids Rob thought Adnan would end up as prime minister or something. Rich, at least. He didn't think he'd be a taxi driver.

When they moved on to Cinderheath High, back then especially, all the Asian boys were meant to know their place, really. They could sit and do their work and get involved with sport, but as far as fighting and messing about and hanging around with the white girls went, that was something else altogether. Rob heard there were schools near by that had things the other way round. When he was growing up, for instance, Cinderheath kids called the school up in Dudley the Ape House, scared of black boys taking their money when they went into town. Somebody always had to be on top, he supposed, some group or other. It was the way the world worked.

He and Adnan grew apart as they got older. Rob concentrated on his football; Adnan on his school work, turning in on himself, sitting at the computer that school had given him when they were getting new ones. He went on to sixth form when Rob went to the Villa: they didn't see each other much while Rob sat miserably in his digs in Wrexham, pretending to be a professional footballer. Adnan drifted along when he finished sixth form – his family assumed he'd go to university like his brother – doing the odd day's work in warehouses and factories, inevitably ending up driving a taxi for Joey Khan. Then one morning he just drove off, disappeared.

Yer cor just vanish into thin air, though, mate, Rob said to Zubair.

He'd had a drink with Adnan's brother every week now for the near ten years he'd been missing. They'd meet at Zubair's office on Wolverhampton Street or sometimes down at the magistrates' court now it had moved, have a couple of pints in Dudley or at Merry Hill, before dumping the car and ending up back in the Lion.

Zubair would shrug, not look at Rob properly. Maybe he knew something more, maybe he didn't. There was family stuff that Rob couldn't really get at, felt he couldn't ask or wouldn't understand, didn't know where to start. Muslim stuff, maybe; things seemed more complicated than they used to.

You couldn't just disappear into thin air, though. You couldn't become nothing.

Rob knew the truth was probably mundane, and tragic, but stories crept in to fill the gaps. Adnan the mujahedin. That was one of the stories. Rob reckoned Zubair knew more than he let on.

A couple of years after he'd gone, Rob read something about the routes into Bosnia, stories of young British Muslim men travelling there to sign up. Get a holiday flight to Italy or Corfu. There were middlemen to sort out a boat across to Albania. Hang around the harbour in Tirana and wait for a bus to a training camp and then the front. So maybe that was it; he was trudging through the mud with an AK-47 or rocket launcher. Or living like a bandit in the dusty mountains of Afghanistan. Or sneaking through the winding alleyways of Gaza. And you had to admit, Rob thought to himself, and only to himself, that there was something in that, something a bit more exciting than sitting here watching it all unfold on the telly, watching everything, your own life included, slide away, turn to rust. Then he wondered exactly who it was he was thinking about.

Nowadays he pictured Adnan bearded and hollow-faced in a cave or dead, under the rubble somewhere, sinking in the mud. Wild fantasies filled the silence. He found himself scanning the faces of al-Qaeda terrorists when they flashed up on the news; the bland, sinister head-shots reminded him of the ones on the football stickers he and Adnan had swapped as kids.

35

Rob thought about Zubair sitting in his office, watching the television he'd rigged up for the World Cup, chain-smoking through matches, leaning back on his chair against the frame of the open window. Thinking about Adnan, his missing brother. Zubair was lonely, Rob thought. But he didn't know how lucky he was: he'd married Katie, a legal secretary he'd worked with; they'd bought a nice house by the park, had a little girl. Rob had bumped into Katie once at a bar at The Waterfront – he'd shagged her mate, but nothing came of it – Zubair had been at home with the baby.

**Mills made a run up the right.** Scholes tried to find him with a pass. England looked in, but the move came to nothing. Rob heard his dad mutter, Unlucky son, to Mills, or more likely to Scholes for spotting the pass.

Suddenly Simeone hit it diagonally, the same kind of ball but in reverse, into the space behind Ashley Cole for Ortega to run on to. Not quite. Another scare. The ball ran out of play.

Thass the ball. Thass the ball they'll atta watch. His dad tapped his arm and leaned towards him as he spoke. They'll atta watch that space in behind Cole, he pushes up way too far, forces it. I doh care how quick he is, I've tode yer.

His old man leaned back then, as if he'd solved a tricky crossword clue.

Rob was suddenly scared that his dad would clap if Argentina scored using that ball inside the full-back, would look around nodding his head, saying, I tode yer, they deserve it.

He wondered what Glenn or some of the others would do then. Maybe they'd just indulge him, maybe not. He wondered what he'd do in return. He'd served that lot with plastic beakers, given himself a glass.

**Jasmine always thought she'd come back to Cinderheath.**
Even getting together with him – and everything that this
had caused – had been a kind of return. Looking back on
the past year, she knew she wouldn't have lost all sense,
the way she did, if it hadn't all somehow led back here.
She would never have hurt Matt in the way she had,
although maybe it had done him some good, if there
hadn't been the idea of some kind of return to Cinderheath, some kind of homecoming, at the back of her
mind. That's what she told herself now; anyway, it was
too late and the damage was done.

There was work to do here. She lifted a pile of folders
from a box, but realized there was nowhere to store them
and dropped them on a table. The tables were all rejects
from other classrooms, engraved with the obsessions of
generations of pupils, hearts and tag names. Jasmine was
startled for a moment to see a bloom of swastikas
tattooed into a desk in the shape of a flower. There was a
lot to do here.

At first, she thought Helena had invented the job for
her. You'd be perfect, she'd said. Ethnic Minority Achievement and a reading recovery programme: a variety of
clunky job titles they still hadn't decided on.

What do you think your job title should be? Helena
asked.

Teacher? she said, bemused.

That's why I think you'd be perfect.

Helena had been Assistant Head at Riverway, the school
in London where Jasmine had taught English. She'd moved
to be Deputy at a school in Aston – she was from Birmingham originally – and she and Jasmine kept in touch.
She'd phoned to say she'd got a Headship, at Cinderheath,
and asked if Jasmine knew it. She'd paused for a long time
before replying.

It's where I grew up.

I knew it! I thought I'd heard you mention it before.

Or rather, when I say I grew up there, my mum's family are from there. We lived there for a couple of years when I was a little girl.

Helena had offered her a job outright. Jasmine was in no condition to think about anything then, after the summer she'd gone through, betraying Matt, leaving him, then being left, betrayed, herself. It was September 11th, the day Adnan let her down, and for her it would always mean that: sitting blankly for hours in front of the television. If he'd done what he'd promised he wouldn't even have been in New York. They'd have been together.

It was at Christmas that it became clear what she was going to do, back at her parents' for the holidays, curled up in the warmth, sleeping and eating finally, reading even, getting some kind of rest, not leaving the house except for a walk into Bridgnorth to pick up some presents, and then along the river with her parents on Christmas morning. It wasn't that she knew what she should do, or even what she wanted or ought to do, but that she knew what she was going to do: the inevitability of it all.

Which left her now, nearly six months on, trying to organize this bare annexe room off the library in Cinderheath High School into some kind of classroom, putting her life back together. In most jobs they'd have asked her to teach right from the start – before September and the new school year – whereas here all she had to do was make sure this space was ready, do pupil assessments, try to meet with parents and do some staff training. She was lucky, even if she didn't feel it.

Jasmine pulled a box towards her and took out some display work she'd saved from Riverway. It amazed her how she'd been aware enough last autumn to pack up these boxes and label them neatly, put them away in hibernation like they used to with the class tortoise when she was a girl, packed away and waiting for the spring, for a new start.

There was a dubious wisdom in decorating this room with reminders of her old classroom – these masks made for the Capulets' ball had hung on the wall next to the door, this *Oliver Twist* poster had filled the space between the two big windows that looked across the docks and down the river. It would have been nice to have some windows here. All she had was this partition of reinforced glass (someone had still managed to smash it into a cob-web of little breaks; they'd replace it before they got children in here) that let her look murkily across a library of unread books and new computer terminals.

She wanted windows, light! She'd had enough of be-ing shut away, buried. Sudden thoughts of the first Mrs Rochester came to mind, she'd read *Jane Eyre* over and over, hidden away as an unhappy adolescent, and then *Wide Sargasso Sea* as a happy student in London a few years later. She wanted light.

The windows of her old classroom opened on to the spaces past Canary Wharf where the clouds broke up, as the river slowly became sea, over the new skyscrapers and crumbling dock buildings. Sitting here in her penitent's cave, she smoothed the edges of the reclaimed posters and thought about those windows. She remembered her shock as a new teacher on looking from her classroom on an un-seasonably warm, sunny September afternoon and seeing bodies, framed against the glinting skyscrapers, paused for a moment, arms raised, before leaping from the bridge over the dock into the water below.

She'd walked down there after school that day. There was a scrap of shingle beach at the cambered end of the dock, and kids playing there, in and out of the water, shouts of, All right, miss? from a couple of those she'd started to teach, whole families down there as well, people holding ice creams and cans of lager, spilling over the dock-side concrete. There was a sign warning people about the water, prohibiting swimming, and behind that a tattooed man teaching a girl in armbands to swim and a dog with a tennis ball in its mouth chopping the water with its paws.

And in the background there were the jumpers, strange and beautiful, with that pause before falling, arms raised in a salute, a body tumbling with sunshine and skyscrapers beyond, planes descending for City Airport. Skyscrapers, planes, falling bodies.

The next day there'd been an assembly about the dangers of swimming in the docks. The pupils were banned; there was a letter going home. Matt gave the assembly. He spoke to them quietly about how it was tempting, exciting, to go down to the water. How people older than them, even maybe mums and dads, uncles, cousins, might say there was no harm in it, and that there didn't seem to be any harm in the sunshine, in the cool water, the ice cream van pulled up alongside the dock, but that it was more dangerous than they thought. Someone had died a couple of years before with the shock of the water after jumping in from the bridge. Some of the kids in that room knew the family. He knew the family. The boy had been a good boxer, had a part-time job on the market that helped his family out, he'd gone down there one summer afternoon, gone off the bridge and never came up. It was a couple of weeks before they found his body. Nobody told you about the rubbish and the rats that were there in the water, nobody told you how dangerous it was. But he was telling them now. They weren't banned for the sake of it, to stop them having a good time. He was asking them to think. They sat there silently, a hundred and fifty Year Elevens, listening intently, some of them nodding slightly. She hadn't seen them like this before, not quite so engaged when someone spoke to them. They were like it whenever he spoke to them.

The weather changed the next day anyway, but Jasmine would watch them the following summer and the summer after that. No one paid any attention to letters or bans, no matter how hard they listened to Matt Johnson when he spoke to them, no matter how much they loved him. It was one of the things he worried about. One of the many. After they got together, it was one of the worries she tried to soothe for him.

He was ten years older than her, divorced, two young girls with his ex-wife in Essex. It wasn't easy. Her parents were wary, to say the least. This was the first time there'd been anyone serious. She'd had boyfriends through university, went out for nearly a year on and off with one of the other volunteers when she'd worked in Ghana, but this was different.

Matt had grown up near Riverway and his family had followed the general eastward drift – parents retired now in Canvey; his ex-wife and girls in Hornchurch – but there was something about the area he couldn't give up. Even at the cost of his marriage. Back then she thought that was committed, romantic even. Now she wasn't so sure.

But you can't measure what difference it makes, she'd say to him. Because you can't measure all the times someone doesn't drown in the docks, or pick up a knife, or get themselves pregnant after you've said something to them. There are other people responsible for them as well as you, you know. They've got some responsibility for themselves. He'd shrug and nod but then carry on as before. And she loved that in him. At first, of course.

Jasmine didn't go down to the docks again, preferred to look from the classroom's big windows, watching the arc of the bodies, little flashes of life against the steel and glass, the water and concrete. Some of them were boys whom she taught – it was all boys and young men – clumsy, inarticulate, angry in school; she wondered what went through their minds. She'd even asked one of them, Freddie Barber, who she knew went down there with his string of brothers, who looked like he'd walked out of the *Oliver Twist* poster, but he was tongue-tied, just shrugged, looked blank, said it felt good. She hadn't pursued it. Maybe that's what it was, a few moments of grace, something that felt good, and then a blankness.

She knew what was coming next with these thoughts. Maybe if all the things Matt said near the end hadn't been so corrosive, if he hadn't been quite so arrogant, so convinced that the fate of Riverway's kids, some of them damaged and dangerous long before he came across them, was so utterly in his hands, maybe if he'd agreed that they move in together, instead of the ridiculous set-up they'd had, then perhaps, perhaps, when she'd run into Adnan, she wouldn't have been quite so reckless herself.

Matt betrayed himself – putting school first was a way of hiding from other responsibilities. She betrayed Matt; Adnan betrayed her. The way these thoughts ran: the jumpers from the towers, a rain of people on to the streets below and then a rain of concrete, steel and glass. Dust and ashes, silence and absence. Where was he? Why hadn't Adnan kept his word?

She thought, of course, that he was somewhere there, underneath the rubble, buried, interred, but she also knew that if she kept working away at these thoughts, in the way she was smoothing the edges of these posters, the way she picked the flesh from around her thumbnails, some other certainty would creep into her thoughts – like a change of light, like a drifting cloud of ash – the certainty that he was somewhere else altogether. The cold, hard fact that a person who could walk out of a life once, without leaving a trace, could do the same again. Maybe one day would have to do the same again.

Before it got too bad, she imagined her mother's voice,

kind and stern, Come on, love, and she laid out the posters and crumbling masks, pulled herself from the chair and opened the library door, off to get some Blu-tack and drawing pins and get back to work.

**They had a throw.** Zubair took it, the first time he'd touched the ball. His belly was sticking out over the top of shorts that were pulled up way too far, like the way the old men who stood at the bar at the Lion wore their trousers. Rob wanted to laugh, suddenly. A couple of girls – women – from down Juniper Close gave Zubair a shout. One of them was Kyle Woodhouse's girlfriend, he thought. Zubair, with the ball resting on the flat of his hand, gave them that look that he'd always had, just staring, a raised eyebrow, an expression he probably used in court, just looking and looking.

What yer fuckin lookin at? One of the girls stuck her face towards his, her face twisting, trying to work up a frenzy. It was just after ten on a Sunday morning, the sound of helicopters overhead.

The whistle blew and blew again. The ref came across in front of Rob, a couple of their players walking towards the touchline. It could have all gone off already. Mark Stanley, the ref, the only bloke who could take charge of this game, got right in front of Zubair.

Get on with it please, player.

Mark was big, mixed race, hair almost an Afro, fifty now if he was a day, worked for the Youth Service, used to get in the paper with his karate, wouldn't take any messing. Mark had been refereeing on the park since Rob was in the juniors. He'd reffed Rob's first proper match, now he was reffing his last one.

Zubair turned and took the throw. The girl was still saying, You fuckin prick, you fuckin prick, but nobody was joining in, at least for now. Zubair threw it for Tayub down the line. Kyle was there, or in the way at least, and the ball hit him, his standing leg, as he tried to kick it, and the ball bounced inside.

Rob was on to it, someone on his shoulder, and he saw, or maybe thought he saw or sensed or just knew, that Glenn's red hair was making a diagonal run into the space that Zubair was never going to get back to, not with that belly, not these days.

Rob struck it, laces, pinged it on a line between their penalty box and the touchline. Too good. Too much on it. Glenn curved his run, but it was away from him and ran on and the defender was across, seeing it out of play.

Glenn turned and put his hands above his head, clapped Rob. Rob put his thumb up.

**Less just read this bit an then yer con play Gulf Strike.**
Rob was trying to get Andre to do some reading with him in the library.

I wanna play now.

Come on, Andre, eh? Just a bit more. Yer know the rule. We'll do our reading an then yer con goo on the computer.

Lerrus goo on now, Rob.

No, less just finish this, come on.

Andre swung on his chair, looking at the computers on the other side of the library.

Fuck this shit, man.

Come on, no swearing. Less read this page.

Rob spread the paper on the desk in front of him and pretended to read that morning's *Daily Mirror*. Andre pulled the chair up next to him.

Would yer gi her one, Rob?

Andre nodded at a picture of a celebrity Rob had never heard of wearing a bikini and dark glasses on a yacht somewhere very sunny.

Her's a nice-looking girl, arr.

44

Her's got nice tits.

Come on, which un dyer wanna read?

Andre pointed at a story.

Goo on then.

Workers at a pub in . . .

Liverpool.

. . . got more than they . . .

Sahnd it aht.

Bar . . . bar . . . brought . . .

Bargained for.

When they . . . catched . . .

When they cleaned.

. . . up a load of old pipes in the . . . car.

In the cellar. Yer know what a cellar is? A room underneath a house. Underneath the ground. A cellar. Pubs have em to keep the beer in.

Andre grinned. I like beer.

An me, carry on, come on. What was in the cellar?

A snake.

Yome looking at the picture. Less read it.

One of the . . .

Pipes. Yow've just read that. Yow ay concentrating.

. . . was a . . . live!

One o the pipes was alive! Busty bar manager, Carleen Doherty, 24, was shocked to discover her boyfriend Tony's pet python, Tyson, had slithered downstairs for a nap. Can yer see, mate, look, there was a snake hiding in all the pipes.

Woss busty mean?

Means yow've got big tits.

Is Miss Quereishi busty?

I shouldn't say that to her face.

Yow like Miss Quereishi, doh yer, Rob?

What yow on abaht? Who's tode yer that?

I con tell.

Me and Miss Quereishi went to school together, did yer know that? We was in the same class as each other for a bit at William Perry.

Andre didn't look that interested.

Andre and Chelsey were both right about Miss Quereishi, of course. He knew he had to stop looking over at her through the glass partition.

They'd had an awkward conversation on her first day, then he'd bumped into her in Dudley outside the library on a Saturday morning. She'd been working in London, but had recently moved back to her parents', out near Bridgnorth. She'd been to university in London, stayed there to teach, east London, difficult schools, a bit like round here she'd said. She'd travelled a bit, taught in Ghana for a while. They'd reminisced about primary school, the couple of years they were in the same class. One time they were the ones chosen to put Atticus, the tortoise, into hibernation. The tortoise, in a panic, had pissed on Jasmine's skirt. Rob had put his arm around her. They'd had their picture taken together for both winning a quiz. Adnan had been unusually jealous at losing out for once. The photo was printed in the *Express & Star*. Rob knew his mum had it somewhere in a box of newspaper clippings, underneath all the scrapbooks of the matches he'd played in.

I didn't know there'd be anyone here that I'd know.

Yeah, loads. He told her he still saw Lee Maloney and Glenn Brown. He didn't tell her he'd gone out with Karen Woodhouse for years, that they'd had a flat together, everything, until that all fell apart. He didn't mention his old man's heart attack and her dad's part in his repair. He didn't tell her about Adnan either, thought she might ask about him. There was all the time in the world for that, he decided. He mentioned seeing Zubair for a drink now and again, but he was older than them, had already left primary school when Jasmine was there; she didn't seem to remember him.

She said she was surprised that he was still around; she thought he'd have moved on. The way she said it stung Rob.

Well, I used to be a footballer.

Was he teaching here at Cinderheath?

Well, er no, he was sort of helping out in PE and as a Teaching Assistant. Just helping out, you know, with having finished playing football, retired really, you know.

She said it was nice to see him; that they'd have to catch up properly when she'd settled in.

After that conversation he'd gone and sat out the back and stared at the canal, smoking, until he had to go and put out the tennis nets for the afternoon lesson.

Those years when everything changed, his dad stayed in bed, didn't speak much, walked down to the shop to pick up a few cans, settled in for the afternoon's racing. Rob'd had a growth spurt and was suddenly playing with the older lads, with men standing around on Saturday mornings nodding their heads at his Uncle Jim, patting him on the back. Yow've gorra good un theer, Jim, ay yer. The scouts, in their long coats, were already having a look, bound to be interested when they knew who his dad was.

This is Jasmine Quereishi, the Head announced in staff briefing. She'll be working with us three days a week and full-time from September. She'll be working on our Ethnic Minority Achievement and setting up a reading recovery programme that we intend to have in place from next year. I'm sure you'll make her feel welcome.

The new Head had a way of speaking that annoyed people. As they left the staff room, Rob heard one of the old teachers moaning, Cos we've not been doing any ethnic minority achievement work up until now or trying to teach kids to read, of course. Rob wanted to turn round and defend her. She did look just out of college, though, didn't look nearly thirty. She looked great.

**It hadn't used to feel like this.** Jim sat moping in the kitchen and was struck with a fond memory of standing with Trevor, shaking hands with Harold Wilson who'd come to thank party workers the year that there were two elections. It had been thrilling being part of all that, central to it. Not like this. They'd all had fish and chips round at Trevor's flat afterwards up at Eve Hill, the flats Jim had helped get pulled down after the drugs and the pirate radio moved in – Trevor now long moved out to a nice semi off Himley Road. It had felt great that night, to be part of something.

Then there was 1997, of course. The landslide. The best night of them all. Jim had been at the count in Dudley, hearing outlandish stuff, rumours that then came true, like Portillo losing his seat. Jim wished his dad had been there. He thought of that story of Maradona in Naples, when he won the league for them, the partying for days afterwards, the graffiti in the cemetery, YOU DON'T KNOW WHAT YOU MISSED.

Jim had paced up and down in front of one of the TV screens, across the lino in front of the dartboard where he'd rested a brandy and a smouldering cigar, playing the part, pacing as if it was on a knife-edge but grinning, slapping people on the back, thanking them for their help like he was Tony's emissary to the people of Cinderheath, feeling like he might burst with happiness.

Even at this short distance, it felt like the few months either side of that election had been a golden age. Michael was doing OK in school, things were going well with Pauline's shop; he'd even got that Wolves scout to have one last look at Rob and they'd asked him to go on trial in the pre-season. Things could only get better.

The undertow of anticlimax was already there, though, even before they'd won it, slowly pulling everyone under. That early morning, five-ish, driving home with Pauline in the back of Joey Khan's taxi, strangely sober but elated, feeling exactly eighteen years younger – they'd looked at the flag fluttering on the castle, crept upstairs for a couple of hours in bed and made love. He lay there while Pauline got ready for the salon, listening to the radio, tears in his eyes; he'd booked the day off, thought he might just wander to the council offices to swan around a little bit, *we're the masters now.*

Revenge. It was what he would've preferred, he thought, in the end; too late to right the wrongs of nearly twenty years, too late to take a different path. That urge to just smash the place to bits: finish the job. In those first few days he'd actually thought they might re-nationalize the railways (he hadn't been on a train himself for years), instead they gave away the Bank of England. He preferred the fox-hunting ban, which was nothing to do with foxes at all, of course. He'd seen a hunt once when he'd still been married to Jackie. They were driving out on a back road near Clent and the horses were blocking their way. The dogs had cornered the fox in the hedgerow and were on top of it, the horses circling and rearing in the road; one of the horsemen trotted in after the dogs, whacking at them. Jackie gripped his arm, her face turned into his chest.

A horse reared again and a woman, a yellow scarf tied at her throat and flecks of mud all over her, waved towards the car, shooing them away and shouting.

Scaring the horses!

He'd seen one of the dogs turn from the ditch with a bloody nose and ear, seen half a fox with purple guts hanging out and had looked at the strange alabaster faces of the horsemen and women in the road, more horses in the field behind, the dogs swarming in the ditch and by the wheels of the car now, before he struggled into reverse and got them away from there. They'd been playing Dylan tapes, he remembered.

Jim breathed a long stream of smoke out through the tiled kitchen. They'd got it looking really nice now, since the extension. That was another thing he'd thought was a bad idea and then had to come round to. It was good now they could all eat in here, together at the table. They should've insisted on it years ago; maybe Michael would've got off the computer, at least up off his arse, taken a bit more interest in everything. Still, Jim only wanted three more years. He'd have his crack at being mayor – that would be nice for Pauline, after having to put up with so much over the years – and then they could go to Spain, maybe. Spend some time in the sun. Sell up and get an apartment some-where, loads of people were doing it.

He lit another cigarette from the end of the last one. He enjoyed doing that; it felt, he was never sure of the right word, opulent? Expansive? Generous? He hated the kind of people who ate half a chocolate bar, drank half-pints. Tight-arses!

He tried to work out how the Arabic squiggles on his cigarette packet said Silk Cut. To Pauline's disgust he'd bought a whole carton from Joey. It made him think again of the fuss over the leaflets. Normally, they'd just print ones saying the same thing in different languages; English and Urdu on the front, Punjabi and Gujarati on the back. This year, though, Jim insisted on different leaflets alto-gether, unofficial, saying different things as well, especially about the mosque or supermosque or whatever you wanted to call it. It was clever – political. The same with the turn-out – the lower the turnout, the better for him because the BNP would get out all sorts of characters who hadn't been bothered to vote before. Nobody ever gave him credit for thinking of things like that.

It was in his blood, though, he told himself. His great-grandparents had been founder members of Cinderheath Labour Party. He'd grown up with the memory of the 1945 election fresh, the previous collision of hope and history, and of the party after the count then. His mother had danced with George Wigg, the new MP. He'd grown up in more hopeful times with thankful stories of Bevan and the NHS, the state of Israel, Indian independence.

There were older stories, too. Of Chartist newspapers read out for the masses in the Lion and other pubs. Of troops sent to quieten striking miners and nail makers. Of God Save the People and After the Revolution. Hope and History.

Jim became a councillor in 1979, against the prevailing mood. He thought he was doing his bit for Cinderheath, Dudley, England, the Labour movement, the working class. He'd noticed people using the term 'working class' again lately, hadn't heard it for years. Blair had got things right in that respect as well as many others: how could there be a Labour Party when there was no Labour left for it to represent? It had to become something else. There were jobs now, of course. The big losses had all come twenty-odd years ago, but it was hardly the same – jobs for cleaners and security men, shop work and mobile-phone sales. Jim was lucky – he'd been at the same place, Smith's, the steel stockholders, for thirty years now, a place that swam against the tide. Even the call centre jobs were going to Bangalore. This was his town's position in the new world order.

He didn't know what to think any more. He felt old, suddenly, he knew that. Just fancied sitting in that clean, white light in Spain, like the world was fresh. He had to summon up some energy from somewhere.

He glanced at the shiny leaflet again. These people couldn't be for real, could they?

Maybe he had got the stomach for the fight, after all. But underneath there was this fear that everything you went through, everything you ever did, made you smaller, wore you out. Maybe our Michael's got the right idea, he thought. Sit on your arse and preserve yourself.

He thought about Rob. He was just trying to do the right thing with this game against the mosque or whatever they were calling themselves (they'd had their own problems). But how did you work out what the right thing was? Jim sat there smoking, thinking of himself as a puddle evaporating in the sun, imagining it raining a long way away.

**The first time Adnan had become someone else Rob was with him,** encouraged him, even. They went on a residential trip to Ilfracombe in their last year of primary school. This was the year after Jasmine had left. The year Rob and Adnan's friendship started drifting apart. The trip was a week of activities – archery, canoeing, rock climbing – some sort of reward for good behaviour. They lived in an old barracks, with other schools from all over the place. It hadn't gone well. The kids from the other schools, with better clothes, generally, and more aptitude for outdoor pursuits, had made them feel clumsy and ragged. It had rained all week and they'd got into fights, with the other schools and each other. Halfway through, on the Wednesday, after the communal breakfast there'd been a big to-do with a school from Portsmouth or somewhere. Adnan got pushed forward to fight another boy. The boy was big, with wild ginger hair and thick glasses fastened in one corner with tape. Adnan tried to knock the glasses off, aimed to stamp on them, thought it might gain him some time before the teachers came, but the boy was stronger than him and the teachers didn't come. He ended up rolling in the wet grass and mud, being pummelled by the boy's heavy fists, ruining the tracksuit bottoms he'd got his mother to sew a Tacchini badge on to. They pulled the boy off him in the end – other kids from Portsmouth, as was the rule with these things – still no sign of any adults.

Fuckin Paki, he'd spat at Adnan as he was led away. He'd heard it before, of course, but somehow in this strange place in this strange accent, the words seemed to give him forewarning of what to expect in life, if he wasn't careful, if he wasn't clever.

No Woodhouse boys in their year group meant he and Rob were the cocks of Cinderheath – as they'd have said then, the eleven-year-olds, at least. Rob, feeling guilty, he imagined, as it had been a toss-up which one of them fought the ginger boy, helped him clean up, got him some cream for his black eye and the scratches on his neck, lent him some spare clothes.

Sick of it all, they'd skived the evening meal, half-hoping to get caught and sent home. They jumped the barracks wall and walked to a chip shop on the front, near the putting green. There were two girls in there, other camp escapees, from a school in Glasgow, equally out of place, sharing a cone of chips and a can of Coke.

Rob had talked to them while they waited for their chips to cook, looking out of the steamy window at the sea. He'd made them laugh, trying their accent.

And what's your pal called? the more talkative of the two girls asked.

Glenn, he'd said. Glenn, before Rob could give an answer.

The girls' names were Elizabeth and Susan. He didn't know which way round.

They sat on a covered wooden bench and ate their chips together. The more talkative girl took a permanent marker from her tracksuit pocket and wrote RFC and NO SURRENDER on the back of the bench. It impressed them. Next thing, she'd sat on Adnan's lap and kissed him. Too quick for him to get nervous or anything, his bruised lips and hers fixed tight together and then open, mouths hot from the chips. Rob and the quieter girl adopted the same position. After a while, the girls got worried about getting caught, having been away for so long, and said they'd best sneak back in. They were leaving in the morning, staying in a youth hostel in the Lake District on the way back up, with food even more disgusting than this place and with even less to do. They arranged to meet up after breakfast to swap addresses, but they never did.

Rob and Adnan watched the girls climb back up the hill, both thinking they should've offered to walk them, both not wanting to go back. Rob pulled a couple of crumpled cigarettes and a lighter from his pocket.

These fell out of his pocket when he was palin yer.

They sat and tried to smoke and felt sick and looked at the sea, musing on submarines and sea monsters.

Turned out all right in the end, eh Glenn? Rob grinned, trying to copy the way he'd seen his dad hold a cigarette.

Adnan nodded, looking out at the waves and the grey squall, thinking about what lessons he could take from the day.

**Zubair had sent Rob a text message.** Simeone's left boot remind you of anyone's? Zubair meant his own, of course, how in the game the other week, he'd arced a pass that dropped over Rob's head for his kid brother to race after. Rob couldn't turn. Zubair couldn't run, mind you, could barely move at all these days, but he could still strike a ball.

Rob wanted to tell him to fuck off, but thought of him sitting there in his office alone and started to write Ha, ha instead.

Sorin got forward, back-heeled it. Kily Gonzalez was on to it. Movement, patterns, watching it was like the pieces of a puzzle falling into place. Kily Gonzalez hit it to the sound of moans. The shot flew wide.

On the replay you could see how Nicky Butt had done enough to put him off, just thrown himself in there to try and close down. That was the stuff that won games, Rob thought, little jobs done properly like that; probably some message for life itself, he thought.

Ha, ha! he wrote. Then, That was close.

**Con I play Gulf Strike now, Rob?**

Rob looked at his watch and leaned back in the chair. Goo on then but first yow've gorra find me a book on snakes from in here an bring it to me.

What fower? I ay doin that.

Goo on, see if yer con find one. I'm thinking o gerrin me one as a pet.

Serious?

Arr, but I wanna find which one to get.

Yow con get em dahn the Merry Hill.

I'm sure yow can, arr.

There were kids who couldn't read. Not those who were dyslexic, or those with other Special Needs (that could mean anything), or kids who arrived only speaking Punjabi or Urdu. No, kids who had grown up in Cinderheath, just like him, and had somehow got to twelve, thirteen, fourteen unable to read more than a couple of words. It was unbelievable. There weren't hordes of them – but neither were there so few you could ignore it and since he'd started looking there were new ones turning up all the time. Some had missed a lot of school – that was how he came across them, turning up in groups that ran for non-attenders – but not all of them. Some of them, like Andre and Kelvin, boys he worked with at the moment, had somehow managed to complete nine years of school each and could read barely a dozen words between them.

Chelsey, for example, had loads about her and was coping so brilliantly in lots of ways, and she couldn't, or wouldn't, read a word. When kids like that kicked off in a class reading *Macbeth* or doing simultaneous equations and threw a chair or called the teacher a wanker, everyone wrung their hands and wondered why.

Anyway, before Jasmine's arrival and any talk of reading recovery, he'd decided to do something about it: teach them to read. Although, that was proving more easily said than done. He didn't know where to start.

The morning he'd spoken to her at the library, she'd got a couple of the headscarf girls from Year 8 with her; she'd met them in her own time and brought them to join the library. Rob thought that was great and told her so, though the reason might have been the way she looked, dressed in a pink summer dress with a cardigan over her shoulders and her hair down.

He'd said he liked her dress and she'd laughed, but looked pleased. She said it was old and then held up her bag, a Burberry check handbag, as if it was a court exhibit.

And this is my mum's, don't get the wrong impression. A lot of my stuff's still in London.

When dyer get the rest of yer stuff from London, then?

She'd waved her hand as if to say it wasn't important.

Oh, some time in the next few weeks, I think.

He'd wanted to ask why her things were still in London. His mind started working on the possibilities. He'd wanted to ask but didn't feel that confident. He was careful not to ask any stupid questions, just grinning a big friendly smile and listening stupidly, a bit daunted, if he was honest, of Jasmine Quereishi, with her posh accent and the unfinished PhD she talked about, and her heart surgeon dad from Karachi, and her mother from Cinderheath, with her dark, shining eyes and perfect hair.

She said they should get together and talk more about

the whole reading thing and that he was right: loads of kids slipped through the net. Then she'd said something about how she had such happy memories of William Perry school. He'd nodded, feeling stupid and dumbstruck, unable to take his eyes from hers, and it was only later that he realized she hadn't looked away either.

See you Monday, she'd said, and turned and smiled as she went back to the girls filling out library membership forms. One of the girls was called Nasima; he'd seen her in basketball lessons and he waved over to them. When Jasmine got back to the table she said something and they all giggled. He found himself hoping she'd said something about him, about when they were kids, knowing the girls would try to tease her for talking to him.

He'd found a reading scheme on the internet for older kids and sent for a sample. It was great – boys always going off down the river to have adventures like Huckleberry Finn, each lesson on different phonic sounds. Structured, ordered. That's what you needed. Rob had learned things himself. The only problem was that it was an American system and cost a fortune. He'd been trying to suggest the school buy it but no one had seemed that interested. He could talk to Jasmine about it, find a way in.

Rob sat there at the window, watching the kids walk up the road. Some days he was timetabled to be on duty on the gates at the end of the day with the senior teachers and police, to keep an eye out for trouble, but not today. The idea was to keep a mix of people out there. This afternoon looked a good one to be doing it though, everyone going home calmly in their little gangs. There'd been a few bits of trouble lately, usually when adults or older brothers came down with some issue or the other. The arrests and now the election were hardly helping things.

He wanted to make a dash for it, as soon as the rush had gone, get up to the sports shop and buy a cheap pair of new boots. His Kings – the last evidence of him once being a decent player – had disintegrated. Then he could get to Tesco before the after-work rush. He cooked for his mum and dad on Thursday nights. He'd always done that, even when he lived with Karen. He'd always liked cooking, would maybe have tried to do something with it if he hadn't tried to make it with his football.

He flipped vaguely through the snakes book Andre had found for him, then leaned back and put his feet up on the radiator and watched the last of the crowds go through the school gates. He was trying to think of how to start a new conversation with Jasmine. He could always, of course, just ask her out for a drink, but he feared that she might wonder what the teaching assistant who strutted around in his football kit all day was doing thinking he had a chance with her. He might be nice to look at and they might have sat in the same classroom twenty years ago but, come off it. It hadn't felt quite like that, though. Maybe she'd like to chat about what had happened to the other kids who'd been in their class, to get nostalgic about when she lived around here. He wondered if she knew about Adnan, if he should mention it. He could dress it up as a big tragedy then offer a shoulder to cry on, or something. Actually, that was probably the way to do it.

A mixed group of girls – headscarves and hair bobbles – hurried through the gates, giggling and holding cooking dishes covered with tea towels.

Working hard, Rob? The new Head strolled past towards the office and didn't wait for a reply.

**When he'd seen the computer had gone from the corner of their room,** Zubair knew that Adnan meant to go for good. He'd been drifting. They hadn't been speaking to each other, but by that point Adnan wasn't really speaking to anyone. He'd do his taxi shift, always offering to work Friday and

Saturday lates, which brought in more money but more hassle too. Sometimes he'd stay to be dealt a hand in the perpetual game of cards that went on in the back of the cab office, but usually he'd just be home to the computer, eating at different times to everyone else, in front of the screen.

Zubair thought he had his own worries then. He'd been about to move out and get a flat with Katie. He hadn't told Adnan this, hadn't told anyone. He announced it one Saturday morning that autumn, with his bags already packed, his parents sitting there not saying anything, like they'd been turned to stone, wondering how they'd managed to lose two sons in the space of a couple of months. It bothered him now, that even amid the agony of his brother's disappearance his big concern had been moving in with Katie, not wanting to lose her. They could've waited, he thought now. It would've helped his mum and dad.

Weeks went by. His parents would look at him like he had the answers; his mother sitting rocking on the edge of the settee, his dad deflating, ageing in his chair. They tried the police and hospitals. There was a procedure for registering a missing person. If a man, boy, nearly twenty, with no obvious problems wanted to just walk away from his life, though, there was nothing much stopping him. Zubair knew his dad had tried stuff through the mosque. He wasn't sure anyone was that bothered, though. Some of them probably thought, bring your kids up as English, bad Muslims, then this is what you get.

In the summer before he left, Zubair remembered seeing Adnan flipping through an old London A–Z a couple of times. He'd almost asked him if he was thinking of going on a trip but they were barely speaking then. Adnan would've probably just grunted, shook his head, turned away. It was something to go on, though. The only thing they'd got to go on. Zubair bought an A–Z, closed his eyes, tried to picture the position of the book when he'd seen his brother looking at it.

On that first trip he'd stayed on Seven Sisters Road in one of the dubious hotels opposite the park. When a big lorry lumbered past, as they seemed to all through the night, the electricity flickered in the building and Zubair thought of the rats eating their way through wiring and then the walls. He ended up sitting in a chair and dozing intermittently in the reddish light that passed for dark, the shadows of vehicles on the main road circling through the room.

When he woke for the final time and pulled back the dirty net curtain, there was Finsbury Park in the bleak morning light, the flow of traffic absent for a moment; he could hear a bird singing, and there in the corner of the park someone had lit a fire, smoke curling upwards slowly, three or four shapes shuffled around it. A man with a huge bushy beard, wearing what looked like a monk's habit tied with rope, pushed a shopping trolley filled with bits of wood down the path towards the fire. He took a swig from a can he'd rested in the trolley's child seat. Zubair shook his head, rubbed his eyes and then his back, sore from his night in the chair. He thought about the way life could swallow people up; he saw it all the time at work. He shivered, showered and dressed quickly and walked to find a café; he needed to drink coffee and make a plan about what to do next, a plan about what to say to his parents.

He got breakfast in a café in Highbury in among road workers in luminous jackets, people in suits shuffling papers and talking too loudly, a young mother trying to man-oeuvre a pushchair. People lived on top of each other here. He could see a corner of one of the stands at the Arsenal ground through the window. The sun shone in across Zubair's coffee and scrambled eggs. The world seemed suddenly more intense and fragile than he could ever have imagined. He thought he might cry.

Zubair had been around, and prided himself in fact on a cynicism that was beyond his twenty-four years. It was turning him into a good solicitor, and this in turn was feeding his cynicism. Every day he sat with kids who'd stolen cars, climbed down through warehouse skylights, cut somebody for looking at them the wrong way, and he had to think of ways to keep them out of serious trouble. That morning, in London, he was conscious of how little he knew about anything.

He rode buses back and forth across the city. The bus from Highbury struggled up the hill like an arthritic old woman and on the downhill felt like it might not stop at all. Out the window, a hotchpotch: crumbling terraces, blocks of flats, grand villas, massage parlours, delicatessens, a Turkish restaurant, a Georgian restaurant, an Ethiopian restaurant, the Inns of Court, Oxford Street, Knightsbridge; it was a ride that became increasingly outlandish. How would you find someone in this labyrinth? How would you begin to look? He stared out of the bus window, thinking about Adnan, about what might have happened – dead in the river, wandering around London like the vagrant he'd seen that morning, amnesia from a bang on the head, mixed up in something dodgy, run away to get married, run away with a man, run away, run away – something had to fill a vacuum; stories would fill the space he'd left. Zubair had to admit there was a certain temptation to let yourself be swallowed. If everything could be so suspect, all certainties and identities so fragile, where did that leave you, where did that leave everything?

**The same ball again.** Walter Samuel hit it diagonally, in the air into the gap behind Cole again. There were groans. Rob took a gulp of his pint. His old man shuffled on his seat, leaned back. Tode yer, he said, thass the ball. The beer made Rob feel cold.

In the game against the mosque, Carl Jones took a throw. Rob dropped off, like he'd done thousands of times before, nodded and blinked at Carl, palms out. He had to take two more strides, say, Yes, Carl, before he got it. He wanted to take a touch, look up, hit a ball towards Glenn's run, but Carl was too slow, and he just had to knock the ball back, one touch, instep, towards Carl – and Tayub was across him, nipped in, out for another throw, a flash of Tayub's red boots, young and quick. Young and quick, young and quick, rattled around Rob's head. He told Carl to put the throw down the line next time.

**Yow've bin smoking in here again.**

I ay.

Jim, yow have. Why dyer lie to me? Havin all the winders open ay gonna tek the smell away just like that, yer know. Iss a nice day an all. If yer must have one, have one out the back. I thought yer was out canvassing, any road. Thought that was the point of having these days off.

No leaflets, nobody to help with the loudspeaker till tonight.

Well, that was a waste of time, then. Dyer want a sandwich? I've onny got half hour. I've gorra two o'clock appointment.

Pauline pulled open the cupboard with a sense of purpose. Yer should o bin dahn the salon. I've had some o the women from dahn the old people's flats in wi me. They've med me head goo rahnd. If I'd known yow was sittin here I'd a phoned an yow coulda done a surgery. Talk abaht moan.

They'm all bloody Tories, any road, Jim said.

Tories? Fascists, I think. Ooh, they think there's a bunch o terrorists plotting out the front o the flats, cos there's a carload of Asian lads that sits aht the front on a Sunday night smoking. It ay very pleasant, I spose, but young lads atta hang rahnd somewhere. Not that colour's anything to do with it. BNP's too left-wing for em. They just want everybody shot, I think. Oh, an they want the Merry Hill buses to stop tekkin schoolchildren, an they wanna know why the flats dahn Willow Road have had theer winders done again when iss meant to be theer turn. Dyer want this corned beef, the date's up today?

Arr, lovely. They might have a point about the winders, everything's gone in the wrong order after that row with the contractors.

Honestly, they moan abaht everything, though. Nothing's any good. I'm just surrounded by people moaning. How am yer, Gladys? *Not too good.* Lovely day, Olive. *Bit too hot for me.*

All right, calm down.

Calm down? Yow ay the one who's had to listen to it all morning or every day more like. Then they got on to the mosque. What am I supposed to say to em?

There were plans for a new mosque and community centre to be built on the Cinderheath works site that had been derelict for twenty years because of endless planning rows. The papers had been calling it a Supermosque. It didn't help that the old church next to the site was lying empty too, because the Church of England was too tight to fix the roof and wanted to pull it down and sell the land for houses or, more likely, to the mosque developers. People were blaming the council for the church as well as the mosque. Jim thought there was enough to blame the council for without picking on things that they had no control over.

The current mosque was in the old Dudley Road school building, but that was way too small and Friday prayers had started spilling out on to the street. At least that was in an Asian area, though. The roads that led up to the works site, furthest from the shops, furthest from anywhere, were the worst in the estate. Jim thought darkly that now they'd finally got a wrecking ball over the works site they could do worse than take the bloody church out and a few of the streets as well.

**There was a roar of approval, laughter and jeering and banging tables.** Batistuta looked up at the yellow card being held aloft by Collina. Collina's eyes bulged.

He's a good ref, him, ay he, Mark?

The best.

Right decision, that.

There was a close-up of Batistuta's face on the screen, his long hair matted and his face hollow like that of a saint. Glenn jumped up quickly, leaped in front of the screen, made his fingers into a circle, moving his wrist back and forth.

Batistuta, you wanker!

He'd jumped in front of the projector and Glenn's shadow appeared across the screen, monstrous, to loud cheers and a couple of voices shouting, Sit down! Rob looked at his dad and rolled his eyes.

**It was all about his standing foot.** People talked about the angle that Beckham ran up at, the speed with which he whipped his foot through the ball, the angle at which his foot made contact with the ball. Rob thought it was about his standing foot, his broken foot, the angle he planted it at, anchored himself. It was his foot that allowed the whip. It was all the other things as well, but it was his standing foot. Rob had been studying it. He reckoned you could prove it, work it out with maths and angles. He thought of Adnan, as always with things like this; you could work it out with a computer no doubt. Or you could stand, hour after hour, day after day, rain and shine, whacking free-kicks on some bleak wasteland on the edge of east London and Essex with no one watching or caring, or at Carrington with Cantona and Ferguson looking on, until it was burned into your muscles, a rhythm you could find in your sleep.

Rob was testing his theory with Patrick Richards and Leroy Moses, the best players at the school. Leroy was on terms at West Brom, Patrick was still playing in the junior teams at Cinderheath, waiting for the scouts to knock. Rob thought Patrick was the better player, for what it was worth; the scouts didn't know everything. They'd taken a bag of balls out to the Astro. Rob laid out an imaginary wall with cones. He'd chalked an X where they placed the ball and drawn a line where he wanted them to place their standing foot.

Patrick's foot went from underneath him the first time; he went crashing to the ground, the ball knocking over the cones like skittles.

Cor I just kick it like normal?

No.

Yome mekkin me look like a tit.

Nobody's watchin, mate. Nobody cares. One day they will, though, which is why we'm doing this.

Rob hit one, not bad, curled it inside the far post. There was definitely something in his theory. They all hit a couple each, trudged together to collect the balls up, walked back to the chalk marks. They hit another set. It started to drizzle with rain, blurring the chalk. Patrick hit a peach, it clipped the bar as it went in. A car horn sounded. It was Jasmine. Rob raised his hand and waved, tried not to look too delighted.

**As a teenager Adnan turned in on himself;** he had no choice, it seemed to him. He went through the motions with his school work, sat in their little bedroom, staring at the computer that had begun to dominate his life, at a torrent of zeros and ones, poring over manuals and magazines, teaching himself Machine Code, teaching himself how to bend things to his will. Work hard, their dad implored them, delighted; work hard, and make something of yourselves.

He'd look at the television, though, at clothes and cars that one day, somehow, he'd make his, pulling on his hand-me-down school trousers, going shiny at the knees, that he'd sewn Farah labels on to himself. His dad told them that hard work made you something, but his dad worked hard, all the hours he could now, since being made redundant and all it made him was knackered. He even said he was lucky, with his new job in a galvanizing place behind the Roman Mosaic when so many were out of work. He picked up some extra cash every now and again driving a taxi for Joey Khan, out until all hours on a Friday night. Work sets you free, he'd felt like painting over their entry wall in a fit of adolescent drama, like in the concentration camp photo in Zubair's history textbooks. It wasn't only this question though, the mysteries of work and money and the lack of any correlation between the two, that nagged away at him. He'd look at Rob and some of the others he'd grown up with, and their everyday glamour – football, fighting, girls – and he wanted that as well. He could make something of himself all right, like his dad said, sit in the corner and do his school work and concentrate on his computer, his zeros and ones, and make something of himself, as much as he'd be allowed to, anyway. More than anybody else he knew, he understood that. He understood how things fitted together; he was starting to understand how the world worked. That was the problem. He didn't just want to make something of himself; he wanted to make everything of himself. He wanted it all. Sometimes he'd look at himself in the bathroom mirror. Fuckin Paki, he'd mouth silently.

Zubair didn't get any of this. They'd stay up late talking across the narrow space between their beds. Zubair said he was going to do Law at university, become a solicitor. Their dad lapped it up. Adnan used to whisper in the dark that it was a good idea but what else, what then? They'd talk about cars and clothes and women, but he knew Zubair didn't mean it. To Zubair they were just dreams. He didn't realize that you could just go out and get what you wanted. Not if you worked hard enough but if you were strong enough. They'd get to the same point in the conversation and Zubair would say that he'd lost him, that he would settle for what he was doing thank you very much, now go to sleep. Adnan would never settle, he promised himself that.

If you were strong enough you could get things, but something was in the way, people who wanted to stop you, he knew that well enough. He read the books that Zubair brought back from college. They'd talk about them late at night. He didn't understand it all but he understood more than Zubair. He read about Germany in the twenties. All the rules the world made to keep the Germans poor. He read leaflets Zubair brought home about Palestine and the refugee camps in Lebanon, a badly copied edition of *The Elders of Zion*. He read about the camps and the ovens, about systems, about zeroes and ones, erasure, people turned into ash and smoke and clouds and then nothing at all. It was metaphor. It was code. People were in the way. It didn't matter who they were: Jews, Muslims, Aryans. It was the idea that mattered. There were people in the way who would stop him getting what he wanted. There were winners and losers, zeroes and ones.

Adnan turned in on himself. He read. He learned his code and practised this language, unadorned, pure, through which you could remake the world in your own image. He thought about erasure, about the transformation that would bring him everything he ever wanted.

**Rob parked on the wasteland at the side of the shops,** a meadow of rubble and condoms that ran down to the canalside wall. Zubair called it the Tourette's Wall. Rob glanced over to it. Someone had written PAKI POWER and painted a star and crescent on it, but at the other end he could see VOTE BNP and NO TO THE MOSQUE and BOING! BOING! It was all in the same red paint. The cans were probably on offer somewhere. Schizophrenia and Tourette's, he'd tell Zubair, try to raise a laugh. Underneath the red lettering and recently drawn tag names there were other fading hieroglyphics, WWFC and a misshapen wolf's head, SHERE-E-PANJAB. And underneath that, the lettering almost invisible but seemingly burned in there, WHO KILLED YUSUF KHAN?

Rob shivered. Zubair had admitted to him that he'd sprayed it up there a couple of times, when he was a student and had a few too many to drink, but he hadn't done the first ones. It had been all over the place for a while, got covered on the local news, got a report in the *Star*. Yusuf Khan wasn't even dead, they'd just kicked him halfway to it, that was part of the story.

This was one of the places cars would go missing from and then turn up with smashed windows and no wheels at the flats or burnt-out down Juniper Close. Rob never usually worried about that kind of thing, but the stolen flag had really annoyed him. From right outside the house. It was probably just some kid messing about, but everyone down the street knew his car. He'd had it long enough, a black Calibra that he'd paid the deposit on when he got a signing-on fee at Hereford. Now it was a bit battered, there was a dent in the passenger door and the wing mirror where he'd scraped a council van trying to park in Wolverhampton and a scratch mark where someone had keyed it. Standing looking at it, he thought he'd give it a wash over the weekend, wax and everything, see if he could get it looking like something. Then he'd put a flag back on.

A lot of the shops had seen better days. A couple of them were boarded up: the place that had been the trophy shop, and the baker's, complete with a rusting stopped clock above the yard gates. The post office had closed as well. There'd been a petition to keep it open that his Uncle Jim had organized. There were clusters of To Let signs on the flats above the shops, where Zubair had first lived with Katie, a couple of them had their windows bricked up. Three boys in Year 10 told him they'd got blow jobs in there from a girl in the year below for a tenner. Rob feared it had been Chelsey. What to say to that? He needed more training.

Was it a tenner each or for the three on yer?

For all on we, but onny Patrick was allowed to come cos her likes him.

There were signs of life as well, though. The pork sandwich shop and the chip shop were always busy. So too the halal butcher's and the launderette. In the middle of the row was Barrys' Shopping City, its sign glowing in red neon lighting that had been installed in the seventies and looked like something from the Vegas strip. The shop sold everything. When the new Tesco opened, everyone said Barrys' would close but it seemed to go from strength to strength, selling the stuff Tesco didn't, like giant inflatable George-and-Dragons, oil paintings of the Golden Temple, illuminated Qur'anic scripts and fireworks, cigarettes and bags of sweets to the schoolkids. Rob had to step into the road to get around the trestle tables sprawling across the pavement with their boxes of coriander and okra and sweet potato garlanded with St George's flags. The family that had started the shop (the Barrys) had all been eccentrics. The last Mr Barry to run it had kept a leopard in a cage on the roof and half the downstairs shop had been a tropical fish aquarium. Rob's mum would bring him down here when he was a kid to look at the leopard and the fish, say it was better than getting on the bus to the zoo and laugh. Rob remembered gazing at harlequins and tiger barbs and angelfish (the tanks were neatly labelled) in among the toilet rolls and batteries and tins of beans. The whole shop had an underwater, marine light to it still, years after the fish tanks had gone. Mr Barry had sold up in the eighties to a Sikh family, but the spirit stayed the same.

He'd just reached the ordered window of Dudley Road Sports – posters of Shoaib Akhtar and Inzaman in among a display of Brazil football shirts – when he first heard the shouts. Little Rhys Woodhouse came charging past him, knees pumping and his shaved head turning every few strides to look behind him. The Woodhouses were always running to or from some disaster. It was as he watched Rhys dodge in and out of Barrys' display that he heard shouts echoing from the flats.

Over the road, from out of an entryway, a boy in a hooded top staggered like a drunk towards the launderette step. There was something dripping from his sleeve. He stood bent over for a moment, one hand on the door-frame, like an old man, stopped short of breath.

It was Andre.

**Lee hacked it out of there towards their right back.** Rob trotted to his left, aware of Tayub alongside him, looked over his shoulder to get Lee and Kyle across with him but they were too slow. Always too slow. The ball went out again, so he could pull them over while they fetched the ball. Joey Khan was getting it. It had rolled in front of the parked cars. Rob had seen the one with the blue strip lights before – trailing him round while he leafleted for his Uncle Jim in an Asian area. There were shapes inside the cars and clouds of smoke from spliffs coming through sunroofs and open doors. Joey was wearing jogging bottoms tucked into his socks, a wax jacket and a checked cap. He looked like a gentleman farmer. Whenever the ball went off the sounds of the helicopter got louder.

**Her taxi driver from JFK was from Karachi.** When he asked her where she was from she said England, London, and that satisfied him for a while but she saw him studying her in the rear-view mirror when they stopped in traffic looking out across the Bedford-Stuyvesant projects, the people tiny on the sidewalks below, everything both strange and familiar, like in all great cities. Like in London, she thought, when she'd had to get a bus through Canning Town or Forest Gate, one foot in the West and one in Lagos or Dhaka. Usually she'd say that was great, such a mixture, a rich soup of people she'd tell her form class, but this brought about an unease in people as well; a kind of vertigo, like you didn't know where you were, who you were.

But your family? Where are they from?

I'm from England, she said, the Midlands, where Shakespeare was from. And Robin Hood. She stopped herself from laughing, that laugh that kept turning into a sob.

Robin Hood?

I live in London, now. My father's from Pakistan, she said. He works in a hospital in England.

Doctor?

A surgeon, a heart surgeon.

England's a great country, he said, like America.

As the traffic moved forward she became aware of the stars-and-stripes stickers in the corners of the taxi windows and the gold Arabic lettering hanging next to the air-freshener dangling from the mirror. She felt the conversation loaded with both the weight of falling buildings and the potential for being quizzed on her dad's background. He'd grown up in Karachi but, as he'd be quick to point out if he said anything about it at all, as a *mohajir*, a refugee. His family lived in India before partition.

How long have you been here? she asked.

Five years.

Have you had chance to go back?

Yes, last year for three months. Two months each year before that.

Do you have family back there?

Yes, my parents, my wife, my children.

That must be hard. Not being able to see them all the time.

I send them money every month. Some time soon maybe my wife can come here with the children. It is hard. Right now, I share an apartment with some other men. When there's enough money, they will come. God willing, he muttered like an afterthought.

When the car stopped again he pulled a photograph from the flap of the sunvisor, leaned back to show her. There was a woman, young and confident-looking, wearing jeans, staring straight into the camera, holding a baby while sitting on some stone steps that went down to the beach. The sea glittered behind them. The eldest child, a boy of about seven, wearing a Big Apple T-shirt, stared toughly at the camera. Next to him, a girl who must have been the boy's younger sister, shielding her eyes with one hand and reaching for a little boy who was trying to crawl away, down the steps to where the concrete ended and the beach began. Across the bottom half of the picture was the long diagonal of the photographer's shadow.

What are their names? How old are they?

This is Imran, eight, Munira, seven, Asif, two years and the baby, Usman.

They're beautiful, and your wife. And you? Jasmine said, pointing at the dark outline in the bottom half of the picture.

And me. I'm a shadow. I'm not good with the camera. Better in a car.

I think it's lovely, she said.

The traffic was flowing again; he put the picture back, began to change lanes.

The traffic's bad here, she said.

Here, yes, but have you been to Karachi?

He laughed softly at his own joke.

I've never been to Pakistan, she said quickly, embarrassed at the way conversations like this always went.

They turned off, zigzagged through the blocks of Polish delis in Greenpoint. She was staying in Williamsburg, a studio apartment of a friend of her friend Emilia. This friend of a friend had gone back to Kansas or Kentucky, Jasmine couldn't remember, maybe for a break, maybe for good, suddenly scared of city life. The attacks had come on her morning off from her job in a jewellery shop near the towers. Emilia told Jasmine the story of how her friend had raced up to Brooklyn Heights to watch the plume of ash.

You here to see family, friends? he asked. It's a good time to come. Cheap.

She couldn't tell if this was a joke.

No. No. I, erm, my boyfriend. He's missing. Was in New York in the attacks. Nobody knows where he is.

I'm sorry, he said.

She shouldn't really have said boyfriend. How should she refer to *him*? Lover, maybe, although that sounded inappropriately sophisticated. That suited him, maybe, but she didn't feel sophisticated. She felt duped, crushed, hollow.

She didn't even know which name she should use. When she thought of him she thought of him as Adnan, but he hadn't used the name for years.

I mean, he's probably dead, obviously. She heard both her parents' plain-speaking in the way she said this, outside of herself, almost. I mean, well I think he's dead but there's no record or anything.

I'm sorry.

They were sitting outside another Polish deli, pulled in against the kerb.

People are still being found, he said. In the hospitals, injured, turning up with no memories, bangs on the head, you see.

Jasmine wasn't so sure about this. She felt exhausted suddenly, wanted to lie down. There was the same kind of light as that morning, the shadows of trees and buildings were stark on the bleached asphalt street. A gull's shadow wobbled across the street in front of them as the bird flew towards the river.

We're here, he said. This is the address, ma'am.

He carried her bag to the shop door. She had to collect the keys from the deli. She paid him, tipped him clumsily.

Oh, what's your name, by the way? she asked.

Sammy.

Again that laugh on the cusp of a sob.

No, your real name.

Samir, he said, Samir.

Good luck, Samir. My name's Jasmine. I hope your wife and children can come soon.

Good luck to you, ma'am. I hope you find what you need.


**David Beckham, side-on to the ball, poised over a free-kick wide on the left,** a hush in the clubhouse. It was all about his broken standing foot. He didn't hit it properly, it

74

went straight into the wall and ballooned in the air. There were groans, Lee swore loudly, the first words he'd said since kick-off. Beckham tore after it, after his mistake, looked like he might go flying in but – shouts and screams – Beckham won the header and Batistuta ran into him. Another foul, a better position this time. Batistuta looked wild-eyed, riled.

Ref, eh, ref!

Jim turned his head and looked at Rob and his dad.

He's gotta be careful, here.

Eh, he's rattled, Batistuta.

Yow've wound him up, Glenn, look.

Good position, this.

Come on England.

A better position this. The ghost of the free-kick against Greece crept into Rob's head, where, when it mattered, his standing foot held firm, his body whipped through the ball, his head down over it. That inevitability as the ball swung through the air, hit the top corner like a bomb going off.

**Rob walked quickly.** Andre slumped on to the launderette step. Nancy, the launderette manager, came out and stood over Andre.

Woss happened, love? She touched Andre's shoulder.

All right, Andre. Rob crouched down in front of him. Woss the matter, mate? Andre didn't speak.

His left arm was hanging limp at his side. Blood dripped from his fingers poking out of the sleeve, a cartoon redness to it, like paint flicked across the pavement. Andre took shallow little breaths, his eyes fixed on the kerb, blinking. He was shivering and a stifled sob came from his chest.

Woss happened, mate?

Rob looked at Nancy, who shrugged to say she hadn't

seen anything. The rhythmic sound of the washers spinning came from inside the launderette. The blood dripped slowly. Andre rubbed his fingers together.

Was there a fight, Andre?

He nodded and closed his eyes for a moment.

Where you hurt, mate?

Again, the same nod. His voice came muffled through the hand at his face.

Stuck me.

OK, where, Andre? Where'd they stab yer, mate?

Rob heard Nancy gasp and saw her hand shoot to her mouth. Rob tried to breathe normally.

Phone an ambulance, Nance?

She held up her phone and took a couple of steps back into the launderette.

Where'd they stab yer, Andre? Wheer dyer hurt?

Andre shrugged and looked at Rob for the first time. His eyes were glassy. Rob thought of the picture of McGuigan losing the world title in the desert, that he'd cut out of the paper when he was a kid.

He felt that strange calm, the sort that descends when something's really bad, that shortness of breath. It was like when he found his dad lying on the front path, trying to work out just how bad it was. Nancy brought some towels from inside the launderette.

Wheer's it hurt yer, mate?

Rob was patting Andre's chest. He looked in his lap and up and down his legs for blood. There wasn't any.

Wheer's it hurt yer, mate?

Andre pulled his good hand from his face. There was a gash across his cheek. There was a line of blood and snot coming from his nose. The snot clung to his hand as he pulled it away. The cut on his face looked bad but wasn't deep.

Is it yer face, mate? Did they hurt yer anywhere else?

Andre looked down his left arm to his bloody fingers. Rob found a hole in the shoulder of his school sweatshirt and pulled at it. Andre flinched. Through the hole, the T-shirt underneath was torn; Rob got both hands at the material, tore it wider. There was a jagged wound underneath, oozing blood, again not deep, across his armpit and high on his shoulder.

Nowhere else mate, no? Yer face an yer arm. Jus yer face an yer arm. Yome OK.

Andre's breath came out in another judder.

Inhaler, he said with a stutter.

Rob patted at his pockets again, felt the lump of the asthma inhaler inside the sweatshirt, pulled it out.

Andre took the thing with his good hand, pumped it in his mouth.

Yome OK. Just try and breathe normal. Just shocked. Thass it. In an out, deep breaths.

Andre nodded, winced.

Iss all right, mate. Yome all right. Rob reached out and touched Andre's head, stroked his hair. There was cold sweat on the boy's head. He was shivering.

There were more people now, the women from the till in Barrys' and the bloke from the chip shop. Rob could hear a woman's voice saying hysterically, Iss just all the while, all the while, this is now. She had a little dog on a lead. It tried to lick one of the spots of blood. There was a siren coming from somewhere.

Another woman appeared. She was wearing slippers and a dressing gown. She came right up next to Rob.

I've just sin em aht the back winder. I was washin me hair. All over him, they was. All over him. On top on him while he was on the ground. They rid off on bikes, the ones that done it, some on em. They was cheering an whooping. Had that camouflage on. I sin em. Had him off his bike. Like animals they was, on top on him. Yer might know who. All over him.

A police car arrived, the siren deafening. Two police, a man and a woman, started asking who'd seen what.

The woman who'd seen something from her window heard someone say he'd been stabbed and now kept repeating, He's bin stabbed? He's bin stabbed? in a high-pitched whine. Rob was looking at Andre saying, He's just hurt a bit. Iss OK, mate. Iss OK. Yow'll be OK.

**Zubair used to joke to him that their dad was a good Muslim because Friday was his holy day:** pay day. Their old man loved work, believed in it in a way that seemed to fill any spiritual gap left by his less than enthusiastic mosque attendance. It wasn't just about money, though – even though he'd urge them that if they worked hard they'd get on – it was as though the physical act of work itself, any work, could cleanse you like prayer was meant to.

The summer he was eighteen Adnan picked up work through job agencies – odd days packing and lifting here and there – which paid for some driving lessons. He hadn't applied for university – his grades were good, everyone assumed he would – just drifted. He didn't like the places the agencies sent him to, units on new industrial estates or factories that had clung on through the bad years, depleted workforces rattling around in cavernous buildings. His jobs – the jobs they called the agency for – were always somehow removed from whatever the normal business was. So in a factory that pressed farm animal feeders he pulled up old carpet in the foreman's office. In a factory that made drinks coolers for pubs he sorted screws into plastic cartons. In a warehouse of flat-packed furniture he spent a day wrapping pallets laden with boxes of chocolate in cling-film. This, combined with the fact that he'd only be there for a few days at most, gave him a sense of separation that suited him. It was an odd time, then. He'd spent the year catching two buses to the old grammar school sixth-form in Stourbridge where the brightest students went, a handful of clever Asian kids all getting the same bus at Dudley bus station. A Sikh lad from Himley Road he sometimes sat with had come up with a collective nickname for them – the Tokens.

Early that summer Rob had seen him at the bus-stop, pulled in to give him a lift in the little car he was obviously so proud of. He'd got through his first year at the Villa; over the loud dance music on the car stereo he told him a story about how skilful Dwight Yorke was, about going for a drink with some of the first team at the Belfry on a Monday night, full of himself. He was about to go off on holiday to Crete with Karen Woodhouse. There was a small picture of her stuck to the sunvisor on the driver's side, her head back laughing in the sunshine, holding a bottle of beer halfway to her lips, her spare hand waving as if to stop the photo being taken, its shadow merging with the photographer's as it fell across her brown legs.

When he got out of the car and Rob pulled away he'd stood on the pavement for a while, thinking about the photo, his clothes prickling on him in the sun's warmth. He remembered a few years earlier when he and Rob had sneaked up the cinema fire exit to watch *Back to the Future* three times in a row. In the film, characters would start to fade from photographs if someone interfered with the past. That was what he felt like now, like he was fading away. He looked at his watery shadow on the pavement. In one of Zubair's history books he'd read how shadows in Hiroshima were burned into the ground, the people who'd cast them blasted into nothing.

Adnan sat apart in work canteens, far enough away to

be separate, close enough to torture himself with the mocking or aggressive looks he got from boys his own age or men as old as his dad.

Wheer yow from, mate?

Dudley. Cinderheath.

No, wheer'm yer originally from?

Me family's from Pakistan. Well, Kashmir, I spose. He pictured his mum mouthing counting games and stories of the mountains in Pahari to Tayub.

Why doh yer fuck off back theer then?

That was a conversation with a bloke with an Elvis quiff driving a fork-lift at a place in Tipton. Usually things were a bit more subtle. If there were women at a place there was more conversation.

Ay it strange for yer, working here, like. Wouldn't it be better with yer own kind?

Dyer like curry, Adnan? I love it, I dun. We have a Chicken Tikka Masala every Friday.

He is good lookin, ay he, this un. Like that cricketer, whossisnaeme, Imran Khan. They send us some lovely-lookin lads from up Dudley, doh they?

He didn't know why he was doing it, what he was looking for. There was other work, office stuff, data entry, where things wouldn't have been such a battle, easier work too, but he always turned that down. He had other money coming in as well. He'd sold a couple of little programs he'd sent to a games magazine, adjustments and cheats for a simulation game where you played God and built a world from scratch. Most of the time he just felt he was waiting for something.

He got a day in a warehouse over the back from his dad's place. He spent the morning loading boxes of hinges into a van. The people who'd bought the site were saving stock before they pulled the factory building down. There were people working on a last order as the place got pulled apart around them. At dinnertime he stood in the queue at the sandwich van and could see right across the yards into his dad's work canteen. He saw him sitting there, at the end of one of the long tables, alone, eating slowly.

Through another door he could see a group of men – white and black, all ages – looking down the table or across the tables, he couldn't see for the wall between the two doors, looking towards his dad, all laughing.

Adnan turned away, looked at the woman cutting sandwiches at the van hatch, blinked. It was all he could do to get his words out when she asked him what he wanted. What he wanted was to grab that knife from her hand and slit her freckled throat. That was what he wanted. Then to do the same to all of them. When he glanced back his old man was standing outside, lighting a cigarette. A group of young white men stood at the other end of the building, doing the same.

Woss yer naeme, our kid? the supervisor had asked him that afternoon, standing on the canal towpath as they filled a skip.

Wayne, he said, me name's Wayne.

**The free-kick came to nothing.**
Iss too much on him. He ay fit, yer know. His dad's voice kept going in his ear. Jim turned, motioned with his pint glass. Rob nodded. Then Owen was away, wriggling clear of defenders, like a little kid running excitedly towards a swimming pool, not completely away, though. Corner ball! Pressure building now.

Come on England!

**Jim sat in his car and looked at the off-white bulk of the hospital looming over him.** In the rain it looked like one of those supertankers you'd see on the news from time to time, flipped over in the sea spilling oil from its belly. He wondered if this was what the mosque would look like, as it was what all new buildings looked like, concrete discolouring in the rain. It would be like dying in a shopping centre or art gallery. Then he thought about the old, dark nest of workhouse buildings at Dudley Guest and Burton Road hospitals, the weeks that summer going back and forth with his dad, and decided that some modern things were better after all.

If the lad died, there were real problems.

Stacey had phoned him from a police car and left a panicked message on his voicemail. Her phone was switched off now.

Jim lit a cigarette and sat looking at the entrance doors, scared to go in. He knew he should've been thinking about the boy, about Stacey at least, but all he could think about was how bad things would get if he was dead. He and Jackie, Tom and Kathleen, had taken turns to look after Glenn and Stacey a couple of times a week when they were kids, when things were difficult. The dad, never around much anyway, got sent down for a long time, their mother implicated as well, running a group of prostitutes in Walsall. Serious crime; serious shame. Their families went back a long way, but there was no need to be so involved now.

This boy Andre was no angel from what Jim could make out – the sins of the fathers, grandfathers, he supposed – not that it meant it was all right for him to get stabbed riding his bike to the chip shop to fetch his mother and sister's tea. You could see how bad it looked. How bad it was.

Pauline was annoyed because she'd made a meal early so they could eat together. It was her college night: aromatherapy. Last term it had been flower arranging. Before that, Beginner's Spanish that she'd tried to persuade him to come to. He needed to learn some, if they were going to move there, but he struggled with languages. He'd tried those Urdu classes years ago and hadn't picked up a thing.

An what abaht yer own son? Pauline had hissed at him as he'd pulled his shoes on. Michael had just sneaked back into the house, two hours late from school, with no explanation, wearing one of those army coats the kids were going mad for. God knows where that had come from. It struck Jim that it might be a good thing Michael had stayed out, instead of his arse being glued to the chair and his eyes to the computer screen, but he thought that best left unsaid. Pauline waved around the knife that she'd been chopping tomatoes with. They'd got salad, part of her continuous health kick.

Iss allus other people's children come first is what I can see.

Wiv had all this before, love. Yer know why I atta do it.

It ull be a bloody relief if yer do lose this election, honestly.

Yer doh mean tha.

Pauline was shaking her head and pacing up and down the hall. He could tell the worst was over. Her temper would blow suddenly and just as quickly subside.

Come here, she said.

Yow ay gonna have a goo, am yer? he said, looking at the knife, a face of mock-terror.

Doh joke abaht things like that, I'll see yer later. She kissed him on the cheek and shouted upstairs to tell Michael his dad had to go out. There was no response. They both sighed.

He'd parked by the side entrance. There was a lifelike sculpture of a dog outside the doors, its nose down as if it had smelled something interesting in the verge of wood-chip and saplings. Someone had rested an empty beer can up against its nose. It looked lonely and forlorn against the giant building. Jim wondered what use it was in the healing of the sick. He patted the dog's head on the way in and walked down the long, bright corridor.

**Zubair went back to London three or four times.** He didn't know what he was doing really; Adnan had gone, he knew that. This was as much about himself. He'd gone through the motions, had taken photocopies of a recent photo of Adnan, gave them out at minicab offices. He'd get back in and his dad would look up from his armchair and Zubair would shake his head, explain quietly what he'd done.

He took Katie with him to London. They stayed in different hotels near the British Museum, rode around in taxis. He was sticking it all on a new credit card, wanted to impress her. One afternoon they wandered into the museum out of the rain. They stared dumbly at the exhibits: smashed fragments from the corners of the Empire. He told her how this stuff was stolen from countries that Britain had invaded, just because he felt he should. She shrugged and tried to make him laugh, impersonating the security guards and Japanese tourists. In the Asian room they stared at a little wooden plaque showing a carved picture of a skeletal god dancing to a band of devils. He told her it came from near where his family was from. They slipped out of the museum, back to the hotel, drank Southern Comfort and Coke in bed and didn't come out until next morning. While they were shrouded in the damp sheets, he told her that he'd look after her, that he'd marry her.

Next morning he woke up thick-headed and guilty, feeling that Adnan was a receding speck.

**There was no shape for ages; nobody could put their foot on the ball,** just got rid of it if it came to them. Whole matches seemed to pass like this on Sunday mornings, whole seasons.

84

Their keeper kicked it straight up in the air.

Rob's ball!

He had to make twenty, twenty-five yards to come and meet it. Paul Hill had to duck with the shout because the ball was coming down straight on top of him but Rob was coming now, and he made it, sure enough, but that was all, he knocked Paul flying. He should've tried to bring the ball down, a player of his so-called ability, but there'd have been no one to aim it at anyway. Glenn was complaining to Mark Stanley about something. The ball went back over the top and through to their keeper who bowled it out to Zubair's feet. Rob had to turn and make up ground to get back alongside the lad with the shapes cut in his beard who'd pushed on, pointing and banging his chest.

All right, Sinbad, calm down, Rob muttered, then felt ashamed, glad the bloke hadn't heard him. He was even more annoyed with himself now, for playing in this shambles at all, for getting drawn into all this nonsense, for not being able to get hold of it, for not being able to bend things to his will.

**Jim was surprised to see Rob sitting in the café that faced the lifts.**

What yow doin here? he said in a too-loud and hearty voice.

All right, Uncle Jim? Yer wouldn't believe whass happened now. Yer know Andre, Stacey's lad. He's got himself in some bother dahn the shops, after school. I was up theer, at the shops, like. He's bin cut with a knife. It looked really bad.

It looked really bad? So he's all right, then?

He's all right. Lucky. It looked really bad. I thought, yer know.

There were two stab wounds on the shoulder. He also

had a gash across his face that looked like it might turn into a scar like Action Man's. That's what Rob had told Andre to get a smile from him in A&E. As well as that, the doctors thought he'd got cracked ribs.

But he's all right?

He's all right, arr. I mean, he's hurt. He ay in danger. They wanna keep him in. He's pretty shook up, yer know, shock an that, I think. What yow here for? Everythin all right?

I'm here for this.

How'd yow know abaht it?

Stacey left me a voicemail.

Rob raised his eyebrows.

I've been helping her with her tax credit forms. Her's in a bit of a mess, tell yer the truth. Got a loan out to get some stuff for the flat. I've sorted her out some work behind the bar at the club. Cash in hand, yer know. Yer know the little girl, summat the matter with her an all, yer know, well, God knows what, tantrums an everything, allus cryin. Her's at William Perry but they cor deal with her. Her needs summat else, yer know, but they cor even figure aht woss wrong wi her. But the boy's all right? Thank the Lord for that.

Jim sat down heavily, shaking his head, irritated now at having raced out and upset Pauline.

What a family, eh?

He looked at Rob's half-drunk cup of tea and began to get back up. Dyer want another cup? I'll text her to say I'm here. Her's up on the ward yer say?

I'll get em. Rob got up, sticking his hand into his tracksuit pocket.

While Rob was at the counter, Jim settled himself. He'd have to stop over-reacting, getting too involved with this sort of stuff. Young lads had always fought one another and anyone who thought knives were a new thing was kidding themselves. There'd always been trouble if you went looking for it.

So, what, dyer work wi this lad?

Arr. To be honest with yer I'm tryin to teach him to read. He can barely read a word.

He's a big lad though, ay he. How's he do his lessons? Jim was looking round for more sugar from somewhere.

He's sent aht on a lot on em, wanders the corridors. Puts his head dahn on the desk if he's in a lesson, gets by, yer know.

What, is he dyslexic or got some sort o problem or summat?

I dunno, maybe. I ay no expert, so maybe he has, I doh know. There must be summat the matter with him, I spose. Nobody seems to think so or do anything abaht it though. But the thing is, there's loads on em.

Loads of who?

Kids who cor read. I mean properly cor read. Nothing else wrong wi em.

What dyer mean? They can read a bit.

A bit maybe, but, I mean, just a few words. I'm talking abaht fourteen-, fifteen-year-olds.

Well, the school's had its problems, but the results am gooin up an they've done well to get this new Head in. We've done well to get her in. Her's worked all over, Birmingham, London. There's allus gonna be some problems an with some kids not speakin English at um.

I ay on abaht the Asian kids. What I mean is, it ay just the Asian kids. Of course, if yow've onny spoke Urdu or Punjabi or whatever at home that might be a problem but there ay many of them. No, I'm on abaht white kids, black kids, English-speakin, yer know.

Jim really didn't want this conversation. He didn't want to hear it. For one thing, the school was improving and had done out of all recognition over the past few years.

There was new building work, the results were up. It was racially mixed, unlike the primary schools. It was a success, a bloody good school. It would do even better with this new Head. They'd been lucky to get her. Rob wasn't a teacher anyway.

Any road, what happened up at the shops, then?

Rob told him what he'd seen.

When he said summat abaht a knife an the state he was in, yer know. Jesus, I thought, this is it, thought it was really serious, yer know.

Jim sighed. So what happens now? Andre brings all his mates an theer dads to get em back.

No, I doh think so. He's a bit of a loner. He ay got no mates, really. He tries to hang arahnd wi kids dahn the shops but they doh like him, to be honest. Iss sad. Iss allus them sort that get it though, ay it? Yome right to worry, though. What if they'd come dahn theer an stuck summat in one of the Woodhouses or John-Paul or Kelvin, other kids I work with, yer know. In fact, I'd just sin Rhys Woodhouse up to no good abaht a minute befower. We'd have a war to worry abaht. Somebody ud get killed. The papers ud have summat to write abaht then. They was pretty much right in the flats. If it was the older crowd that come up theer an had bin caught, well.

Rob blew his cheeks out. Jim hated this idea of separate areas but it was true: a gang of Asian lads turning up for a fight at the flats was a real problem. Half the estate would come out after them. He sipped his tea.

Glenn?

What dyer mean?

Dyer reckon he might start tekkin an interest in his sister, all of a sudden, now his nephew's bin stabbed, or whatever yer call it? Especially with all his new mates.

Jesus. I dunno. Iss bin a long time. He stopped speaking to her long before her even got pregnant, yer know. We hadn't left school when he stopped. Her never used to have any dinner money an Glenn ud have some off his grandad, but wouldn't share it. Wouldn't look at her. Mom used to give me a bit extra to give to her some days.

I know. I gid it yer mother.

Jim enjoyed telling him this as it came out of his mouth, then regretted it immediately. They sat there quietly for a while.

It ull suit that lot dahn to the ground though, woh it? Asian gang rampaging into the estate, law and order and all that. Rob smiled and shook his head.

Thass what I'm worried abaht. What abaht the police?

They was theer quick. The woman that sin it phoned em. An Nancy, yer know, our Nancy, from the launderette, phoned an ambulance.

What they said?

They've took statements. I've given one. It was short though, cos I day see what happened. I doubt if Andre's gonna wanna say much. He's bin in trouble before an that.

Yer doh say.

Jim leaned back, feeling claustrophobic in the the small, fixed plastic chair and flickering artificial light. An old couple walked past slowly towards the lifts, the man in a shirt and tie, the woman with some grapes. They lived in the Priory Court flats, the old man had come to see him about the lighting on the back steps and Jim had got the housing association to sort it out. They said hello to him. The woman called him councillor. It made him feel good.

Ah, keeping it quiet ull be for the best, maybe, he said, stretching his arms across the back of the little chairs.

Thass great, except somebody walks rahnd with a knife havin nearly killed a kid this afternoon. Woman that sid it said there was loads on em. Andre had a fight with a lad called Jabar back end o last year. I know Jabar's brothers. I assume they did this, like.

Meks it worse sometimes though, doh it? Teks months to come to court, the risk of other stuff happenin, it ull all be in the papers.

Maybe the Woodies have got it right then, eh? Keep yer mouth shut and sort yer own problems out.

Woodhouse was one of the notorious names of Cinderheath, a huge, sprawling family of endless cousins and step- and half-siblings, not just a name now, more like shorthand for a way of life. They'd been around a long time. An older Woodhouse had been a bareknuckle fighter years before. He turned up in articles in the *Bugle* every now and then and there was a picture of him up in the new Wetherspoon's next to the Slasher.

Jim knew this was a touchy subject with Rob. He'd lived with Karen Woodhouse for years. She was a lovely girl, lovely looking. She'd left him in the end. It was after that that Jim had phoned Steve Cummings to see if there was any work down at the school for him. Before that Rob wouldn't come out of the house, his football going nowhere, his mother worrying herself sick.

Still, everyone had their bad times. Before he'd met Pauline, after Jackie had left, Jim had gone to pieces. He'd been younger than Rob. Where did the time go? He'd filled his days with party meetings, football, drinking, whatever overtime he could get. Filled his time, otherwise – otherwise it might've been really bad.

He used to turn up at his mum and dad's for a decent meal a couple of nights a week. The Winter of Discontent they called it now. Those months were the worst. It was how he'd ended up a councillor. He'd started to go to more and more party meetings to keep out of the pub for as long as he could; threw himself into it, playing less football as he reached his thirties. As the pain started to get easier, he thought he might meet someone else like Jackie. It didn't work, not in that sense, anyway. He met

Pauline much later, when she came in her little van to do his mother's hair.

Sometimes you just atta be brave, yer know, he heard Rob saying, waiting for a response. Rob had been dwelling on things more and more, lately. That had been his undoing as a player, Jim reckoned: over-thinking. You needed to get on with things.

There's a lot of things yow atta stand up to, mate. Yer just have to pick the battles yer can win, he said.

Jim wanted to sound as if he knew what he was talking about, but he wasn't sure what he meant, what he thought, at all.

**The Argentinian keeper, Cavallero, was suddenly underneath the ball** as a cross swung into the area. He got a punch on it and Ferdinand went in and flattened him. Something went through the crowd in the Cinderheath clubhouse, like a change in the voltage, with the sense that things were building here, an England goal was coming.

There'd been jeers for the prostrate keeper but it was Hargreaves, in close-up on the screen now, still shaking his head, who was limping off.

He's finished.

Thass a loss, Hargreaves gooin off, thass a big loss. Glenn was talking loudly again to whoever might be listening.

Trevor Sinclair was going to replace him. He looked nervous. Fair enough, Rob thought.

It makes yer think. There's some lucky players on theer, yer know, Danny Mills, Trevor Sinclair, some lucky players with the injuries. I mean, we ay got much strength in depth, have we? I spose Sven knows what he's doin. I quite like that Danny Mills, mind yer. He's havin a decent go of it today, iss the left-hand side thass bin the problem. He's game enough, but winning the World Cup? I doh know.

Rob turned to his dad, surprised by this lengthy speech.

Rob could never really tell what was going through his old man's head. He knew he liked Sven, essentially believed that all Europeans, foreigners in general, had an innately superior knowledge of football than the English. But of all the players on show, Danny Mills was perhaps least like the type of player his old man usually rated: no first touch, all hard work, graceless, shaven-headed and menacing, the old image of English football abroad – before Beckham and Owen turned them all into the Beatles – the very opposite of the kind of player the legendary Tom Catesby had been.

**The night Tom Catesby saw Puskas and Czibor, Machos and Kocsis at Molineux** was the moment everything fell into place for him. There were fifty-odd thousand at the ground that night but Tom thought they were playing just for him, just to show him what it was his life was for.

That first half, sitting in between the apprentices and the older squad players who hadn't been picked, Stan Cullis's back to him as was usual, might have been the happiest in his life. Monday 13th December 1954, Wolves v. Honved. The unofficial European Cup Final, the unofficial club championship of the world. The way the Hungarians moved, the way one minute Puskas would stroll out from the middle of the park to be here on the wing and the way there'd be someone else to take his place, that movement, and the way he might trot back again and take about three markers with him and the ball would end up in the space he'd left, at Czibor's feet, was mesmerizing. Puskas waddled, pot-bellied, pointed, then would ghost into position, take a touch, strike it clearly and purely out of the mud. Instead of the stop-start, bang, bang, huff and puff stuff that was played up and down England there was this. Football like water, like dancing, like light.

Honved were two-up at half-time. It had been the most beautiful thing he'd ever seen. Cullis got the Wolves organized in the second half; they huffed and puffed, and the crowd roared, and the Hungarians' legs got slower in the Molineux mud. The Wolves players, good players, great players some of them, Tom knew that, were stronger. The Honved players were at the end of a world tour. When Shorthouse banged the third in, people were going crazy – Wolves, the best club side in the world – but it didn't matter to Tom. They could have scored ten in that second half. He'd seen his future in the first.

There'd been jobs to do at the end. The place was going berserk. He'd wanted to get near to the Hungarians, maybe even try to get Puskas's autograph. Instead, later, he swept out the dried mud from the Honved dressing room, wandered around the grandstand's empty insides. As he was sweeping, moving lighter and lighter on his feet, even in the heavy boots he was wearing, he felt like he was barely touching the ground at all, like he could run across the Molineux mud and leave no footprints.

He was the last to leave and floated up to Dudley Road to get the trolleybus, the crowds long gone. As it rattled along uphill, Tom remembered the feeling, like the trolley-bus itself was suddenly floating above the cobbles, as if everything was capable of moving like the Hungarians, as if everything was suddenly lighter – and of course it couldn't be – but he could be. This knowledge hardened into certainty as the trolleybus made a little whoosh down the hill into Gornal – how it could change his life, take him away from here, turn him into something new.

**What abaht this game? Jim asked.** Yer still playin? I'm sorry abaht havin a goo at yer this morning.

Rob looked uncomfortable and shrugged. I'm gonna play in it. I meant what I said. It is just a game. It is ower team. He shrugged again. I might pack it in then, though, call it a day. I've had enough. I'm thirty next year.

Thirty's no age, son.

Depends how you look at it. I could probably book a holiday and not have to worry about anybody ringing me up for pre-season.

Am yer gooin on holiday, then?

Rob smiled and shook his head. They sat and watched the people hurrying for visiting hours.

Stacey emerged from the lifts. She looked tired and pale. Without any make-up on she looked young, younger than she actually was. Too young for all this anyway, Jim thought. She'd had Andre when she was fifteen. It had caused a lot of fuss at the time. Her hands were tucked into the sleeves of her red hooded top, little wisps of tissue paper coming from the end of each sleeve.

All right, she said quietly.

All right, love, Jim said, and touched her arm gently.

Stacey nodded and stared at Rob. She'd already given him a mouthful of what she thought of the school at Andre's bedside in A&E, barely looking at him.

Doh, Mom, Rob's all right, Andre had said, through dry lips.

Police have onny just finished, she said, still quiet but spitting the words out now. Wanted a statement off him. Stood guard while we waited to be sin. I'm surprised they day arrest him. He's bin blamed for everything else why not gerrin stabbed?

They'm keeping him in, ay they?

Arr, but I'll atta fetch Gemma now.

The doctor and health visitor kept fobbing Stacey off about Gemma. Jim thought he might go with her to the surgery himself, insist they refer the girl to a paediatrician or somebody. Gemma would go wild, flinging herself around the place, hurling herself into walls and doors, screaming, kicking, biting. Stacey had told Jim how late Gemma'd been to sit up, walk – but that nobody would listen to her.

What did the doctors say about Andre? Jim asked.

Said he's OK. He's lucky. Depends how you look at it, I said. It ay that lucky havin a load o kids jump on yer and –

She began to well up. Jim put his hand out to her but she waved him away, fumbled with her tissue.

I'm all right. Iss all right. They just wanna keep him in for observation. The policeman's still standin at the end of his bed. I've tode him not to say nuthin. They've glued his face, said it woh scar as much as stitches. It looks bad where . . . yer know . . . iss weeping rahnd the stitches on his shoulder. Iss all jagged on his shoulder an tha. He's bin pestering abaht where his bike is, so he must be all right. She smiled, took a deep breath, smaller tears than before rolling down her cheeks.

What abaht now?

I'll atta fetch Gemma in a minute. Her's wi me neighbour. Yer know, Gloria, the nice one. I've said I'll come back here fust thing in the morning. They've got me mobile number up on the ward. I'll atta get Gemma back an settled.

Nobody could have her tonight?

Stacey shook her head. Jim thought briefly he could offer to look after Gemma or have them both round for the night. He pictured what Pauline's face would be like when she got in and found out. It would be her doing the looking after, admittedly.

All right, I'll tek yer back.

Iss all right. I'll do it, if yer want, Rob said.

Actually, if that is all right, Jim said. It meant he'd beat Pauline back from college. He might even be able to do a bit of election thinking or try a conversation with Michael.

Stacey shrugged, nodded, stopped crying.

**Owen was in again, this time, clear through, yes!**

Yes! Jim leaped forward in his chair and in front of Rob, who didn't see the ball as it hit the post. Beer splashed across the tablecloths. A woman screamed from the back of the room. Rob jumped up and the ball wasn't where it was meant to be, wasn't nestled in the back of the goal. Instead Owen was looking skyward, jogging back, his mouth a kind of rictus. Rob stayed standing. There was no one behind him here, next to the bar, just the fruit machine blinking with the gold of a pirate's chest. He reached for his cigarettes and lit one, dragged on it heavily. His dad glanced up at him and then back at the screen, shaking his head slightly.

Jim had slumped back into his chair, a big hand patting his chest then reaching out to right the spilled drink, his own, calling to Stacey, who was chewing her nails behind the beer pumps, to replace his pint. Rob watched Stacey as she turned to pour the pint, her body moving under her top.

That might have been it. The one chance. That might have been it in a game like this, cagey, jumpy, nobody really at ease. Rob sucked so hard on the cigarette it gave him a headrush, like that first time he'd tried one on the seafront with Adnan.

**A taxi driver got kicked nearly to death.** It was a few weeks after Italia 90. The things were linked in Adnan's mind because of the way he found himself – involuntarily it seemed – leaping with excitement when Cameroon had gone two-one up against England in the quarter-final. Zubair looked at him askance. Before that he'd been delighted when Platt scored his miracle goal against Belgium. He was his mate Rob's team-mate, club captain, after all, and he grasped at this vicarious sense of belonging. But when Cameroon surged forward against England he couldn't help himself, spurred on by the agonized groans he could hear coming from houses and pubs through the tiny bedroom's open window, thrilled by the shiny black bodies that overran England, the looks of horror on English faces.

Zubair looked like he was going to kill him and punched the air in front of his face when England equalized and then scored again. They never talked about it afterwards. They were talking less and less. Adnan settled for feeling quietly satisfied when Pearce and Waddle missed their penalties against Germany, became as subdued as his brother, who sat there with his head in his hands, thinking about defeat.

Yusuf Khan got pushed round in a wheelchair making grunting noises, got fed through a tube. His teenage wife had to learn to change his catheter and colostomy bag. It had been on *Midlands Today*. The mosque was raising money for him. Adnan saw them sometimes. The wheelchair was hard to steer over the broken pavement; it was too heavy for her. He'd lurch about in the seat like he was doing a dance.

There was a Black Country story from the war. Adnan had read it in the library. A woman's body was found in a hollow tree trunk on the Clent Hills near the gypsy camp. Her hand had been removed, the way that witches do for spells. About the time the woman had been killed, two German airmen had parachuted into the woods. There had been a spy ring in the area, guiding bombers to munitions factories. The body was never identified. There were all sorts of stories: gypsies, witches, spies. Then graffiti started appearing in Hagley, in Stourbridge and around, up in Dudley, WHO PUT BELLA IN THE WYCH ELM? No one knew who was writing it. It had continued, on and off, for forty years. No one knew any answers. Stories filled the gaps.

Adnan bought a can of green aerosol from Barrys', crept out one night and wrote in neat letters, even though his legs were shaking, on the old dairy wall, WHO KILLED YUSUF KHAN?

For a while it took on a life of its own. Like the Bella graffiti must have done, he supposed. Some of the university students took it up as a slogan, in a half-hearted campaign to look for the attackers. One night Zubair told him that he'd sprayed it on the wall by the bridge that ran down to Dudley Port. Adnan didn't say anything, for the first time in ages feeling a bit of control.

**They walked across the car park.** She still hadn't looked at him.

Andre's reading's coming on, he said, for something to say.

Doin him a lot of good. Start working with him when he's nearly thirteen. We'm the back o the queue as usual. They have reading groups for the ones who doh spake English right from the start.

Rob didn't reply, instead he nodded towards his car and paused to let a 4x4 drive past. The woman at the wheel turned and aimed a slap at two boys squabbling in the back seat. He could hear them all shouting as the jeep slowed for the exit gate.

Stacey had gone ahead of him. She walked up to a shiny silver BMW that was parked next to his car. Rob just walked to the battered Calibra and only looked at her when he had the driver's door half-open, smiling.

She almost smiled back at him, mouthed, Sorry, pushed some hair back from her face and smoothed it behind her ear.

I thought yow'd a bin drivin a fancy car, what with yer football an all that.

This used to be a fancy car.

Used to be.

I used to be a footballer.

We're gonna let you go, Robert. Ron Atkinson had looked at him, right at him, in the eye. Rob couldn't even be angry with him, not like the others coming out of the office, crying and swearing or both. The gaffer had the guts to say what he thought, straight to him, better than false promises, better than the waiting. Rob had trained with the first team a few times, even played in a couple of the Friday five-a-sides, had a run in the reserves, must've been close, must have been. The last thing the gaffer had said to him before that was when Dave Sexton had got Rob with Earl Barrett practising banging crosses in one morning in March. That's a lovely ball, son! And again! Great stuff, Robert! He must have been close.

It's your job, though, son, to prove me wrong.

But he never was going to prove him wrong because he wasn't good enough. Not quite good enough. Not at that level, not at any level that mattered. He felt like he'd been found out. He drove around for ages afterwards in his little Fiesta – he hadn't long bought a stereo for it – drove back from Bodymoor Heath and parked by the ground, at the top of Trinity Road. A group of boys wearing mirrored waistcoats and prayer hats kicked a deflated ball along the street on their way to or from the mosque. He listened to the Portishead album all the way through. He got out and, to his surprise, was able to walk through an unguarded turnstile, and up the Holte End. Empty stadiums were lonely places. He watched the light fading over the North Stand and the brown hump of the Rowley Hills in the distance.

We've had a call, Robert, from an interested club. You're in a much better position than a lot of the lads. I'm not telling you you haven't got a future in football. You're a hard worker, a bright lad. Just not here, son, not here.

For a minute he thought it might be the Wolves. That he could go home and say to his dad that he was going to the Wolves, could ask him about it, make everything all right.

Wrexham.

He drove to his Uncle Jim's, wanted to find his mother there and talk to her first, wanted to talk to his Uncle Jim. It would've been better if his old man blew his top, at Rob, at Big Ron, at life in general, but Rob knew he wouldn't. He'd nod his head, say a few words, maybe even say, Never mind, son, but his eyes would slide away. His dad always knew he wouldn't be good enough.

Wrexham was half a season in the reserves, out of position, right-back in the rain, then half a season of nothing at all.

You're shite, son, utter shite, one bloke's voice from the tiny crowd every time he put the ball up the line.

We're letting you go, son.

It went on; so that each substitution, each time he was dropped, each bollocking, each time he heard we're letting you go, became a relief, another step closer to the end. There were brilliant things, of course, like playing the game of his life in that Youth Cup game against United, or later, getting phoned out of the blue for a pre-season at the Wolves, when it all felt like it was going to happen, even if his old man did show about as much interest in it as if he'd told him he was popping up the road to buy a pint of milk. Now here he was at the end of it all, without the faintest idea of what he was doing. His uncle was right about that much.

Stacey walked over to the Calibra and as the stream of hospital visitors drove past, Rob pictured them as others might have. A couple returning from visiting a parent or grandparent, an old aunty, somebody, not a stabbed kid anyway, smiling shyly at each other, comfortable with who they were and what they were doing. Maybe calling for a takeaway and a couple of cans on the way home, watching one of the soaps that she liked, that she'd taped, while they ate. He might flick through the paper. A few minutes at Sky Sports and then up to bed, to make love and then talk softly of the holiday they'd booked, the house they'd move to, the children they'd have, eyes bright with possibility in the darkness.

They didn't say much on the way back. When he pulled up in front of the flats, he said, I'm sure he'll be all right, yer know, it'll be OK.

She nodded, twisting a tissue in her hands.

Thanks, she said quietly, looking away.

Dyer need anything tonight, now? Dyer need anything doing?

No. She shook her head. I need to goo and sort Gemma out. Thanks, though, Rob. Thanks. All her anger about the school had gone now, probably didn't seem that important.

As she got out of the car, Rob looked at the line of a black G-string above the waistband of her jeans, forced himself to turn his head. He'd looked at her, thought he'd felt her look at him, even in the state she was in, but then he thought of Glenn and that made him pull back. Well, that and her two problem kids. He wouldn't have minded pissing Glenn off. He smiled sadly to himself and looked away past the row of flats, over the railway line. Still, she was all right.

A cloud of dark smoke, burning tyres maybe, rose and merged with the clouds over Great Bridge, Dudley Port, then he looked back. He watched her as she punched in the code to open the communal doors. She turned and waved. He waited until she appeared on the third-floor walkway. She walked with her arms folded then knocked on the second last flat to the end. Hers was the end one. Jim had helped sort that out, years ago. The flats had a reputation. It was where the council put you when you couldn't pay your rent elsewhere. When he saw the door open he turned the car around. He looked back up and saw she was holding Gemma with one hand and had the key to their front door in the lock with the other. She rested her head just for a moment against the door's frosted glass window before going inside. He waved even though she couldn't see. He'd phoned home from the hospital and said he'd call to the chip shop on his way back if they were OK to eat late. That's what he should've done, he thought, called to the chip shop with Stacey or offered to bring her some back. That's what he should've done.

**The ball was at Zubair's feet.** Rob could see what he was going to do, what he was trying to do. When he hit it, Rob thought he'd head it, although somewhere inside himself was the picture of taking a couple of steps back and taking the ball on his chest, stepping out with it or looking for a pass, like Beckenbauer or Sammer, or like something McGrath would've done on the odd days he trained at Villa. Somewhere inside him Rob had a picture of exactly what he could do.

He knew Tayub was outside, somewhere on the left, conscious of red boots and a willowy shape that moved like Adnan used to when they played as kids, like a ghost. Zubair had hit the pass, stood like a golfer having hit a tee shot he liked, perfectly still and watching it, and the ball that Rob thought he was going to head, deep down wanted to take on his chest and step away with and show his contempt for this game he'd somehow ended up involved in, was suddenly on him and he'd taken a step towards it to head it, but it was floating, floating, and was going to drop over him and instead of jumping Rob had to turn, which he couldn't do, not any more with his disintegrating knees, and scramble after it, and the ball was dropping over his head. He stumbled as he turned and the ball had already bounced as he completed the turn and had to start running almost from standstill and Tayub was running next to him, quick, young and quick, and where was the left-back, Carl

Jones, who'd wandered upfield and let Tayub just stroll past him? And Lee, asthmatic and heavy and wheezing, and slower than Rob, who put his head down now to tear after it, thinking quickly that he'd bring Tayub down, getting sent off would end the agony, but he couldn't even get near enough to slide in after him, those red boots mocking him. Chrissie came out to narrow the angle, wasn't that bad a keeper, really but Tayub had got it under, one on one, and he hit it wide of Chrissie, on the floor into the corner, a great finish, and wheeled away with his arms out-stretched shouting, Yes, yes, yes, and whoops of delight from his team-mates and the cars on the sideline. Rob's tongue was flopping out as he slowed to a jog, his arm raised half-heartedly and looking towards the linesman – the first time they'd had proper linesmen in this league, ordinarily it would've been one of the Woodhouses stick-ing a flag up when Rob told them to – but the linesman had already turned away and Mark Stanley had blown for the goal and was running to stop them celebrating so much, something he'd talked about with the police and the captains before the game.

Glenn was swearing from the halfway line. Chrissie slapped the ground with his keeper's gloves. Rob was trying to swear, but his breath was coming out in shreds like torn newspaper. He wanted to tell Tayub if he did that again he'd break his leg but knew he wouldn't catch him even to kick him, wouldn't really want to do it anyway. Zubair had trotted over to join the celebrations but got there too late and just ended up ruffling his brother's fancy hairstyle, with Mark Stanley shouting at them to remem-ber what he'd said before the game about booking people for celebrating. Joey Khan was doing a little dance on the touchline. Glenn was walking towards Carl Jones, who looked like he wanted to hide.

Fuckin hell, Carl, every time. Yow've gorra goo with

him. Just fuckin stay with him. Instead o just letting him run past yer. Fuckin hell. Wiv gorra sort it aht at the back theer. Yome just givin it to em. Fuckin sort it aht, eh.

Glenn glared at Rob, who looked away. There was no point saying anything.

There were the usual shouts of Heads up, and Straight back at em, and Come on. Rob's breathing got a bit easier.

If he comes past yer aht there, just tek his legs, Carl, we'll defend the free-kicks, Rob said, and the young lad nodded, looked as sick as Rob felt.

**Trevor Sinclair got the ball straight away, went past a man, got his head down and ran at them.** They didn't like it, you could tell, not that it came to much. With his head down like that he had the same shape as Glenn, the way he'd stick his nose over the ball and go tearing off with it, trying to weave through the defenders in front of him, no tricks or anything, as if force of will alone would take him through them all.

It was what he did straight from the kick-off after the goal. Off on his own, straight up the middle, like a kids' game. He beat a man; inevitably it ran out of his control, but he nicked it in front of the lad with the beard, rode the challenge, touched it too far again, so it ran towards Zubair. Glenn was already off the ground, launching into the challenge before the ball reached Zubair, who just flicked it with the outside of his boot and jumped to get out of the way of Glenn's studs. Glenn caught him on the foot as he jumped, slid underneath him. As Zubair landed he let his foot come down on Glenn's ankle, stood over him for a minute.

There were shouts of Ref! from both sides; the whistle blowing, Mark Stanley in there, ushering Zubair away, and the other lads beginning to crowd round.

Free-kick.

You fuckin prick, fuckin stamped on me, ref, fuckin look at this. Glenn had jumped up pointing at his ankle. Mark Stanley muscled between the pair of them and led Glenn away, his face as red as his hair.

Mark was talking quietly to him with Glenn still moaning.

And what about the foul there, eh? What abaht that foul?

Mark had got his cards out, looked like he was shuffling them.

Rob heard Lee say, He's gonna send him off. For a second Rob thought he was. That would have been it, then. Glenn would've piled in. Game over. Abandoned. A few of them down the police cells. The helicopter was drowning out the sound of what was being said.

Mark Stanley's voice boomed now. Two-footed challenge.

He was making a big show of writing Glenn's name in the book, lifting the yellow card; he was making a performance of it but it was slowing things down. Thank God he was refereeing. A bloke who looked off his nut on something had chased that young ref around the pitch after an hour of the game against Royal Oak. Cinderheath had been about eight-up by then. Royal Oak got suspended from the league.

Glenn was limping and swearing. His sock was torn at the ankle; the white of the shin-pad like the white of a bone with the flesh torn off. Zubair could handle himself, that was for sure, although he was stepping gingerly where Glenn had caught him. They could both handle themselves, that was one of the problems. Rob decided he'd just try and split it up if it went off between them. He didn't care what anybody else did.

Rob called to Glenn and tapped the side of his head.

Just think, eh? he said quietly. Glenn wouldn't have heard. Glenn nodded his head. Rob could hear Chrissie clapping his gloves together behind them, Come on, lads!

The lad with the beard was talking in Urdu to Zubair. Zubair's Urdu was about as good as Rob's.

**There was no one in when Jim got home.** He'd made the mistake of driving the quick route back right through the estate. There were flags everywhere. On Juniper Close there was a house with red, white and blue bunting up, as if dropped in from the Shankhill Road. He reckoned the red, white and blue were BNP and the St George's were football ones. There were some BNP posters, not just the ones on lampposts and street signs; he'd seen three tonight in people's front windows. One of them was in Nancy and Wesley's front window, and she was his bloody cousin! Mind you, he'd never liked Wesley, he had to admit, and had never bothered to help him when he came to complain about the kids making a noise out at the bus-stop in front of their house.

In a bad mood about the posters, Jim opened a bottle of wine, picked out his *Madame Butterfly* CD and went upstairs to get five minutes on Michael's computer. Jim loved opera. He'd got into it in his forties. When he'd been with Jackie they'd listened to Dylan, Neil Young, Van Morrison and he'd loved that stuff then. It was too much for him now. One morning recently at work he'd heard the organ at the start of 'Like a Hurricane' from the radio and had to walk out to the yard with that pain in his chest, thinking about playing that album over and over at a cottage Jackie and he stayed at near Aberystwyth, the year of that great summer, when they'd slept naked with all the windows open and a breeze blowing through from the sea. Before he'd met her he'd preferred R'n'B, Blue Beat,

Ska, Motown, that they used to play on Fridays in Dudley. He'd gone to see Stevie Wonder once at Dudley Plaza, seen him led on to the stage like a lost little boy.

Pauline liked pop – all sorts as long as it was cheerful. She had the radio on all day at the salon but could never name the songs and that was OK, but Jim liked throwing himself into things. He started liking opera when the Three Tenors sang at the World Cup Final; before that he'd sort of assumed, as people did, that it wasn't for the likes of him. He began getting CDs from the library and then started to learn more about it. Now, he liked nothing more than getting in on a Friday, or maybe some time on Sunday morning when he was doing odd jobs, and putting the stereo on and turning the sound up with the windows open to the whole street, blasting out a bit of Puccini or Verdi. They were his favourites.

That was a trip to plan, when he'd been mayor and retired from the council. Or in a few weeks when he'd lost his seat, he thought darkly. He would've liked to go to Milan, to the opera house. He imagined a weekend taking in *La Bohème* at La Scala and the Milan derby at the San Siro. Cigars and good suits, red wine and pasta. Or to Verona and that festival they had in the amphitheatre. Yes, a cheap flight to Italy and they could spend his stash of money he'd put away after a couple of lucky bets, intending at the time for it to be for when – if – Michael went to university. For a moment, he felt quite bright about losing the election.

Michael's stereo had a better sound than the one downstairs. He'd found a game Michael had been playing where you were a soldier running around shooting people. There were a lot of people he felt like shooting and it got things out of his system. So he sat there, knocking back some cheap French wine that Joey Khan delivered in crates, the aria drifting out of the window and across the houses and gardens bedecked with flowers and flags, wrestling with the mouse to get his figure to forward roll and jump and shoot and dodge in and out the burning buildings against a bright, dusty, mountainous background somewhere in the Arabian desert, instead of ringing Bill or going through the postal votes list, or any number of jobs that he'd planned to do while watching lorries coming and going into the yard at work earlier that week.

**Batistuta lost Campbell completely.** It was inevitable, really, that they were back at the England end, the nervous ebb and flow of a game like this. England hadn't capitalized on their little spell.

He moved across Campbell. The ball came in and he flashed a header goalwards, his long hair like an explosion around the ball. More screams.

Great save!

His Uncle Jim threw his head back. Rob leaned against the fruit machine, like he was burrowing himself away from the screen, through the wall into the street outside. His dad sat like a statue. Batistuta looked reborn suddenly, eyes bright.

**After the computer he had a cigarette in the conservatory and listened out for Michael to come back,** realized he should've been more worried than he was, with everything that was going on.

Michael's key sounded in the door at five to nine, five minutes before Pauline was due back.

All right, mate, where yer bin?

Aht.

I know, but where out?

Just aht.

Oh. Was yer playin football? I sid there was a game gooin on at the park when I drove past.

No. Michael moved to go upstairs. Jim thought he heard him mutter, I doh even like football.

Onny yer need to be careful, me mate, with everything thass gooin on. Yer know wheer I've been tonight?

No response.

Dahn the hospital, thass wheer. Yer know Andre Brown from yower school, he's Stacey's son, who yow've heard us talking about. He's younger than yow, yer know him, got attacked tonight, stabbed, the back o the shops. Yow've gorra be careful, mate.

Mom tode me. Is he all right?

Michael looked at Jim for the first time, worried. Jim was relieved, thought that even this news might have been met with a shrug.

Well, he ay great. He ay gonna die if thass what yer mean. He'll be all right. Iss his arm and shoulder an a mark across his face. Imagine that, eh. He'll be scarred across his face. He's in shock. Still in the hospital tonight. Imagine how his poor mother feels.

Michael shook his head vaguely.

Nobody was sayin nothing at school today was they? About a fight or nothing. I know how these things goo on.

Michael shook his head again. Yer know who it ull be, he said. They'll have all come up from Dudley Road or summat, probly.

Well, yer shunt just assume that, Jim said. There was something in his son's tone: *they, them, yer know who it ull be,* that sounded borrowed, reminded Jim of all the voices on the estate he'd hear at his surgery or at the bar in the clubhouse or sitting down for a sandwich at work. *Them who get everything, yer know who that ull be for, yer might know, them, them, them.* Them and us.

But yer day hear nuthin abaht what was gooin on? Nor tonight when yer was out? I'm surprised people wor talkin abaht it. Yer know what folks am like.

Michael shrugged.

Jim decided he didn't have the energy, tried a different tack.

I got to the bridge on Gulf Strike but got shot. I was a ghost for a while and found out where all the terrorists were.

This caught Michael out and his face brightened. For a moment his face was open and happy and the cloud seemed to lift.

Yow always play as the goodies.

Well, yer know, get the girl an kill the baddies. Thass what it's all about. Iss just like life, son.

The cloud started hovering again.

Gulf Strike. Ay yer got council work to do or summat?

I'm doin it now.

What he was doing was doodling a map of the ward. It helped him think. There were just under ten thousand people in Cinderheath ward, of those, two thousand were Muslim, the vast majority of the rest were white. The Muslim population was younger than the white one – say five hundred were kids, so couldn't vote anyway. That left fifteen hundred, say turnout would be thirty-odd per cent, if that: that only left five hundred people. Even if all five hundred voted for him there were still a couple of thousand votes in the rest of the ward. Most of them should've been Labour voters. In fact, they all should have been Labour voters, allowing for a few hundred Tories around the park, except now suddenly they were all going to vote BNP. It was a fashion. It was ridiculous to even think he might lose. It wasn't just the posters – Wesley and Nancy, for God's sake – it was a strength of feeling, an undercurrent, a lingering resentment that Jim could feel, throbbing from the streets all around him, from people he'd known all his life, and getting into his head, *us and them, what they get, what we doh*. He rubbed at his temples and stared at the map.

The turnout would be bigger because of the BNP. Maybe it would mean more Labour voters would come out too because of the threat of losing the seat, but he wasn't sure people were that bothered. Why should they be, given the evidence of what use it was to them? There'd be loads who'd never voted before, not kids but young ones in their twenties and thirties, queueing up to vote for Bailey. He'd asked Stacey the other night if she'd ever voted and she just looked at him blankly, like he'd asked if she'd ever been to the moon. Mind you, if he was being honest, it had never bothered him that much before. People would tut about the turnout at the count and in the days and weeks afterwards, but what did it matter, really, if you got elected? In most wards you knew exactly what was going to happen. Who cared if two-thirds, three-quarters, four-fifths of the population couldn't be bothered to vote if you knew you were going to win?

Jim pictured queues of people at the polling stations, minibuses flying St George's flags running up and down Juniper Close ferrying people back and forth. No, you reap what you sow, he thought for the second time that evening, even muttering this as he carried on drawing on the map, worrying that he hadn't checked up on the postal votes at the old people's flats because he'd been busy at work – some bloody problem caused by the price of cheap Chinese steel. Yes, you reap what you sow, he decided, drawing a line of question marks around the old Cinderheath works-cum-mosque and then tapping his pen to the rhythm of the angry American shouting that passed for music snarling from Michael's room.

**Zanetti hit another cross.** Campbell was nowhere again. The ball fell for Kily Gonzalez. Rob tried to push himself back through the clubhouse wall. Kily Gonzalez volleyed it – Rob had spent the whole season watching him do this, had loved the Valencia side that had done so well that year, loved sitting watching them on Champions League nights with his dad – but there was Beckham closing down, working hard, only one foot or not.

Thass great stuff from Beckham.

Yow cor fault his effort.

**On the Friday, Glenn arranged some training.** Glenn had got them sprinting up and down on shuttle runs when Rob got there, having to swerve around piles of shit and people walking their dogs. Rob had arrived late on purpose, trying to miss the running. He was Paul McGrath at this level, he told himself, didn't have to do any running.

Also, this was what you might do in July, not with a game of the season left to play and with a title to decide. A bit of ball work would be fine. Get the people who'd be playing together in the match playing on the same side now with a bit of five-a-side, get their confidence up, no problem. Instead they were sprinting up and down the park with Glenn staring at a stopwatch.

All right, Glenn.

The park changing rooms were locked. They'd been exiled from the clubhouse just behind the far fence when Bailey bought their new kits. There was a pile of clothes and bags where Glenn stood, not lifting his eyes from the stopwatch.

All right, Rob. I'm abaht to stop this now and get some ball work going. (Thank God for that, Rob thought.) Dyer wanna do a coupla laps just to warm up?

Not really, mate. Rob slipped off his trainers and pulled on what was left of his boots. His sock poked out of the split right boot like a lizard's tongue. I've just come from football wi the kids. I bin outside all day, pretty much.

Important game, Sunday, Rob. Couldn't be bigger.

Glenn looked at him from underneath his eyebrows.

Running a team that was doing well and now getting involved with all this political stuff had gone to his head. He got things organized, Rob would allow him that, and always had enthusiasm. That was how he'd ended up in this BNP business. Rob could imagine him drawing up little maps of the estate and ticking off voters and those who needed to be seen. Planning everything as a proper campaign, like you were supposed to. He could probably even get the trains to run on time. Rob smiled to himself, imagining Glenn in a uniform with a big hat. It was nothing to smile about, though.

Glenn was still staring at him, while Rob flicked a ball up.

All right, Cloughie, he laughed and set off on a desultory jog around the park. He tried to attract Lee's attention as he trotted off but his mate was bent double next to one of the cones, throwing up after a sprint. He'd probably had a couple of pints after his shift.

Rob actually enjoyed the run, and at the far end of the pitches strode up the bank and alongside the fence to look into the gardens of the big houses that backed on to the park, had a glimpse at the lives inside: a woman washing up and looking out of the window, two kids wrestling over a toy car, a girl, still in her Cinderheath uniform, her face lit by the glow of a computer screen, talking on her mobile phone. Where he turned to run back, he could see the roof of Zubair and Katie's house. He and Karen used to walk along this way on Sundays and imagine living in a house like one of these, maybe not in Cinderheath. If he made it somehow as a footballer it would be somewhere else, but there were worse places to live. It was a small ambition, he thought now. Back then, even when he was dropping a league a season, when he was twenty-two, twenty-three, he thought it would still come together. Failure hadn't seemed so inevitable then. He and Karen bought a new flat by the canal with the promise of her money from the beautician's – she was already managing it – and a deposit from her grandad. There was money left over from years before, from cash that her grandad had buried when he robbed the post office. He'd kept quiet about where it was, served the full sentence and then dug it up the night he got out and went and deposited it in an account at the same post office. Rob had thought then that he'd be able to tell their kids about how they'd paid for their first house with buried treasure. He'd have done anything to be able to buy a house by the park now.

As he ran back in, Glenn was explaining a routine he wanted them to go through. He'd put a couple of cones down to make a goal and ordered Chris between them. Chris was another odd character to be playing for a team that was being run by the BNP, an art lecturer at the college who smoked roll-ups. Rob went to join the others in one of the lines, but Glenn stopped him.

Right, wim gonna do this against a defender an all – Rob, yome defending – the attacker starts here, knocks it out wide – yome running already – and runs into the goal-mouth to look for the cross. Rob's job's to keep yer out. Got it?

Everybody nodded. Rob trotted back to the goal.

All right, Chrissie.

Chris smirked and lifted his arm in a Hitler salute and nodded at Glenn.

Right, I'll run through it fust as the attacker. On yer toes, Glenn shouted at Kyle Woodhouse who was at the front of the other queue. Kyle had got jeans and a jumper on, with his jeans tucked into his football socks and foot-ball boots. His head was shaved and he'd grown a wispy moustache since last week's game. Rob and Karen used to babysit him on Thursday nights when they'd first been going out and her cousin would be going to bingo. Rob had given him his old *Star Wars* figures. Looking at him now, Rob felt old.

Right, go!

Glenn mis-hit the pass towards Kyle. A hospital ball, and even though Rob had been rocking on his heels, he worked out he could take off, nip in and get to the ball before it even reached Kyle, even if it meant sliding through him and everything else: all this in a fraction of a second. Not even a coherent thought, really, an instinct, a memory of all the times he'd made that kind of equation before. Slide through it and send the ball flying up the park to show Glenn what a pathetic excuse for a pass – he couldn't even kick it five yards – and a training session this was; how utterly far beneath him it was to be kicking a football around the local park with a load of grown men, who should've been old enough not to have cared less about a shit game in a shit league, when it was causing all sorts of problems, really was.

Rob's legs went completely from underneath him and he hit the ground with a crash. These fucking boots! The chaos of the other night meant he hadn't bought a new pair and with the ground still damp from the rain he'd lost his footing. The moulded studs had worn away to nothing.

Kyle waited for the ball to arrive and tapped it back into Glenn's path, who took great delight in placing it past Chris into the corner of the goal. Only then did Glenn wheel around and offer a hand to pull Rob up.

Rob tried a sheepish grin. He looked down at his boots. Jesus, he muttered.

He could hear kids' laughter as well and looked up to see Patrick and Leroy, his football boys, strolling past the end of the pitch. Rob grinned at them and waved half-heartedly.

All right, try it again. Glenn beckoned a different pair of attackers. Go!

This time the pass outside was firmer and Rob snapped into concentration, bent-kneed, side-on, he put his arm out to feel where Neil Twigg, the attacker, was. The cross came in along the floor towards the near post. Rob got his body between Twiglet and where the ball was coming from and took a couple of steps towards it.

His legs went out from under him. This time he landed on his back, which knocked his breath away. It was all Twiglet could do not to stamp on him as he tumbled across him.

Shit, sorry. Rob got up, shaking his head. He could feel Glenn staring at him, was aware of Patrick and Leroy looking as they walked away. They hadn't stopped to watch, at least.

All right, Rob, serious this time, eh, Glenn said, and clapped his hands. Rob told him to fuck off under his breath.

The pass went out again. Again, a couple of steps towards the ball as it came in and bang! Head first this time, but at least with his hands out to break the fall. His right hand slapped down on to a pile of dog shit. He stayed down on his hands and knees for a moment, fuming. He rarely lost his temper these days, not since starting at the school, in fact, not like when he and Karen used to row and he'd smash his fist against the wall in a rage, but he was angry now, disgusted with it all. It wasn't just the boots. He could feel himself deflating, any ability he'd once had leaking slowly out of him. There was no use pretending any more. Even as he'd slipped through the leagues he'd kidded himself he could play a bit. Now he thought it was a miracle, a fluke, or just because of his surname, that he'd got anywhere in the first place.

Bloody hell, Rob, have a break, ull yer? Lee, mate, come an be the defender for a bit. Wim gerrin nowhere wi this.

Yow'll atta get some studs in yer boots, Rob. Yome like bloody Bambi on ice.

Withdrawn from a pointless little training exercise like this, with a handful of shit, was a new low. Rob wiped the palm of his hand methodically on the grass before standing up with as much dignity as he felt he had left. What was worse was that no one was laughing, just staring at him, apart from the two schoolkids, who were now a long way down the other pitch sharing their cigarette and laughing their heads off.

Fuck this, Rob said, and he walked slowly but purposefully past the two lines of players without catching anyone's eye. A couple of them began to call after him as he walked towards his car. Glenn's voice was loudest but Lee, knowing his mate a bit better, said, Just leave him, he'll be all right, yer know what he's like.

**They were back up the other end.** Another England free-kick. Beckham's familiar stance, his curved run, a much better strike. Somebody headed it up in the air and the ball dropped towards the edge of the box. Beckham was after it and threw himself into a challenge, Kily Gonzalez again, his arm flailing. Beckham flattened Gonzalez. Rob's eyes snapped towards Collina and just for a moment thought somehow Beckham had done it again, was going off again, and what that would do to him.

No, Rob said under his breath, took a few steps back to the table. Nobody else seemed to see it. There was blood. Gonzalez was standing now, his nose bleeding. People in the clubhouse were cheering.

And it was fine, no card or anything. Rob sat heavily back on his chair, took a few mouthfuls of his pint, remembered he was trying to take the drinking easy because of later, and turned to ask Stacey if she'd pour him another pint.

**Rob appeared at the conservatory window.** He still entered the house the way he had when he was a kid, through the side gate and round to the back door, where he'd rattle into the kitchen. He was wearing his football kit, no shoes on his feet, no sign of any. He padded across the tiled floor in his socks and asked if he could use the shower.

Jim could hear him now, opening the bathroom door and walking across the landing. He put the kettle on, pushed away the notebook in which he'd been writing a letter about the new mosque. As he was writing he'd realized that he'd based all of the 'community opinions' he'd referred to on a drunken conversation with Joey Khan in the clubhouse a couple of months before, told to him at least second-hand anyway, as Joey was hardly a regular at Friday prayers. It would've been easier if the other Labour councillors had still been speaking to him. Not that anybody had said that they weren't, but it was there in the way they wouldn't look him in the eye at council meetings or in the silence regarding helping him out with this election campaign. Not that he'd been too willing to accept any help, this election or any other. He used to pride himself on being a bit of a maverick. He was stumbling over the letter, though, because the truth was he didn't even know any Muslims, not really.

He knew Joey, obviously, and Mr Ali from the Muslim Parents Association, whose son had been questioned after the Tipton arrests and had now gone off to Pakistan. There were people he came across in various groups and meetings, people in the Labour Party, of course; the two other ward councillors, Abdul Haq and Sajid Mahmood, were Muslim. Nobody he could really talk to, though. And it got embarrassing, because he ended up pretending he knew more than he really did, about Islam in general, about Cinderheath in particular, about everything, and what was worse was that he suspected that everyone else did the same. Anything but lose face and talk about things honestly.

This was the chink – no, the bloody great big hole – in the armour that the BNP could exploit.

Yome looking better than when yer come in, Jim said to Rob as he came down from upstairs. I've put the kettle on.

Ta, Uncle Jim. Rob was towelling his hair off and had changed into a T-shirt and tracksuit bottoms with still no sign of any shoes.

Yer lost yer shoes?

Sort of.

What dyer mean?

Throwed em in the cut. Rob sat down, smiling to himself and shaking his head, his earring glinting in the sun coming in through the window. Jim noticed he'd helped himself to his aftershave.

Eh?

We was meant to have training tonight. I doh know. Iss ridiculous. Grown men chasing arahnd the park like kids. With kids. I lost me temper, just left. Threw me boots out the car winder when I got to the bridge. Me trainers am still on the park. Lee ull pick em up, I hope.

That was a bit of a saft thing to do, wor it?

The training or throwing me boots away?

Yome a bit old for this, son.

The boots was split, any road.

Jim got up to make the tea. Calling by when he was in some sort of trouble or things were on his mind was also something Rob had been doing since he'd been a kid, protecting his mum and dad, working out how to soften the blow. Jim remembered washing a bloody school shirt for him once, not asking any questions; remembered him sitting there when the Villa let him go, when Karen left, working out what he was going to say at home.

Does this mean yow've changed yer mind abaht playin next wik?

Rob shrugged. I'll atta play, woh I.

Yow woh atta do nuthin, son, if yer doh want to. Yow ay got no boots now, any road. Jim tried to make light of it.

Maybe they'll drop me now, after tonight, storming off.

Arr, course they will.

Maybe it'll get called off. Iss too risky in loads o ways. Stirrin up trouble.

Maybe, maybe. Do us all a favour if it was. Well, do me one, probably. Be one less thing to worry about.

Yer doh think they'll call it off, though?

No, not now. I've phoned the league and the police, expressed me concerns. They think iss a bigger risk not to play it. Means they'd atta give the title to yow lot without yer playing. Unless the Gurdwara score a hatful – I'll talk to yer abaht that in a minute. I told em back in January to throw yer out the league when it became clear who was paying for everything.

I know, sorry.

Back in January, when the original game had been postponed and the Sunday team expelled from the official Cinderheath Football Club, after the BNP had bought the team a new England kit, Jim had tried to get the league to throw them out as well. They were too scared or lazy to do anything. Then and now.

Listen, yer doh atta play in it, yer know. Yer can just walk away like yer did tonight.

I've gorra play in it. Iss ower team.

It ay ower team no more. Wim just gooin rahnd in circles, wi this. Woss yer dad say?

Not much, as yer know.

Maybe yer should try askin him.

He woh say nuthin. He'll shrug, tell me to do what I

think. He's thinking o voting for em, to hear him carry on lately.

Doh joke, son.

I wor.

**Glenn was fuming after training.** He'd had it all planned out and Rob had ruined it. He was lazy, that was Rob's problem. Everything came too easy to him. He'd never had to work for anything so when it came to it, if you asked him to dig a bit deeper, there was nothing there. It was pathetic. Spineless.

The rest of Rob's family were the same, Glenn thought. His Uncle Jim was the worst. They thought everything would come to them. They were wasteful with their friendships and their attitude to life. Rob going off and having a drink with his Paki mate, his Uncle Jim cosying up to them all at the council, spending his council tax on the Rastafarian centre and Asian women's groups and on the wages of those people sitting up in the council offices doing nothing for their own kind.

He'd admit that they'd been good to him, really helped when he was a kid and things were bad – he used to go round there a lot – but that was part of his point, they were too nice to everybody, too soft. He'd driven past Pauline's salon the other day and seen Rob's mom talking to his sister Stacey outside the shop. Stacey had got the girl with her. He'd seen Kathleen give her some money, a couple of coins.

He'd spoken to his sister just once since she got pregnant the first time, to ask if she'd come and see their grandad before he died. She hadn't. It had all started with the big row about the type of bloke she wanted to hang around with. It ay right, his grandad, had said. It allus ends in upset. Yer should goo with yer own. He'd gone on on that theme before. Stacey had a go back at him. He'd called her a slut, hit her. She spat at him. Glenn hadn't known what to think. She was fourteen, he was fifteen. He thought they'd been through the worst. Next thing she was pregnant.

The first bloke was never going to stick around, not at that age. She lived with their mother and the baby. Then, what a surprise, their mother threw Stacey out and she ended up on her own up at the flats. Jim had probably sorted the flat out. Eventually there was another bloke on the scene. Probably loads of them. Not for long, though. It never was, was it? Long enough for her to be pregnant again, though. What were you meant to think? It had all ended in upset. His grandad had been right about that.

It was actually Stacey who wasn't talking to him. If she backed down a bit, admitted her mistakes, maybe they could do something – those kids were his flesh and blood after all, although the idea of it made him shudder. He thought his wife Anne spoke to her occasionally, but she didn't say anything to him. She protected him, he supposed. If Stacey backed down, maybe they could sort things out. It was ridiculous now she was working behind the bar in the clubhouse. Jim had probably done that on purpose to force him out. He wasn't having it. It made trying to buy a round a problem, though.

The boy had been in that bad fight up at the shops. A knife, he'd heard. He thought about Andre. He'd actually seen him a few times. When Stacey was still at their mother's he'd call round to visit sometimes, timing it to avoid his sister, she was doing a cleaning job, working shifts. The baby boy would grip Glenn's fingers tightly as he lay there in his pram, Glenn tickling him with his other hand. Jordan was going up to the school in September. It would be nice if she had an older cousin around to look after her.

It would cost them all in the end. They'd learn. Their stubbornness and laziness would cost them all. What with his sister and Rob and Jim on the one hand and families like the Woodhouses on the other, just running wild, no discipline any of them, people who should have known better. In the end, they'd have to realize whose side they were on. They'd have to choose. A change was coming.

**The summers he was sixteen, seventeen, eighteen, he would work late at his computer.** Zubair was out all the time now with university friends, or a girl, Adnan reckoned. His brother didn't say much when he got in. He'd often had a drink and would be trying to hide it.

Sitting alone, Adnan would sometimes be woken from his dream of zeros and ones by shouts from people on the main road, drunken calls from late-night kebab punters, young lads singing football songs, or by the tapping of moths attracted to the brightness of his desk lamp. He kept the window closed, the curtains open. The moths would batter the glass at first and then flutter their wings, increasingly gently, craftily, against the metal frame, paint flaking, as if trying to feel a way in. They would rest eventually, as if tired by their efforts, and Adnan would look at their alien heads pressed against the glass and transfixed by the light.

In the end it was a choice, he decided: between having it all and settling, between winning and losing. He could work hard, he could get on, like his dad said, like his brother was, like he himself was doing – getting on the bus every morning and heading off to sixth form, but in the end, he was on the outside, he was the clever Paki boy in the corner, never quite getting all the others' jokes, never quite wearing the right clothes.

It hadn't always been like this. As a kid it had been different. You could have it all. He liked football and fighting and computers and drawing and acting in plays and reading out stories at school to all the other kids sitting on the story-mat. He liked everything. He liked the world and the people in it. But slowly your options shut down, the choices became one thing or the other, a whole string of zeros and ones, a narrowing of the world as the years passed. God knows what being a proper adult would be like, in a world as narrow as a coffin, as narrow as this space between two beds.

He sat on the same side of the bus every morning, head pressed against the glass as it pulled on to the Stourbridge ring road, and always looked for the same thing: two girls from his maths classes who would take turns in driving each other to college, Jessica and Rachel, perfect hair tied back, dressed in their cardigans and short skirts, seventeen with cars already, a Renault 5 and a Fiat Uno. Some mornings he'd see them across the traffic through the dirty glass as they pulled into the slip-road and the bus sailed past for the station, and they'd be laughing or singing along to the radio or just looking blankly at the college buildings and he would ache and look at them like they were something he had lost. They sat in the row in front of him in the lecture room on Thursday mornings. He'd always try to wear a good shirt and put on some of Zubair's aftershave. He'd hear snatches of their conversation, about university applications and some boys they knew who played rugby – always rugby not football – and a trip they were planning to Greece. He wanted to speak to them.

Stuck-up bitches, Ayesha, one of the girls who'd get on the bus in Dudley, used to mutter about them, and he'd laugh with the rest of them at her indignation, but really, just like Ayesha, he wanted to be part of that world and knew that from where he was starting it wasn't going to happen.

He was the moth, of course. Alien head pressed up against the glass. And he thought about how caterpillars grew into moths, and in a wild daydream he saw them keep changing: moths becoming crows, eagles, pterodactyls, B-52 bombers, X-wing fighters out in deep space. Why not? If you accepted the outlandishness of the moth's head, resting now, trying to eat the tiny flakes of paint that drifted off the window frame, you could accept the outlandishness of the whole world – and why not transform?

He would leave. He would become someone else. His own dad, after all, had walked out of his village one morning, a village not even there now, drowned under the waters made by a massive dam, a village he barely spoke of, and walked out of one life and into another.

Once, when he'd been a little kid, they went to a massive wedding in Bradford, some cousin's or other. He'd overheard his dad telling the story of how he'd been headed for Dudley Hill, Bradford, and ended up in Dudley, still Worcestershire then, how all these places seemed the same at the time, and how he ended up staying there, just that little but further, just that little bit more distanced from the ties of home. By the time he'd realized his mistake fully, he'd sorted out a job, somewhere to live. He'd done it on purpose, Adnan knew that straight away. His dad told the story in his joky way, apologetically, to these smiling, bearded men who all looked like him. Just that little bit more distance. People did it all the time.

Adnan wasn't going to settle and he wasn't going to be the person people wanted him to be. He would transform himself. And he worked away at this problem, as he sat staring at his computer screen and the moths flitting outside the window, his options narrowing, the walls closing in.

**England were on top again.** Rob drummed on the table. Sinclair had got it again, that run with his head over the ball, like Glenn's.

Goo on! He and Glenn shouted at the same time, a touch of incredulity in their voices, given their thoughts about Sinclair. It came out to Scholes.

A couple of years ago Rob had asked his Uncle Jim what modern player his dad had been most like.

Scholes, maybe. I'm serious, son. I doh know. Maybe a bit lighter weight than that. I doh think I ever sid him mek a tackle. Valeron, maybe. Bergkamp. Light on his feet, like a ghost. He was the best player I ever played with. Remember this is after the injury, he couldn't walk for six months after it. It ay like now where they'd a flown him off to some specialist somewhere. No, he had to practise hobbling up and down Cinderheath Lane on his own. Born at the wrong time, maybe, I doh know.

Scholes hit it. It came back off Heskey who'd been trying to run across the defender. It bounced around, came to Owen, inside the box. Owen with the ball in front of the defender, then he whipped the ball away. Owen went down. Penalty.

Penalty!

The game had stopped. They were all on their feet. He'd given it. Collina was pointing at the spot. Jim was punching the air. Everything slowed down. There was a gap for Rob, between the penalty decision and realizing Beckham would take it. It must have been the same for the rest of the room because the cheers were strangled, muted, as the camera swung to Beckham's face. Rob could hear Stacey asking if it was Beckham who had to take it, could hear the commentator saying something about what a moment, a chance of redemption.

Owen was asking Beckham if he wanted him to take it. He waved him away, stepped up for it.

**Tom Catesby was the best player Jim ever played with.** That didn't make him the best man, though. There'd been times in the years since when it had crossed Jim's mind that introducing his little sister to his older mate hadn't been the best decision he ever made. It struck him that back then, when he and Tom played together for Cinderheath in the late sixties, he was as much in love with Tom as Kathleen was. They used to have a few pints in the clubhouse after the game, listen to the results on the radio. If they'd played away, they'd get a lift back to the clubhouse or climb into Tom's Hillman Imp and have a couple with the reserve team before meeting Kath and one of her mates and heading up to Dudley or out for a meal. Tom was ten years older than Jim, turning thirty, the aura of his years at the Wolves wrapped around him like the dark overcoat, blue suit and shiny shoes that he'd wear at the weekends. Cinderheath were doing well, up near the top of the Southern League, had a great set of young lads together in their late teens and early twenties and then Tom, set there like a jewel in the middle of it all, strolling around, not tackling, not running back, walking into space and demanding the ball and then hitting a pass that no one else could see, not at that level, limping near the end of games, walking on tiptoe on the heavy pitches they played on; Jim doing the running for two, young and game, Tom just coaxing him through it.

Jim learned more from Tom in that couple of years they played together than he ever learned from anyone: when to run, when to stand still, how to hold yourself, not just on a football pitch, everywhere. Tom was slender and silent; there was always something a bit removed about him, always a sense he was holding something back, waiting. With Jim, what you saw was what you got: big, clumsy, talkative, eager to please. Jim tried to be like Tom, the way he'd wear his clothes, hold his drink, stand at the bar or at the edge of the room as if waiting for something, watchful. The years had made Jim think that what he'd believed was Tom's authority, confidence, had always been something else, something darker, a silence, a fear, a kind of reckoning up of the world. There was a cynicism that came from this reckoning, some assessment that the world wasn't going to turn out how you wanted. If Jim had recognized it at all back then he'd have thought that maybe it all came from Tom's injury, but he wondered now if it had always been there, in some way, this ego, this selfishness.

When Tom and Kathleen became a regular fixture on a Saturday night, when Tom became a regular at the Sunday dinner table where they all ate together at the old house on Cinderheath Lane, when the date was set for their wedding up at the old church, it felt to Jim that this was some kind of affirmation. Of what he wasn't sure: of him, of his family, of their way of life. More ego, more selfishness, on his part this time.

In the years after Tom and Kath got married, though, it all seemed like a happy ending. Tom never played football as a married man, said he wanted to spend time with his wife, something Jim should've learned from when he got together with Jackie. When they had Robert they couldn't have been happier. From what Jim understood, it had been touch-and-go whether they could have children and when it happened there was a sense, you could tell, that they felt doubly blessed. Tom was already thirty-five then, after all, in those days ancient to be a first-time dad.

They'd settled into a way of life. Tom worked hard at Cinderheath, was respected, people whispering in the background out of earshot about his football, Tom just saying that was a long time ago now if anyone ever mentioned it to him. He'd been great with Robert in those early years, Jim thought. That was something he should've copied; he wished he could've been as close to Michael. It was when the works closed that it all went wrong again. As if everything was as fragile as Tom's right knee. Tom had always liked a drink, but he lost himself in it then. Slowly, though, quietly, over time, a long withdrawal from the world.

Jim reached for the notebook between sips of tea and pulled a crumpled copy of the league table from it and put it on the table between them. Here yam, look at that.

| | P | W | D | L | F | A | P | GD |
|---|---|---|---|---|---|---|---|---|
| 1. Cinderheath Sunday | 17 | 12 | 5 | 0 | 67 | 33 | 41 | 34 |
| 2. Cinderheath Muslim Comm'ty | 17 | 12 | 5 | 0 | 55 | 31 | 41 | 24 |
| 3. Gurdwara | 17 | 13 | 0 | 4 | 58 | 33 | 39 | 25 |

Nobody's said anything abaht the Gurdwara, look yer.

No, I know. Complicates the picture a bit though, doh it. They've gorra win, what, by ten, ay they, an then we've gorra draw. Be like a kids' game, even in this league teams doh get double figures.

Rob looked at it a bit more, shook his head and smiled. Thirty-three goals we've let in. Two a game nearly, and wim top of the league. Think they need to get a new centre-half, to be honest.

It ud be double that without yow an they wudnt be worried whether they was gonna win the league or not, they bloody would be letting double figures in.

Who've they got, the Gurdwara?

Castle Villa.

No chance of em getting ten. That Luke Wilkinson runs em, doh he. He used to play for the district wi me when I was at school.

Iss interesting though, ay it. If yow was to draw, like.

Onny if somebody pays Castle Villa off. Rob laughed. I think we'll beat the Mosque easy, to be honest. Be nice to win summat, for a change. I doh even think there'll be any trouble. There's other stuff to worry abaht. Iss just a game o football.

Doh kid yerself, son. I think yower lads could turn nasty if yow lose, especially if the BNP lot am dahn theer stirring it up, which yer know they ull be.

We better win then.

They sat quietly for a while.

Have yer heared from Stacey at all, about Andre?

Her texted this morning to say he's bin discharged. He's back at um with her now.

I tried her this morning but the school's got the wrong numbers. I was gonna go rahnd there but I wanted to check fust.

What they said at school today?

Nothing. The Head said summat in the staff briefing abaht if anybody heard anything. They ay said nothing to the kids. Iss all they'm talking abaht, though.

I thought they might have done an assembly or summat.

This new Head. I mean it day tek place on school grounds or nuthin, did it. I doh think her's that bothered.

For a second, Jim squeezed the mug handle and thought please, please, please don't let this Head be a disaster as well. He'd really pushed at the interview that she was the one for the job.

Maybe thass the right thing, he said, doh mek a big deal of it, keep it low profile.

Push it under the carpet, Rob said.

Iss where some things am best left, son.


**The pictures of the missing were already fading,** disintegrating with the weather, like it was already too late. They bloomed at intersections and on hospital railings like shrines she'd seen travelling in India or on back roads in Sicily, the faces merging together to form strange gods or saints. When she added his face to the collage, when she stood on street corners handing out the information leaflet she'd made, she felt fraudulent. The voices of sympathetic people that stopped for her – as much for themselves as her – told her their own story of that morning, those days; others with people missing or who had known someone who died. Jasmine wanted to say, But I'm not really sure, not really part of this at all, I think he might just have run away.

She skirted the site, sometimes heading up into Midtown, sometimes close to the cordon. Trucks rumbling back and forth waved in and out by police and fire officers.

The city had a gift for naming things: New York's finest, New York's bravest. There at the heart of it all, Ground Zero. A perfect name because that was what it represented: nothingness, oblivion. She wandered the streets with thoughts like this mumbling through her head. Nothing comes from nothing; a huge zero in the middle of the city. What was it he'd said to her about belief? That when it came down to it, it was all just zeros and ones; that was all we were. Then she'd catch herself, the further from the site that she got, when looking up and seeing the sun sparkle on the Chrysler Building, glancing at a skirt in the window of Banana Republic, at a woman and little girl holding hands on Broadway, thinking that everything had changed for ever, maybe like the city itself, and then realizing that there was a lot of life that would just go on, whatever happened.

The next day Jasmine stayed in Brooklyn, exhausted by everything; she walked up to Brooklyn Heights and wandered around cafés and bookshops, deciding that there was as much chance of bumping into him as someone recognizing his face from one of the leaflets. She sat for ages over a coffee, fantasizing about what she'd do if he just strolled in there, had indeed just walked out of one life into another. Here she was, sitting at one end of Gatsby's island, after all. Paul Auster lived around here. She thought of Fanshawe in the *New York Trilogy*, walking away from his life. That book had been on her mind. She toyed with the idea of tracing the strange routes she'd taken while handing out leaflets, to see if they spelled out any meaning.

Matt loved that book. He'd lent it to her when they first started seeing each other. She decided she'd go to one of the bookshops she'd passed and buy a copy. Her old copy was at Matt's flat. She'd been thinking about Matt as much as she had about Adnan.

Later that afternoon she wandered further still, down towards Red Hook, thought about her classes at home, teaching *A View From the Bridge*. She thought she'd be returning to Riverway then. Even if it would be awkward, to say the least, with Matt. A breakdown was practically a badge of honour at that school. It was a difficult place. She'd be welcomed back. She took some pictures of the docks, of the cranes, imagined showing them on the board in her classroom. One of the reasons for teaching the play was the similarity of location, the similarity of situation, a clash of cultures, the bridge between a new life and an old one. What was it Alfieri said in the prologue? About settling for half, about liking that better now. She sat and looked at the bridge and across to the skyscrapers and the smudge above the tip of the island that might have been cloud or smoke or ash. She'd never really understood that line until then.

**Simeone walked in front of Beckham.**

Bastard, Rob muttered under his breath. There were shouts across the room. Beckham didn't look at Simeone. His face was blank, concentrated. This was taking ages. Rob tried to empty his head, the way Beckham must've been doing. Think of nothing, just put the ball down, get up to it, stick it in the corner. Nothing else, don't think about it. The trick at this point was to let go, to not want it too much. To relax. Rob thought about whether to look or not, could see that Lee had half-turned his chair round and was looking at the doors. Rob concentrated on Lee's tattoo of Stevie Bull on the inside of his forearm. That preseason at Wolves, he got shoved upfront with Bully for twenty minutes in a friendly at Chasetown. He thought they'd seen enough, decided he was in. He'd flicked a cross on and Bully hit the post. He hadn't had much of a clue upfront apart from doing that. It had been the hottest day of the year. He could barely run. Bully told him he'd done well at the end, said he'd worked hard, thanked him.

Glenn was standing up. His Uncle Jim had his hands over his face. His dad sat motionless. Rob tried to empty his mind, tried not to want it too much.

**Zubair was careful about what he said about London or where he thought Adnan had gone.** He was selective about everything he said, was tentative around the pain of the whole thing like someone cleaning a wound. He told his dad about the London *A–Z* Adnan had been reading, that it was the only thing they had to go on. His parents looked at him blank-faced and questioning, as if they expected him to know the answers, to know more than he could give them. He'd come in through the door and their faces would be expectant, hoping for a scrap of news and he'd shake his head.

But why would he want to leave?

I don't know, Mom. What more can I say.

He could've started to try an answer, something about how Adnan must've felt hemmed in or had somehow hemmed himself in. That it was bound to be difficult for someone like him, like the child he'd been, to not have things going the right way. That he must have felt frustrated. None of it would make much sense. His mom and dad shook their heads, shattered, stunned. He was surprised that he was angrier with Adnan than he thought they were. He was selfish. He'd run away. They considered the possibilities of him just coming back. He saw it in his mother, the myth of return, whenever the door went.

He moved in with Katie a few weeks later, into a grim flat above the shops on Cinderheath Lane until they could get something better. His dad was diagnosed with lung cancer late in October, already a long way gone. That winter was one of driving his mother back and forth to the hospital, holding her hand when they got back in, holding his dad's as he got weaker and weaker. He made it through to spring, died on an unseasonably warm day in April, the sort of day people aren't meant to die on, crying out for his own mother and his missing son, thinking he was in the village he'd had to leave, that was drowned in the waters of the dam project, said he could see mountains at the end. There was so much now that Zubair knew he hadn't asked him. He married Katie in the June at Dudley Register Office.

Weeks and months went by. Nothing happened. His mother didn't mention Adnan. She didn't mention much any more, with one thing and another. Zubair talked about him occasionally to Rob. He and Rob had slipped into the habit of meeting for a couple of pints once a week. The anger – at his brother, at the stupid boys and their parents that he defended, at his dad's death, at the way the London sun might slant through a café window, at himself – leaked slowly out of him, like from an unchanged battery.

**She didn't seem that interested at first.** It had taken Rob ages to decide to go over there, sitting watching the clouds move over the estate, biting his nails, then suddenly getting up, like when the referee's bell would sound in the dressing room and there was no more time to waste.

He knocked on the door, even though it was propped open with a fire extinguisher to dilute the paint fumes. The room looked totally different from when she'd started. White-painted walls, dry now, posters up around the room.

The desks had been sanded down and the smell of the wood mixed with the paint to make the smell of something new, something hopeful. It was the smell of the entrance hall of the flat Rob and Karen had bought. There was even a bunch of flowers on a side table, a couple of computer terminals being put together.

The bell had just gone. She'd let the two Year 7 girls who she'd been working with go and was putting their work into folders.

Hi Jasmine, he said. It looks great in here now.

Oh, thanks. She touched her hair as she turned to speak to him.

It's about that reading scheme, he said, motioning with the papers he'd printed out.

Oh, yes.

He started to tell her about it but he thought she wasn't listening, was distracted; he'd pretty much dried up when she interrupted him.

Rob, that sounds great but there's a lot of planning to do, so I can't commit to anything.

Here we go, he thought, a polite but firm knock-back, for the reading scheme, for any ideas he might have had.

Have you got any time later this week we could talk about it properly? she asked.

Sorry, what?

Have you got any time later in the week we could talk about it properly?

Erm, yeah. Thursday, after school?

I'm not in on Thursday. Doing my part-time bit still, remember?

Oh.

Oh, hang on, I'm going shopping with my mum on Thursday. I'm meeting her at Merry Hill. I don't suppose . . .

We could meet there?

Yeah, before I meet my mum, obviously. Unless you

want to come shopping? She looked at him and smiled. It would mean we could get it done and maybe we can concentrate more away from here.

Yeah, of course. He tried not to sound too delighted.

He ran out to tidy up the PE stores after that, collected a couple of footballs from out on the Astro, couldn't resist flicking one of the balls up and volleying it towards the goal, smashing it into the top corner.

**Now it was just Beckham standing there, waiting for the whistle.** Rob looked up at the screen, down at his shoes, back at the screen, trying to empty his mind like Beckham had to, thoughts creeping in, the sending-off, the free-kick against Greece, We're letting you go, Robert; hopes and fears.

The realization that it came down to this. He'd either score or he wouldn't. There was something artificial about a penalty. If he scores this we'll win the whole thing, Rob told himself, looking, not looking. If he scores this there's a happy ending. You either scored or you missed, zero or one, nil or one: that belied the game's complexities, that was outside all the subtleties of movement and decision and action that really formed the game.

It came down to this. He remembered hearing about a team that used to refuse to take penalties, would miss them on purpose, saw them as alien to the spirit of the game.

**Who killed Yusuf Khan?**

Lads appeared from nowhere. Friends of the Woodies and others, older ones, some of the gang that used to hang around the canal tunnel with glue bags. Rob didn't know where they came from, they hadn't been with them before. The taxi was rocking. Someone was shouting and laughing, Turn it over, turn it over, come on! Rob scrambled to get out, scared of getting hurt and feeling sick all of a sudden, the beer up in his throat, the car rocking. It had just been a bit of a laugh. They couldn't believe it when the taxi pulled over. They weren't meant to do that. They'd all been out that afternoon, drinking cans round at Glenn's and then down by the tunnel with a bigger group, couldn't take their beer, really, just out of school. They'd put their arms out, trying to get the taxi to stop, just for a laugh. Next thing it had pulled over and they were all piling in, seeing how many of them they could get in there. The driver looked terrified, realized he'd made a mistake but was stuck now, stuttering his few words of English.

Rob got his shoulder out and across Glenn's legs. Glenn was trying to get out as well but now Rob was on top of him, swearing and shouting, scared. The door slammed against Rob's shoulder and bounced back open, bodies up against it as he forced his head through. Nobody was laughing now, there was this other sound, lower-pitched, like animal noises. Rob crawled his way out. He remembered the way the gravel stuck to his hands, somebody sitting or sliding across his back, it might've been Glenn, and his face going right down on to the floor and thinking all at once about his contract at the Villa, realizing he should've thought of that earlier, and not wanting to get hurt, and whether his face would be scratched from the gravel so people would see he'd been here. He knew it was bad, already, deep down. All this must've just been a few seconds. The smell of the rough ground like after rain, although it hadn't rained for weeks. And just before pushing himself up from the floor, thinking that he could just lie there and go to sleep, drunk and really tired. They were all at the front of the car now.

But he did push himself up and as he was getting up something hit him hard. Grazed his ear and caught him full, high up on the arm. He didn't know if it was a kick or a punch or somebody throwing a half-ender but he turned to have a go back and right at that moment they'd got the driver through the window, his legs were coming through the window, his foot catching on the glass, and leaving him snagged there, and then he was out and they were holding him, three foot off the ground, three or four of them on either side.

They were getting the driver out of there for a laugh. Or to drive off with the taxi, burn it out down by the old works. All the Woodhouses were there, including Alan, Kyle's dad, the one who died. They were all there. Later, going through it, over and over and over, it reminded Rob of when they pulled the Ayatollah's body out of its coffin and tore it into the crowd. Then the hands that were snatching at the driver let him drop to the floor and they were on him. They swarmed over him, kicks and punches. They were off him for a second and there he was lying still on the ground. Rob turned and caught Glenn's eye and they took off, ran away, and he didn't think he'd ever been as frightened as right then, across the car park and the uneven ground, thinking don't fall over and don't fall because they'd be on them like they were on him.

Glenn fell over, tumbled and did something like a forward roll and was up on his feet again almost and Rob grabbed his arm and they got to the end of the shops. They turned to look and they were back on him again, but there were others running away as well. Some lights from a car on the main road illuminated them all for a moment and then they were all running but Rob and Glenn had got a head start at least and were off, zigzagging away through the estate.

When they got to the canal they jumped it, didn't walk up to the bridge, pulled themselves up the embankment on hands and knees and stopped at the phone box by the Perry Street flats, asking each other if they were OK.

Rob had some change in his pocket. They agreed to get

an ambulance. Rob was shaking so much he dropped the coins as he got them out of his pocket, but Glenn remembered you didn't need money for 999 and he went in the phone box. Rob looked around wildly to check there was no one around, still hearing the echo of their footsteps against the flats, the light from a telly flaring from one of the windows. When he looked down he thought he was bleeding, his leg all hot and then he realized that he'd pissed himself.

It might be that they saved his life. That was one way of looking at it. There was another call as well. From the woman driving the car that had turned off the main road, but she might've made it after them because she drove to her mother's bungalow down Chestnut Avenue first. They might have saved his life. After they'd tried to kill him, of course.

Who killed Yusuf Khan?

They stopped running after the phone box. Just walked a big loop, coming out by Dudley Port, walked the long way up along the main road. A police van even passed them on the bridge, but they were walking the wrong way then, or looked innocent, or whatever, and they got back to Glenn's and stuck Rob's jeans in the washing machine and sat drinking tea with six or seven sugars in to stop themselves shaking, and talking about whether he was dead or not and how quick the police would come.

But the police never came. Not to anyone. Now they'd have CCTV and everything, but it was before they'd started doing that. They hadn't got anything to go on. No booking at the taxi office. No witnesses. Nothing. Rob didn't know at the time what he was more scared of – the police knocking the door or one of the Woodies or their mates, but nothing happened. Nobody said anything. Like it was a dream. Silence. Their own little law of *omertà*. Years later, occasionally, there would be whispers, rumours, about who had done it and after he died people tended to say it was Alan Woodhouse, because he was dead and that was convenient, as if he could have done all that damage himself. Alan was already way gone by then. All skin and bones.

There'd been appeals for witnesses at first and reports on *Midlands Today* and in the paper, but that soon died away. His only family here were his in-laws. He'd only been here six weeks. That was why he pulled over. He'd come over from Pakistan with his new wife, a girl who'd been at Cinderheath High but who'd left a year early to go back. Rob kept forgetting her name. It all faded away more quickly than it might have.

Rob had chipped a bone in his foot somehow as they ran away, or when he was struggling and kicking to get out of the taxi, the second metatarsal in his left foot, same as Beckham's. At least he thought that was when he did it. It got sore during his first couple of months at Villa. They found it with an X-ray in November, said he must have done it in a pre-season game. He ended up in plaster for a month, started training again in Christmas week. He wondered sometimes if it might've been that that set him back, made the difference in the end. Plus the fact that it was on his mind all the time, of course, when the knock at the door was going to come.

Some time after Karen left, late, late one night, drinking and not able to sleep, drinking tea and a bottle of vodka that was left over from Christmas, he'd even phoned the police station, but it went to an answerphone, wasn't open at that time, and he chickened out or saw sense and he hadn't done that since. It was all about him, though, his own guilt, nobody else.

Rob pictured the girl – it bothered him that he couldn't remember her name – wiping the dribble from her husband's feeding tube or changing his nappy.

It was when Rob had come back from Wrexham, had

pushed it from his mind, and had got together with Karen, that he saw it on the wall of the old dairy. WHO KILLED YUSUF KHAN? And it was like it was almost worse because he wasn't even dead, just useless, pushed round the cracked pavements every now and again in his wheelchair with his blankets and feeding tube and woolly hat that guarded him against the Midlands cold he'd never got chance to get used to, by his still-teenage wife – and they'd done it, he'd done this, was part of it, anyway. Painted there in green spray paint. And it appeared all over the place for a couple of years after that. All over Cinderheath. Sometimes in Dudley, Tipton, Great Bridge. Still none of them said anything. Never would. Silence.

**Corinthian Casuals.** As the name came to him he realized to him that Owen had dived. If he hadn't dived as such he'd bought the penalty, invited the foot forward so he could fall over it. They were different things. Diving was cheating. This was professional. It was why the hand had been such an affront. There was no pretence. If there was a hand, it was the hand of God. Beckham looked up at the keeper – a good sign – and down again. This was taking for ever now. The half itself had gone so quickly, disappeared, and now this was taking for ever. He looked up at the keeper, down again. That was how time went, life passed. Suddenly you were here. A point of no return. He would score or he would miss. This was clearer, though, of course, real life didn't really offer this, no matter what people said. Apart from the way it stopped now.

He stepped forward. Hit it. Terrible contact. Rob watched now. It went low. Everything speeded up. It hit the net. The keeper hadn't moved. It was in.

There was a pause, then a low roar that seemed to come from outside of them all, not the normal Yesssss! of a goal but fragmented, individual, a split second when people were on their own, checking it really was in, it was there in the net. The keeper hadn't moved, just had his arm stretched out to his side, his weight all on the wrong foot, and Beckham running now towards the corner, on his own as well, arms held strangely down at his side, shouting from down inside himself. He got to the corner, leaped with clenched fists, the other players catching him up.

The shouts came all together now, beer flying everywhere. Jim's arms were aloft, Glenn was on his knees in front of the screen. Yes! Yes! Yes! Rob's fists were clenched in front of his face, doubled over almost, he turned now to his dad, still in his seat but his mouth open, his head going back and forward, as if shouting but not making any noise. Rob grabbed him, kissed his cheek, his dad gripped his arm, then he turned to the fruit machine, banged it with the flat of his hands and set it rocking, turned back towards the screen.

There was chaos around the room, the whooping of delight, a short-lived Eng-ger-land chant went up from the other end of the bar. Argentina were kicking off, but suddenly it must be nearly time, the whistle was going and Collina was pointing towards the tunnel and it was half-time and what a time to score.

What a time to score, eh! What a time to score! Jim and Glenn danced with each other around the tables.

# HALF-TIME

**The salon was on the corner of Dudley Road and Juniper Close** in a green dip in the road before it forked for Dudley and Tipton. Everyone called this row the little shops. There was a newsagent on the opposite corner and a council estate office next door. Over the road was a children's playground. Pauline had nagged Jim about getting a safe, springy surface laid in place of the gravel. Behind that were big ash trees, from where the crows flew back and forth between the park and their nests.

The buses to Dudley and Tipton and the new one that did a circle of the estate before going off to Merry Hill all stopped a short way up the road. That was one of the things they'd thought would make here such a good spot. It had been hard work, taking on the salon after her mobile business – she used to just get in her little van and drive to her appointments – and there'd been times since when she'd wondered why she'd let Jim talk her into opening a shop. You had to get on, move up, apparently.

It was worrying her this morning. Lisa, the girl who had worked with her for the last couple of years, had left to go to Karen Woodhouse's place. It was the third time this had happened, if you counted Karen herself, who'd driven around with Pauline in the school holidays and then come to train with her when she took the shop on. She wanted to feel angrier than she did but that was what it was all about, she supposed, getting on. Karen would pay Lisa more than minimum wage and she'd get to work with – and on – girls her own age. She'd get to do more cuts than pensioners' specials. Pauline had realized the other day, at Gornal crematorium in fact, that her clientele was in danger of dying off. She didn't know what she was going to do about getting someone new in. She'd started a new Saturday girl, who was no good, and she didn't know if she could afford anyone in the week. The extra work was going to kill her, though. It was hard enough as it was, with Jim and Michael, and having to do more these days for her own mother and Jim's mum. She'd thought she should wait until after the election before saying something to Jim; now she thought she'd wait until she didn't know when, after the World Cup she supposed, after they'd got everything with Michael sorted out.

Sensing this, Kathleen had been helping out a lot in the last week. She had her own problems with Tom and Robert. You'd think things would get easier as they got older, with husbands and sons, but she wasn't so sure. Kath had been coming in, doing some cleaning, popping back later in the day to sweep hair up. Pauline was going to try to force some cash on her later, easier said than done. She'd become a good friend, her sister-in-law.

It was Kath who had suggested them getting together this morning. It had actually meant more work. Pauline had to drive to Gornal to pick her own mum up and then back round to the flats to meet Kath, and then the rigmarole of getting Evie into the car. Jim and Kath's mum had lost her leg, had it amputated after a blood clot during a series of illnesses a couple of years ago when it had looked like she wouldn't make it. They'd spent that Millennium New Year's Eve holding her hand as she drifted in and out of consciousness, thinking she was talking to her own parents, talking to people who were long gone. She'd had scarlet fever as a young girl; she kept calling out like she was in that soaked-sheet room in a long-demolished house among erased streets. It had been weird that night, fireworks and celebrations through the window, flickering images of the first moon walk and the Berlin Wall and the entry into Auschwitz on the television, and a monologue from Dudley in the thirties that none of them ever talked about except in moments like this, last days, last hours, from the hospital bed, time bleeding in different directions. Evie was a miracle, really, to look at her now, her hair freshly done, eating a chocolate éclair, talking about David Beckham, swinging her one leg like she was taking the penalty.

Pauline had done three cuts so far today, but none of them for paying customers. She was doing her own mother now, had got her under the drier. Evie had actually given her a fiver. When Pauline had protested she'd grinned.

From that nice Mr Brown, she'd said. Yer wanna put yer prices up for these pensioners.

It was true about the pensions. Gordon Brown was as popular as David Beckham in the Cinderheath flats.

Kath brought a half-time cup of tea out for everyone. On and off through the morning they'd been talking about their sons, husbands.

He has mentioned someone lately. This was Rob, now.

Has he? Who's that then?

Kath leaned towards her, conspiratorially.

Yer know Pamela Thomas who become a nurse?

Who married Mr Quereishi. They said this together. The surgeon had achieved a kind of fame through keeping various family members alive. They liked him because they knew a little bit about the story of him marrying Pamela Thomas, a girl Kath had grown up down the road from, and because he wasn't always off playing golf when you tried to make an appointment like some of the consultants they'd had to deal with. They'd become experts, over the years.

I know how the heart works, he'd said to Kath, sadly almost, half-smiling and patting her hand when she got upset at the end of a chat when he'd explained the procedure he was going to perform on Tom.

Well, their daughter, Jasmine, who was at the school when they was little and Mr and Mrs Thomas was still alive, has gone back to work at the school. And I think Rob, yer know, might be keen.

I remember her, course I do. Lovely little girl. And what about her? Is her keen on him?

I think they might have been out a couple of times, only after work, for a coffee, yer know. I spose it might be nice for her to have someone her knew there at the school. London, he said her'd bin working at a school there, an abroad, I think he said.

Pauline was delighted with this news, a little stab of hope about things, something good.

Fingers crossed, eh?

What yer whispering abaht? Evie shouted.

Nothing, Mother. Kath laughed, turned to Pauline and blew her cheeks out; fingers crossed, she nodded. She looked tired, Pauline thought.

Yow've got all this fun to come with Michael. You'd think it ud get easier, wudnt yer? Kath said to her when they took the tea things back to the sink, the television going through the move that led to the penalty from different angles.

Pauline rolled her eyes. She didn't want to talk about Michael, not after his behaviour. Yes, you'd think it would get easier. She tried to think of something else to say.

**As the players walked off, Simeone offered his hand to Beckham and they shook.** Rob banged his left hand on his thigh, took a sip from the pint in his right.

Dyer want anything, Dad? I'm gonna stretch me legs. See how Mom's doin.

Tom shook his head and Rob got up and weaved towards the door, away from the rush to the bar. He considered for a minute whether to go and help Stacey, but saw that his Uncle Jim and Lee had gone round. As he got to the door he felt a hand on his shoulder.

Dyer want one?

It was Glenn. Rob flinched. For a moment he thought he was going to take a swing at him. It was the first time they'd spoken since the election.

All right, mate, yeah. Same again.

Glenn had an old England shirt on, an Italia 90 one. The sleeves were tight against his biceps and a George and Dragon tattoo showed underneath the blue pattern on the sleeve. The beginnings of a belly stretched the material above Glenn's jeans.

I ay sin that shirt for a bit.

Dug it out from the back o the wardrobe. Thought I'd wear it for luck.

Rob could've sworn he was wearing it that night on the car park. Yusuf Khan. They looked at each other, the weighing up of something, both of them trying to think of what to say next.

Yow all right? Glenn said.

Arr, I am mate, arr.

I'll get yer a pint, then. I'm half pissed already, tell yer the truth.

They gorra hang on to this, ay they?

They stood like boxers, rocking almost on the balls of their feet, not quite square on to each other, Glenn south-paw, which gave them an awkwardness.

I think we'll get another. Butt and Scholes have got hold of it in the middle. Veron ay got the bottle for it. There'll be more chances with Owen.

Think it was a pen?

What yow on abaht? Course it was. I know what yome gonna say.

Never touched him, mate. Doh get me wrong, he should goo dahn but he never touched him.

I ay listening to yow. Bloke ud have to have shot him for yow to gi a penalty. Yow sayin yome a better referee than Collina?

I'm sayin I ay bothered. Yow think Kily Gonzalez woh goo dahn if he gets past Danny Mills?

Arr, well they'm cheating bastards, ay they.

Yow should hear what they'm sayin abaht Owen in Buenos Aires, mate.

I couldn't care less.

They both smiled. For a moment things felt OK.

Am yow two gooin to the bar or just standing canting? a big bloke shouted from behind them. Rob didn't know him. He was wearing an even older England shirt – Spain 82, the Keegan one – stretched across a much bigger belly.

All right, big mon. I'd like to see yow when wim losing. Cheer up, Glenn said, and started to move towards the bar. Rob leaned out of his way as he squeezed past.

Eh, Mark, Glenn shouted towards Mark Stanley. This un reckons it wor a penalty. A few heads turned towards Rob who just shook his head and grinned and walked out into the car park.

**It was at a friend of a friend's thirtieth birthday party in Shoreditch.** They were people from university. She wouldn't have gone but she hadn't seen them for a while. Barristers, journalists, New Labour researchers: she wouldn't get a word in. Matt had got the girls for the weekend and they were still taking her contact with them slowly. Even after four years. She'd asked him during an argument whether he thought things might have moved a bit more quickly with his family if she'd been completely white. She'd only said it to hurt him. It was a line the kids at school would come up with.

It was the first weekend of July, almost the end of the school year. The teachers were talking about long spells away in India, Morocco, Brazil, or weeks of doing nothing at all. Matt was going to run the summer school, and spend a couple of weekends taking the girls away. Jasmine wasn't going to work during the summer this year, she needed a break.

Coming to a night like this was easier without Matt. Maybe it was the age thing beginning to show.

If they were chocolate, they'd eat themselves, he said about her university crowd and shook his head sadly.

They're just a bit naïve, she'd say.

That's right. And in a few years' time they'll be running the country.

He'd got a point. She might have said as much herself, but the cynicism was something new. She'd fallen in love with him because of his lack of cynicism, for the fact that he was so obviously someone who believed that whatever you did had an impact, made a difference, good or bad. He'd applied for Helena's job when she left – never got a look in. It was hurting him, watching people who he didn't think cared as much, just said the right things, getting promoted, getting on. He wanted to be a Head. She'd begun to think the trick was not to care as much – she didn't tell him that, though.

She shared a crowded taxi with Emilia and some others. Jasmine told them all a horror story about Rukshana, a Bengali girl in her tutor group, chased down to the river by a gang of Somali boys with knives, saved by her brothers screeching up in a car. A gun had been fired. Stories from the wild side: so much for not getting a word in. She went quiet for a moment. Matt had gone round to Rukshana's family's flat that night, said he was worried about her brothers, wanted to stress Rukshana had done nothing wrong. He said it had gone well. Jasmine had been angry with him because he was late back and the family had given him food. They were meant to have been going out for a meal.

Is Sally's dotcom millionaire boyfriend going to be there tonight? Emilia asked.

The one from the States?

He only works in the States. He's English.

I don't think he's her boyfriend. Just someone she's seeing. I'm not sure he's a millionaire either.

What's his name?

Yusuf.

I heard a story he changed his name.

Strange.

People do, I suppose.

Yeah, people do.

He was standing at the bar when she saw him. He stood holding a credit card lightly between his long fingers, smiling at the barman. The glint of a gold watch-chain showed from the cuff of his white shirt. For a moment she thought she recognized him from work or through Matt or that he was someone famous, vaguely, from a magazine. There was a second or so when she thought that. He was turned halfway towards her. The way she remembered it later was that she'd recognized his long, slim hands first. It was like everything had stopped, like the building was coming down around her.

Oh my God, Adnan!

**Charlie the burger man was busy.** Rob raised a hand to say hello, messed with his phone with his other hand.

The radio commentary was playing from inside the van. A voice was saying, I think it was a soft penalty, but, hey, who cares?

He'd said he'd phone Zubair at half-time.

Doin OK, ay they?

I tell yer, mate, I think we can win this. Not just this today. I mean the whole thing.

Jesus, Zube. Long way to goo yet, mate. It ay even bin that good a game.

I'm serious. I think we can do it. Yow've gorra have the luck an all. Was a lucky penalty, wor it.

Rob laughed. I think so, mate. Everyone else thinks it was nailed on. Doh matter now, anyway.

Thass the thing, though. The luck's gotta be with yer as well. Beckham, Owen, Eriksson, there's a luck about them. Batistuta looks fucked.

I still fancy him against Campbell.

I'm sober, remember. I know what I'm on abaht.

Yer had chance to watch it properly?

Arr, course I have. Even if there's kids out up to no good the police am all watching this, ay they. It's dead quiet.

Thass good.

What dyer reckon, second half?

All right, I tode yer. We'll do this. They'll atta watch that ball behind Ashley Cole, yer know that diagonal ball for Ortega, they've tried it a few times.

I think we'll score again. Wass it like dahn there, by the way?

All right, packed. We've got seats so it's OK.

God save the Queen?

It ay bin too bad.

I bet.

Me dad's come dahn with me. Iss all right, yer know.

Thass good, mate. Say hello to him. Zubair paused for a moment before saying this and in the brief silence Rob wondered whether he was thinking about his own dad, Adnan, loneliness. There was something that caught in his voice.

Still on for a pint tomorra? Rob checked.

Course. Well, I better get some work done.

Yeah, right.

Tomorrow, look, there's summat I wanna talk to yer about. I'll talk to yer tomorra.

Rob was distracted, trying to get around the corner of the building, half-undoing his fly.

All right, no problem. I might ring yer at full time.

Tomorra, yeah, I'll talk to yer about it tomorra.

Rob guessed what it was about. Something about Katie, probably. She'd probably left him, gone back to her mom and dad's. That had happened before. Something, Adnan, loneliness.

He stood pissing against the wall with a cigarette clamped between his lips, careful not to splash his trainers. He could be seen from the road from here and realized that he was feeling the drink. He pictured himself, pissing up the wall of the football club, legs astride, fag hanging out of his mouth, Eng-ger-land shirt on his back; laughed quietly, thought how it would make a good picture. He rocked back and forth, finishing off, let himself consider the idea of England winning the World Cup. His headache had cleared. He actually rested his head gently against the wall, feeling a kind of strange peace.

**Mark Stanley blew for half-time just after he booked Glenn.** It felt too soon, a half gone already, the league title – shit though it was – slipping away. Rob wandered towards the others as they made their way to the far corner. There was a circle around Glenn, a couple of the hangers-on joining in, new faces, Glenn's BNP mates, a bloke in a suit walking across towards them, Bailey, the candidate. Rob looked around, hoping he could maybe go somewhere else, realized his Uncle Jim was, unusually, nowhere to be seen, realized he'd got some sense after all. There was a policeman strolling near to the circle of players. Glenn was opening a tub of oranges. The water was being passed round. Zubair walked past Rob, equally late and slow to his side's team-talk over by the souped-up cars. His friend winked at him, looked delighted with himself, held his hand out to shake. Rob touched it briefly then tapped Zubair on the arse as he walked past him.

Long way to go yet, mate, he said.

One-nil, Zubair said.

Come on, Rob, get in, ull yer! Glenn shouted.

All right, all right, he said as he reached them.

Glenn was waiting for people to have a drink and catch their breath before saying anything. He told a couple of the younger ones to shut up when they started moaning about other players. The helicopter buzzed over, almost right on top of them, and they winced and looked up at it.

Who yow shekkin onds with? a voice said in Rob's ear. One of the hangers-on – a bloke in his thirties who looked like he'd got a false eye which gave his face a strange, fixed look, wearing a black jacket and England cap – was leaning into him. The cap's peak was nearly touching his face. Rob had never seen the bloke before.

What? Rob said, as if he hadn't heard.

I said, Who yow shekkin onds with?

Me mate on the other team.

We decide who yome shekkin onds with an when. Just remember that.

Fuck off.

Yer wanna watch yerself, sunshine.

Who am yow? Wanna watch myself?

Rob turned back now, square on to him. This seemed to take the bloke a bit by surprise because he took a couple of steps away, turned his head to look at Rob with his good eye.

Who the fuck am yer, any road? I ay sin yow dahn here befower.

There were various cries now of, Leave it, Rob, All right, Rob, Leave it, Kenny, it ay wuth it. The police looked towards them.

Rob settled his voice down a bit. Lee had got his hand on his shoulder, he could feel big Chris standing next to him. Wheer am yer from, mate? I ay sin yer dahn here befower. Tellin us what to do, how to behave.

The others in their caps and jackets were leading him away. One of the other men, who Rob thought he'd seen at a school parents' evening, was talking softly to him; Rob heard him say, Calm down, Kenny, eh. Not here, not now, remember what we said.

Bailey, with his suit on and somehow not a splash of mud on it, had walked off down the touchline.

Just watch yerself, eh, the man called to Rob, turning with his good eye again.

Prick, Rob said, mumbling that he should fuck off back to wherever it was he'd come from, that he hadn't seen him down there on a Sunday before, stamping down a divot, angry with himself for getting involved.

Come on, come on, it ay wuth it, settle down, eh, we got a game to win here, a league to win. The players fussed around Rob until they were all facing Glenn again, sucking on oranges, taking swigs of water.

Glenn began the half-time speech he used when they were in a bit of trouble. Rob was shaking. He glanced over at the group of men in the corner of the field now, caps on, smoking, cracking a few jokes with Bailey who'd rejoined them. Big Chris patted Rob on the back a couple of times.

I doh know abaht yow lot but I ay come this far this season to lose it now to that lot. I doh care who they am. For the next forty-five minutes yow've gorra ask yerself dyer want a winners' medal, dyer wanna goo um this afternoon sayin, we've won the league, or not.

I do, Glenn, said Twiglet.

Rhetorical question, Twiglet. I'm hoping we all do. Rob?

Glenn had started asking Rob to say a couple of things at half-time. He'd been flattered at first, now just wondered how he'd let himself get so caught up in this. He had to steady his voice, was still shaking as he started to speak.

Right, we've gotta tighten up at the back. Lee, that big fella's yower bloke, man-to-man, nuthin fancy this half, just stick to him. Carl, same thing with the lad in the red boots, he's quick, so yow've gorra get right up his arse; if he turns yer out theer we'll atta fetch him down, we can defend free-kicks but not a foot-race with him. Their outlet ball, their onny ball, is through Zu – is through their left-back – Twiglet, Paul Hill, is yower job to close him down much quicker if he wants it from the keeper's hands. Everybody, the way for us to win this is for us to hit Glenn's feet a lot quicker, he's mekkin some great runs an he's got the beating of em when he has a goo at em. Rob took a deep breath. They were all looking at him, concentrating. For a moment everything else had disappeared.

Lads, one more thing, in a football sense wim givin em too much respect. They'm a better side than we've played this year, we know that, but we'm a good side too – he stopped himself adding, at this level – a better side, I think. Have a bit of confidence in yerselves. Winning the league should be enjoyable. So less enjoy it, eh, and, last thing, less keep this shut this half. Rob put his finger to his lips. Meself included.

Mark Stanley was blowing the whistle to get them back on. Everyone was clapping. Come on, Cinderheath. Come on the whites. They ran back on.

As Rob trotted towards the penalty area, forcing himself not to look over at the men standing around Bailey in the corner, Chris put his arm round him as he ran to the goal. They'll be bloody voting for yer next, mate, woh they, great stuff!

Rob shook his head and smiled. He was still shaking a bit, but did sneak a glance over at the corner now.

Doh worry, mate. It had to be said. Doh worry abaht that lot. Chris was clapping his hands, marking his goal out.

Come on, lads! Big effort!

The man with the glass eye, face strangely blank, drew his finger across his neck and stared at Rob.

**He slept in the taxi for three, four months.** That's what he told her. She wasn't sure now. One morning in June, nineteen years old, he drove his taxi off the forecourt and all the way to London without stopping, without ever looking back. It was easy, in the end, he told her, that part at least.

He kept his money in a bag, kept it with him, eked it out. He'd been paid for a couple of programming jobs, had just picked up what he was owed from Joey Khan. He'd almost felt rich, more money than he'd ever seen then, a few hundred quid in an old football-boot bag on the passenger seat next to him. He knew he had to make it last, though, so he slept in the car for three, four months. There'd been some terrible rift. That was the impression he gave that night. Something had happened at home that made him run away. He'd used a different name and now that name had become his. Yusuf Khan. He hadn't spoken to his family since. He had tears in his eyes when he said this. She started to cry.

He moved every few days at first, found the emptier parts of the city: Park Royal, the wasteland behind King's Cross, Carpenter's Road, Clays Lane on the marshes, the back end of Canning Town by the scrapyards, Silvertown, North Woolwich by the airport and the flood barrier. He moved east for cheaper food. Romford Road was good, he'd said, smiling. She shuddered every time he mentioned somewhere she knew, held his hand a little bit tighter, thinking how she might've walked past him, how their paths might have crossed before now.

He said the strange thing was that he had neighbours in some places. Other men – always men – older than him, usually, wary obviously, sleeping in their cars. Some of them went off to work on the sites. He'd known people slept rough, shop doorways, the edges of parks, but he thought the car had been his own idea. He had some changes of clothes on hangers in the back. At night he'd tie the bag of cash to his ankle.

He told her things to lighten the story. In the place he stayed the longest, for a few weeks, near the freight terminal in Stratford, flowers bloomed in the patch where he used the toilet. He kept himself clean. There were showers at the big railway stations. The mosques had crossed his mind, just as quickly faded from it. They weren't in this story. He didn't believe. He believed in what was in front of him, that we were just zeros and ones; he believed in the human imagination.

She told him where she'd lived, worked, mentioned Riverway. He knew it. He knew all the places.

You know everywhere, she said, amazed.

He'd walked for three, four months. Before that he'd memorized the A–Z, had thought he might fall back on driving a taxi if things didn't work out. When he wasn't walking, he'd use the libraries, he could use the computers there; that was a lifeline. He walked and thought about the things he was working on. There was this idea that the web would connect everyone. It was like the streets of a city. It was like the diagrams of the human circulatory system he'd had to learn at sixth form; his dad wanted him to be a doctor, of course. To get to places, you had to know your way around. He knew these things were linked, thought about them in all sorts of ways as he trudged the streets. There were hermits, monks who'd shut themselves in caves to find enlightenment. Maybe it was a bit like that. He smiled. She couldn't tell if he was serious.

After three, four months walking, thinking, plotting, planning, he got the break he'd been waiting for. Regular work for a small start-up, writing software that made predictions on industries in the developing world – Honduran timber, Congolese bauxite, Uzbeki gas – predicting where the money would go, where investors should follow, now you could move cash with the click of a mouse. It could be the force of enormous good, he'd said. He asked her if she remembered that time in Miss Johnson's class, they'd had to walk it all the way through the tunnel, gone to visit Cobb's Engine House, had a picnic in the long grass by the ruins; she smiled and laughed, it was something she hadn't thought about for years. He talked about the way technology was changing the world in the way industry had then, or rather how this was another wave of technological change, another revolution.

He was restless, he said, unfulfilled. The work he was doing helped hedge-funds move their money around in milliseconds, but that just kept the money with the rich. Well, and with him. He laughed. He made a lot of money, he said, with a wave of his hand, like it was nothing. There were ways, he said, that the world might change. Say you were a cocoa farmer in Ghana, he said. She'd told him about her time teaching there. Say you had this small cocoa crop at the whim of big corporations in faraway countries. She'd taught her form class about some of this on charity days. Except this wasn't charity. If you had the training, the knowledge, you could turn things round. This hypothetical cocoa farmer they were suddenly so engrossed with could turn technology, the new pace of the world, to his own advantage, invest the money straight away in something else, Mexican honey for instance, keep it moving, money just made more money; next thing the cocoa farmer's building a school and a clinic for his village, a group of cocoa farmers are improving the roads. His eyes were shiny as he said this. It was a revolution. No guns, no bombs, just zeros and ones.

The digital revolutionary. She laughed.

The digital revolutionary. He nodded. I like that. That's what I'm doing. That's who I'm going to be.

160

Later she wondered if it was just another story he'd told her.

He said over and over again how amazing it was to see her. She told him her story since she'd last seen him those years ago at primary school. She thought now about little embellishments she might have made, little half-truths. She'd barely mentioned Matt, for instance, and she thought now about whether, if you change a small thing, there was such a big jump to changing the story altogether.

He'd been lucky during those first few months. He hadn't been robbed. One day he got back to find somebody had tried to set fire to the car, scorch marks up the side, but it had been too wet to take or someone had disturbed them. He said that near the end of his time, his meditation as she came to think of it, he woke after the first cold night of the year with the doors frozen shut. He'd got a room in a house in Forest Gate, moved soon after to a one-bed flat in Hackney, bought a place in Shoreditch, near the office, work going well, timed for the boom, had sold that, bought his flat now in Primrose Hill. He spent part of the time in New York, part in California.

He shrugged, like he was embarrassed. He'd told her all this in the back of a Turkish café on Kingsland Road, after they'd slipped away from the others, drinking coffee and Efes beer.

It was light when they left, just edging light with grey clouds billowing out east, the clouds she'd watch from her classroom window as they moved towards the sea, inevitable now that she'd get a cab back to his new flat. She drifted off to sleep on his shoulder as the taxi edged through a five a.m. traffic jam in Camden. It all seemed natural, inevitable.

He said of course he'd thought about going back, of course he had. And the long hours and travelling and material success itself could be lonely. He was lonely. He'd dream about just walking back in as easily as he'd left, trying to make everything good. Going back was harder than leaving, though, but maybe one day, maybe. He'd like to.

This was the story he told her.

SECOND HALF

**They brought Aimar on.** People were still settling, coming back in when they kicked off. The doors were open and they couldn't see the screen for the kick-off itself and when the image on the screen became clear, there was Aimar running at them, and suddenly Rob felt sobered; there was a whole second half to go yet, and here was Pablo Aimar skipping along with the ball, another of those Valencia players that he and his old man had spent Wednesday nights in the season in front of the telly cheering on.

I doh fancy him runnin at us for forty-five minutes, Rob said to his dad.

Tek his legs, Jim shouted.

Just fuckin get into em, Glenn said.

Watch yer language, son. Jim leaned across to Glenn and touched him on the shoulder. Glenn apologized.

Thank the Lord for that, Tom said quietly. Rob couldn't work out if it was because Aimar had lost the ball or for Jim finally saying something.

**It was seven weeks between her meeting Adnan – she couldn't call him Yusuf,** although that was the name he used – and telling Matt. There were two weeks of the holidays left. Matt had been at school every day running the summer programme. He'd taken the girls away twice as he'd promised. She and Matt had managed a weekend in Southwold: long walks in an empty landscape and an aching for Adnan, a physical sickness that made her think she was actually ill. The last night there she lay on the hotel bed and Matt stroked her hair, knowing that something was wrong, starting to explain that things would be different when the girls were older, how he loved her so much and understood how she'd put up with a lot in the last couple of years, and how brilliant it would be if they could just get a house together and get on with their lives. Normally, she'd ask, Why don't we then? And they'd spend hours

agonizing over his daughters and the fragile state his ex-
wife was in and how it made sense to take things slowly,
that enough damage had already been done. That night
she didn't ask anything. She just looked forward to the
next morning when Matt would get up and go out to
school and she could pick up the phone and ring Adnan.

She told Matt everything that had been going on, start
to finish.

Do you love him? he'd asked quietly, his voice a whisper.

She said yes. It was very sudden, she knew, but yes.

He said good.

In the end it was easy, she thought, to walk out of one
life into another one.

The way Matt spoke to her that night, quietly, plainly,
made her think of the reasons they'd been together in the
first place. It came back to her weeks later, lying, wailing
on her old bed at her parents', about how she was sorry
for what she'd done, and her dad trying to comfort her,
stroking her back and quietening her as she sobbed, telling
her it would be OK, she would be OK, quietly, clearly,
then, an old joke, saying he knew she would be OK because,
after all, he knew how the heart worked.

She hadn't told Adnan much about Matt. Not as much
as she should have. He knew she was seeing someone, but
hadn't asked many questions. Not about that, anyway.
They'd taken to meeting at strange times; one of them
would text the other. He'd have a meeting in Clerkenwell
or the City or Kensington and they'd work out somewhere
near where they could meet up. She'd change plans with
friends, with Matt, all to see him. They'd eat, walk, talk,
filling in their stories since they'd last seen each other,
when they were ten years old. She didn't ask him why he'd
left straight away; he skirted around it. She thought it would
all come out in time. They had all the time in the world.

So you're free now? he asked, looking at her, after she'd

spent a long afternoon walking by the river telling him about Matt.

Well, it wasn't a prison sentence, but, yes, she was.

And we're free to be together?

She nodded. That's what I thought we might do.

**His mum didn't even like the bingo.** She'd decided it was the only way she was going to see her old schoolfriends, Carol and Sandra, regularly, so she gave in. They talked between games and in the bar at the interval. Rob had gone with her a few times when he'd first moved back home. He'd enjoyed it more than her. He liked sipping his pint while the numbers were called out blandly. He liked the hush and murmurs of the crowd as they got close to sensing a 'house', especially when the 'National' was called.

I never thought yow'd see me off to the bingo. It is sad. His mum grumbled, tidying her hair in the mirror. She was in her fifties now, looked younger, especially tonight, done up to go out, with her hair done, wearing a skirt and lipstick.

Sandra sounded the car horn outside and his mother grabbed her handbag and kissed his dad before heading for the front door. Seeing their faces together made the comparison stark: like she was kissing her own dad goodnight, not her husband.

I'm just off dahn the shop, Dad. If his old man was going to have a drink, Rob decided he might as well get something reasonable.

His old man muttered a benign reply and shifted in his armchair, scratched the bare skin showing between his trouser bottoms and slippers.

Rob could hear kids shouting somewhere, thought about Andre and how scared he must have been when the knife appeared. The leaves on the big ash tree behind the shops were thickening and Rob watched a crow fly from the off-licence roof and disappear into the tree. There was a nest there. On mornings on his way to work, he'd watch the two crows that lived there swoop down from the nest to the roofs or into the gutter to tear through the chip wrappers and other detritus from the shop. He noticed things like that more and more as he got older, invested some nameless meaning in them. He only knew it was an ash because he remembered his dad telling him once when he was a kid. They'd stood out the front on a summer night. He must have been pretty young, they mustn't have long moved there. He remembered, or thought he remembered, standing with no shoes on, his feet on his dad's feet, his back resting against his legs, and they'd pointed to all the trees and bushes you could see from there and named them.

There might have been crows in the ash tree every year, for all he knew, but this year he'd kept an eye on them, back and forth from the tree to the shop roofs to the gutter. They'd caw at other birds as they flew past. The crows now flew quickly from their branch, black sparks rising from a fire.

The shouting and laughing was coming from the bench outside the shops. He was crossing the road before he realized who was there. His cousin Michael was sitting with Chelsey, sat perched on the upper part of the bench, her feet on the seat next to Michael. She was stroking his ear. Michael pulled his head away uncomfortably when he recognized Rob. Mohammed was standing with them pulling at a fighting dog straining on a lead, its front two legs in the air in front of its nose like in a boxing stance. On the other side of the bench, sitting on a ped-bike was a boy called Baldy. They were all watching something on a mobile phone that Michael was holding out.

Like the kids who couldn't read, there were kids on the estate who just didn't go to school. Not loads of them, but a few. Occasionally, Chris Bald's name would appear on registers and Year lists at Cinderheath. He was meant to be going to something called Inclusive Provision with the Youth Workers, where they played pool and did art therapy at the community centre, but Rob knew he didn't go to that either. Michael pressed something on the phone and put it in his pocket.

Dyer like me new dog, Rob? Mohammed reared the dog a couple of inches higher, its muscles bulged.

That ay yower dog, mate, is it?

Nah. Mohammed grinned again. Pakis doh like dogs, yer know that. Iss his. He nodded at Baldy.

Nice dog, Rob said, for lack of anything else to say.

Iss a Staffs cross, Baldy said. He had a high-pitched voice that didn't match his little barrel-shaped body.

Great. Rob shuffled from foot to foot. Well, everybody all right? He looked at Michael as he asked this. He would definitely say something to his uncle now. It was still early, but this was no company to be hanging around in.

Arr, sahnd, yeah, came a chorus.

Good.

As he went to walk into the shop, Chelsey jumped from the back of the bench and put her arm through his, holding on to it as he pulled his hand from his pocket.

What yer buyin me, Rob?

Nothing for yow lot, yer know that.

Goo on, Rob. Just for me. Get me a WKD.

No. He tried to laugh, untangle himself.

Goo on, Rob.

I've said no. Firmer this time and he yanked his arm away.

All right, fuckin hell. I was onny havin a joke. Chelsey glared at him and stamped her foot. She left a footprint on the dirty lino. There was water seeping from the fridge, which was making a high-pitched whine. Tears formed in Chelsey's eyes and she turned and left the shop.

Rob called, Chelse, and thought about going after her. To say what, he didn't know. He stood in front of the wailing fridge for a moment, gathering his thoughts. He hadn't intended drinking tonight but now he was here, well. He picked up four cans of Carling, decided he could do with them.

He bought a half-bottle of Bell's for his old man. The bloke behind the counter didn't speak to him all the time he was in there, didn't even look at him, just pointed at the green digits on the till to ask for the money. The shop had changed hands a few times recently. Rob felt like nodding over the road to the salon, explaining that it was his aunty's, explaining that he belonged here.

Ta, my mate, Rob said exaggeratedly, but the man's eyes seemed somehow to slide further away from him.

Outside, Chelsey was nowhere to be seen. Baldy was revving the ped-bike up.

Seeya, lads, Rob said without really looking at them.

They mumbled replies. He didn't look back as he walked up the slope back home, but thought about Chelsey and the bloke in the shop, some half-thought, some idea forming just out of grasp, his finger flicking the ring-pull on one of the cans as he walked up the garden path.

**Jim was delighted that his letter was in the paper.**

*In response to Mr Bailey's letter of the 21st, the building of a new mosque on the former Cinderheath works site, rather than fuelling Islamic extremism, will go some way to combat it.*

*As anyone who lives in the area (unlike Mr Bailey) will attest, the current situation at the Dudley Road mosque is entirely unacceptable both for residents and worshippers, as at busy times worship has to take place in the street. A more sinister development in*

*recent months has been the presence of representatives*
*of radical Islamic organizations in the street outside,*
*canvassing local young Muslims and promoting*
*messages of extremism and anti-Western feeling.*

*A move to a secure, contained new site will not*
*only be of benefit to Dudley Road residents (Muslim*
*and non-Muslim alike), but will also mean the*
*moderate local Muslim leaders will be able to have*
*more control over the message being given to the*
*younger and more impressionable members of their*
*community, that of peace, tolerance and submission*
*(the literal translation of Islam).*

*Furthermore, development at the site – that the*
*council is wholeheartedly committed to – will include*
*a new community centre and childcare facilities that*
*will be of benefit to the whole community.*
*Councillor Jim Bayliss (Labour),*
*Cinderheath Ward, Dudley.*

He read it through three or four times, sat back and reached
for his cigarettes. Not only did it get the point across and
respond to Bailey's letter, it did so with the gravitas
expected of an incumbent councillor, Jim told himself. He
was especially pleased with his translation of the meaning
of Islam being included (they'd often edited things like
that out of previous letters). It made him sound like he
knew what he was talking about. He also liked the way he'd
stressed the council's commitment to finally doing something with the works site after all the years of wrangling.

Pauline walked into the conservatory. He hadn't heard
her come in.

I've just gorra give up saying anything abaht yer smoking in the house, then. Yow've med yer decision.

Sorry, love. I'll give up again after the election, promise.
He leaned back further in his chair, blew a stream of

satisfied blue smoke into the air and handed Pauline the paper, folded to the letters page.

She stood in front of him and read it through, then put the newspaper down on the table. Very good, she said before turning to go back into the kitchen to put the kettle on.

Iss great, he said . . . peace, tolerance and submission.

Dyer think iss a good idea drawing attention to the mosque at all? It might just put people's backs up.

What dyer mean?

Well, thass what they'm saying, ay it, the BNP? Look at this council, they ay done nothing wi the site for twenty years and now they wanna build a mosque on it when it could o bin anything, houses for people, Tesco's, a swimming pool, a factory, God forbid, if the council hadn't med such a mess o things. Yer said yerself they'd gotta point. Yow've said it at council meetings yerself.

I know, arr, but iss gonna be the mosque now an thass it. Better to be upfront abaht it. Better there's summat there an they need a new mosque.

Better not to draw attention to it, if yer ask me. An I thought yer said there was just a few boys from the sixth form handing stupid leaflets out? Yer mek it sahnd like Osama bin Laden's dahn theer or him, the one wi the hook, from dahn London.

Jesus, I was onny sayin they'll have more control if they ay got nutters hanging arahnd outside recruiting for suicide bombers an they have their own proper building.

Pauline laughed. At least yer day write that. They'll all be dahn theer, looking for terrorists. Mind you, they already am, half the time.

While she was saying this, Pauline was chopping some tomatoes. Mek us a cup o coffee, love, will yer? she said in a softer voice.

Jim sank low in the chair. She was right. What if the BNP

all went down there instead of just handing out leaflets at the shops? It was as if he'd issued a challenge. All bloody Abdul Haq had told him was that there'd been a bit of bother with a few students not from the area coming down to hand out leaflets and things. In fact, he hadn't really told Jim directly. Jim had overheard him in conversation with Sajid Mahmood outside the council chamber one night and sort of butted into the conversation. Abdul Haq had been very animated when he was talking to Sajid – Jim heard him swear: fuckers! – which is what got his attention in the first place:

And then they still wouldn't listen to me! The fuckers wouldn't move.

He quietened down when Jim joined the conversation, waved it off. They were talking about that new mosque, somewhere over by Queen's Cross in Dudley, he was sure. He liked both men but he found it difficult to talk to them. Especially Abdul. They'd chat and Abdul would ask Jim what he'd done at the weekend. Jim would start to tell him about his Saturday morning surgery, about going to the football at Cinderheath in the afternoon, a few pints after that, watching telly, the Lottery, and then a film with Pauline. He'd tell him about Sunday morning: usually a bit of work around the house and then a row with Michael about whether he was going to eat his Sunday dinner at the table with them, which he'd normally lose, some roast pork cooked to perfection by Pauline and falling asleep with a glass of wine at some point in the second half of the game on Sky TV that he always watched with Rob. Abdul would look at him blank-faced. Jim thought he was being judged. The thing was, though, he wouldn't want his weekends to be any different. He had a nice life.

**He saved her from being beaten up once.** Cinderheath hadn't been all sunshine, much as she'd loved it. Far from it. She reminded him while they were having a picnic on Hampstead Heath on one of the first days after she told Matt and she felt like she was floating with the relief of it all, kept looking at Adnan to check he was really there.

Karen Woodhouse and her friend, Janice Moses, a black girl who lived in a family of all brothers opposite Jasmine's gran's house, had dragged her into the alley at the side of the school next to the bins. Karen had grabbed a fistful of her hair and was twisting it round and round.

Leave me alone! Jasmine had said as bravely as she could, and the other two mocked her voice and she and Karen went round and round like in a dance, Karen twisting her hair harder, Janice thumping her on her back a couple of times with her big fist. The punches made an echoing sound in her chest and made her want to cough. She'd never been punched before. I'm only ten, she wanted to say.

They were only doing it because Jasmine had answered all the questions in class that afternoon and Karen was jealous. Karen was jealous too because she used to get all the attention from Adnan and Rob and the other boys by doing handstands up against the wall at break-time when the football went over the fence, but now Adnan and Rob liked to talk to Jasmine instead.

Adnan jumped down from the wall behind the bins all of a sudden, from nowhere. Like Spiderman, she thought afterwards, and grabbed Karen's arm, twisting his hands back and forth in a burn. There was a tug of war with Jasmine's hair for a second and then a scuffle like they were all dancing now. Then Janice pushed Adnan hard and he raised his fist to punch her and she burst into tears. They ran off then. Jasmine gasping for breath, the echoing feeling still in her chest, trying to keep pace with his long legs and grabbing his hand so he pulled her along. They remained holding hands while they got their breath back, walking past the works gantry, looking up towards the castle and the zoo, trying to spot the camels from a distance.

Jasmine moved school not long after that and found out it had done her a good turn. She'd been teased for being posh at William Perry Primary and then for not being posh enough at Little Malvern Girls' Day School, where she'd ended up, her mother relenting to her dad's insistence they go private. They teased her there, that is, until she grabbed one of her tormentors by the hair and twisted it round, battering her fist on the girl's back. Nobody bothered her much after that.

Adnan winced at first as she remembered the story and then laughed along.

Karen Woodhouse, he said, shaking his head like he'd never given her another thought. You were lucky, he said, leaving when you did.

Was I? Jasmine asked. I don't know. I really liked it. It felt like, you know, home. We'd moved around a lot before then.

She turned around on to her front, aware of her body moving under her summer dress, lying across Adnan, watching his smooth face as he looked at the sky.

Why did you leave? she asked.

Because of that fight. He smiled.

Seriously, why?

Seriously. I had to avoid Janice Moses's brothers for the next nine years.

They were quiet for a while; he put his hand to her hair, the sun went behind a cloud briefly and then it brightened again.

I drove one of them in the taxi once, actually, took him to court. Clive, I think, his name was. He asked me when I pulled up, Yow went to school wi me sister, Janice, day yer? I said yeah, thought he was going to mention that fight. He didn't though, just said, Sound, man, sound, and touched fists. He got sent to prison for six months, I saw it in the paper that night. You should've heard what they used to call them at the cab office. The Moses family. Black people in general. That really was one of the reasons I left. I couldn't bear it. The small-mindedness of it. Why I said you were lucky was as I got older it felt like the world was closing in, you know. Like everything was planned out in advance. Like everyone was playing the part that had been given them. Mine wasn't what I wanted.

That's it?

It's enough. I was unhappy and now I'm happy. He leaned on his elbow and looked at her. I'm happy now.

As simple as that, just flick a switch?

It is as simple as that. Well, maybe not as simple but, yeah, why not. You can be the person you want to be. That's what we got promised in school assemblies. I became the person I wanted to be.

What about your family, your home, though? Why can't you see them? What have they done?

Nothing, he said. Maybe one day I'll go back. We'll go back.

She could feel his heart beating as she lay across him, leaned over and kissed him.

**Owen went clear, hit it wide.** Next thing, Mills had it down the right, Owen was on the floor this time. Heskey had a shot. Scholes had got it, volleying it; the keeper punched it away.

They were all over them at the start of that second half. Zubair had tried the same ball again straight away but Carl Jones was keeping pace with Tayub this time and blocking his run and this time Rob watched it properly, took a step, took it down on his thigh, stepped away past Tayub and Carl Jones, fired a ball into Twiglet's feet.

176

Calling, Out, out! This time Lee and Carl and Kyle Woodhouse all came with him. The ball was cleared, came loose in midfield again, got picked up by the lad with the beard and Rob was in on him, he'd knocked it a touch too far and Rob stepped in, timed it, taking the ball, flattened the bloke with his shoulder; Mark Stanley shouted, Good tackle, play on, to counter any appeals. Rob drilled it into Glenn's feet and pulled the bearded lad to his feet. Glenn turned on the edge of the box, got a shot away, hit the top of the bar. A minute later he harried down their centre-half, nicked the ball, put the chance a yard wide.

It's coming, it's coming. Rob was shouting now, clapping his hands.

**The boys had been playing for about two minutes when Marcus Moses,** Leroy's brother, not as good a player though, called little Abid a Fuckin Taliban and kicked his arse. Rob whistled and brought the ball back for a free-kick, said he wasn't having that sort of carry-on and that if it continued they could all go home and there'd be no more after-school football. When the game restarted he pulled Marcus to the side.

Marcus, be honest with me. What would you have done if he'd called you an effin Jamaican?

I am Jamaican.

Am yer Jamaican?

Me nan's Jamaican.

Fair enough – but Abid's not from Afghanistan, is he? Seriously, what would you have done?

If he called me a fuckin Jamaican?

Yeah.

Beat him up.

Marcus looked at Rob with pity, as if he'd asked him the most obvious and most stupid question in the world. Rob was inclined to agree with him and wished he hadn't started this conversation. He thought again how much he needed proper training.

Exactly.

Marcus looked totally incredulous. But he cor beat me up!

Thass me point, Rob said, realizing as he said it that it wasn't.

Eh, Si, Marcus shouted over to his friend. This one reckons that lickel Taliban can beat me up!

Calling adults This one or That one was a new, infuriting fashion at the school.

Marcus started giggling.

Marcus, yome just bein silly now. You of all people should know that yer just cor say things like tha. Iss racist. Anyway, when did I become This one?

I cor be racist, Rob. I'm black.

Jesus, Marcus. Iss racist. Dyer wanna goo home?

No, I wanna play football.

Well, get yer act together then an stop acting so saft. Goo on. Rob nodded for him to go back on.

Rob, Marcus shouted over his shoulder.

What?

Me nan says yer shudnt say Jesus like that.

I'm sure her does.

Was it something to worry about, really, whether the sides were mixed or not? The boys had organized their own teams and were ready to start when Rob got out to the courts. People spouted a lot of rubbish about race and you were bound to mix more with your own kind. He wasn't sure these segregated sides could be right, but it was how they had wanted to play.

The problem was that what you ended up with was the game on Sunday and all the problems that brought. Where you ended up was the estate being a no-go area for Muslims and then the other end, anywhere near the canal or in the old terraced houses between the main road and the mosque a no-go area for whites: the situation they were in. And yet, not even that. There weren't any signs up. You could go where you liked. It was a free country. With unspoken rules. What you ended up with was separate lives. Take Glenn and Lee, he thought. They'd grown up with Asian people all around them and probably couldn't tell you the name of a single one. They'd even pretend to have forgotten Zubair and Adnan, who they used to play with as kids. In fact, Rob thought, maybe they had genuinely forgotten, somehow wiped an inconvenient truth from their minds. Not that it was only the whites to blame for this separation.

It had been a long time coming. When he was at school, playground games had been a variation of the one in front of him now. They'd called it Blacks stick Whites then. At some point in the ten years between his leaving school and coming back here to work, the black kids seemed to have changed sides to play with the whites, but that was just due to numbers, to even the sides up. His Uncle Jim had a rant about it, one he could never get away with up at the council chamber or at Labour Party meetings, but that he'd deliver on a Sunday afternoon sometimes before settling down for the football or even at the bar in the club if he'd had one too many, about money being pumped into Asian women's groups and the like, and it being wasted and just creating more division. It was depressing.

Rob looked out across the playground at the boys scampering around after the football, not a care in the world, decided not to blow the whistle, but let anarchy reign. At one point little Abid tackled Marcus and sent a wild shot flying over the fence. In the break, while he fetched the ball, the boys all lay on the floor, all of them, laughing and staring at the clouds overhead, enjoying themselves. Jasmine drove past on her way out and smiled and waved.

That last week of the school holiday they went to Crete for the week. Adnan had booked it secretly. They ate at the Greek restaurant in Primrose Hill, near his flat, at a table by a window with the shutters propped open over the London street below and he pulled the tickets from his shirt pocket and put them down on the white tablecloth. Someone he did some work for had an apartment in the old town in Chania, would she like to go?

For the first time that afternoon the dread of going back to Riverway had begun to creep into her thoughts, like one of Dickens's fogs, coiling up the river to swallow her. She didn't want to face Matt. And to be honest, didn't want to face the work any more. She wanted to do this. Eat at beautiful restaurants; fly off to Crete at a minute's notice.

I'd love to go, she said.

It was everything she could've imagined. The apartment was in a crumbling building just back from the old harbour. In the mornings, they opened the bedroom shutters and let the light come flooding into the room and looked across to the lighthouse as they made love. They'd swim for a while – the place had a pool of course – lie out in the sun and then go for a salad and a beer in the late afternoon, watch the men bring in their fishing boats. They talked about the beauty of the light, talked about everything. One day they went to Knossos, wandered around the ruins, thought about the labyrinth.

That night, eating squid and drinking retsina by the water, Adnan paused from telling her about some work he'd been putting off in New York, where he'd have to go in the next few weeks, took a deep breath and told her the story of Yusuf Khan.

It was the first time he had offered anything about his leaving without her having to ask. She held his hand as he spoke, sipped at the retsina. He looked out across the water, talked about how he used to think about what went on below the surface, sea-monsters and submarines. Then he told her about changing his name.

I don't know why I decided to use it, really. I mean, not really. I'm not sure it means anything.

I'm sure it means a lot, she said, quietly shocked, not so much at the story, she was used to horror stories by now after working at Riverway, but at the depth of his feelings, his reaction.

She kneaded his hand as he remained looking at the water. Then he seemed to snap out of something.

I left partly because of Crete, because of here.

She couldn't tell if this was a joke now, or not.

I thought you hadn't been before?

I haven't. It was worth the wait. One time in Cinderheath, before I left, I got a lift from Rob – you remember Robert – he'd got a car by then, we were seventeen, eighteen. I hardly ever saw him by then. You go different ways, you know. He was about to go on holiday. He was taking Karen Woodhouse to Crete!

He laughed briefly. She still couldn't see whether he was trying to be funny or not.

Karen Woodhouse?

Yeah, it's funny, isn't it? They were going out together. Anyway, I wanted to go to Crete. I couldn't see how I was going to get to Crete. Not from there, anyway.

I don't think that's such a big ambition, she said, dulled by the retsina and the sun. I mean maybe not here, like this but I'm sure you could have –

He waved his hand impatiently, the way he did sometimes. No, no, I don't mean it like that, I mean –

Crete as metaphor, she realized.

Exactly, yes. Crete as metaphor. It could've been anything. I think I ran away on the strength of Crete and a pink Le Shark cardigan that Rob once wore when we were fourteen or so, that there was no way I was going to afford, or if I did, that no one would take me seriously wearing, not by then.

He shook his head. He looked at her now.

We could go back, he said, more decisively than he needed to. I mean, I could go back, to visit, to make amends.

She leaned across the table and kissed him.

You could hold my hand, he said.

**Campbell won a header, beat Batistuta.**

Well up, Sol. He realized that he, Lee and Glenn had said this together.

He's finished, Batistuta, Jim announced. Bottled it. Next thing Batistuta had it at his feet, sent a wild shot into the stands.

Doh speak too soon, Jim, eh?

**The things he'd deal with (the things he'd deal with well)**, like Stacey and her tax credit or that young Woodhouse girl who was pregnant and applying for a flat or whether Sid Lovell's grandson, who'd been in a bit of bother and been thrown out of school, could get in at the parks department, seemed somehow to be looked down on by them. By Abdul, particularly. Jim thought he was a clever bloke and always supported what he said at council meetings, but he hated the way he was so superior, telling him about his two daughters at university, spending his time at the mosque when he wasn't at council. It felt like a judgement. They weren't being that helpful with this election either; in the past they'd organized a minibus to ferry some of the Muslim men to vote, organized the postal votes for the women.

Jim got up from the chair and put the kettle on, muttering, I was onny tryin to get some o the initiative back. Anyway, they do need a new mosque.

I know love, iss all right, calm down. Pauline patted his arm. Here, I'll do this now, just sit down and relax. I shudnt a said nothing. Nobody reads the letters, any road.

I onny did it to reply to that bastard Bailey's letter.

I know, but yow agreed wi most of it.

And that, really, was the problem. In the letter Bailey had lambasted the council for an endless mismanagement of the works site/mosque débâcle and gone on to make some general criticisms about housing allocation, maintenance and young boys making a nuisance of themselves at the shops, all of which were spot on.

Come to think of it, his letter had been three times as long as Jim's and he bet they hadn't cut any out of his. For a moment, he wished he could lose this election just so he could turn around and say to that smooth, perma-tanned face, Iss easy to knock, now you try workin wi this bag of weasels.

Except, what would happen is, the other parties wouldn't engage at all with a BNP councillor and the bloke wouldn't be able to do any job at all, let alone the one he was elected to do and that would leave people in Cinderheath – white, brown, red-in-the-face, whatever – with one less functioning councillor and even more cut adrift and ignored than some of them thought they already were.

**Some months before, Zubair had offered his own take on the state of the world.**

They should just have a wank.

Yer what?

All this talk of these virgins waiting for em if they die on jihad. They should just get a couple o magazines, have a wank.

Zubair was drunk. Rob had been late to meet him and he'd had a couple sitting reading the paper about suicide attacks in Jerusalem and Haifa. There were pictures of

183

bodies and blood, twisted steel. He was wound up anyway, following an afternoon over at Brinsford, talking to a
kid who'd run a woman over in a stolen car, who wouldn't
make eye contact with him, just sucked his teeth and looked
at the tiled walls.

Look, I'm trying to help you, he'd said.

The lad had looked at him then, come to think of it,
and had smirked and shook his head slowly and let his
eyes slide away, like he'd never heard anything so stupid.

There's a link between bombings and orgasms, I swear
to God.

I'm sure there's more to it than that, mate. Rob felt
uneasy and wanted Zubair to keep his voice down. You
couldn't tell what he was going to say in this sort of mood.

Of course there is. But there's something in it. Educated
people say that iss because they'm so desperate blah, blah,
blah. He waved a copy of the *Guardian* around. They am
desperate, course they am. The whole situation's evil. Doh
mean to say they ay just being used, kids, explosions and
the promise of sex and life in paradise, what fifteen-year-
old boy wouldn't go for that?

Jesus, Zube.

Rob took a breath.

What about Adnan?

What dyer mean?

Well, dyer think that's what he might've gone for?

For a minute Rob thought Zubair might have taken a
swing for him. He saw his hand tense around his pint, then
that look, staring at him, looking right into him, the kind
of thing Rob expected he must do in court, questioning
some policeman, or more likely in the office or a bleak interview room somewhere, an incredulous, combative look
that asked, did you really just say what I think you said?

Gone for what?

184

Yer know what I mean. Dyer think he got mixed up in something? Went off somewhere. Yer know.

He'd never asked him anything about it outright. Zubair was quiet for a bit.

I think he's too clever for that. What do you think?

I doh know. Maybe. I hadn't sin him for ages before he left. He was always interested in politics and stuff. I mean, yer cor just disappear. Thin air, yer know. He musta gone somewhere.

What, an yow think he's gone off to join al-Qaeda? Just cos he's supposedly a Muslim. Just cos he's supposedly a Pakistani. Thass what everybody tells us, anyway.

No. I doh know. Some kind of political stuff or summat.

He never went to mosque. We used to have to drag him if we ever went on a Friday.

I never said he did. I said political, any road. Not just religious.

Same things, these days, mate. Zubair shook his head and took a drink of his pint.

Look, I doh know. If you ask me, we have to think he's dead. I've said that to me mother. I've said, Me brother's dead. There's no other way to think of it. I doh know where he is. Probably we'll never know. I doh think he'll be back now. There'll be a body somewhere, yer know. Some back-street somewhere, stuck him in the canal, out in the forest, somewhere. Thass what'll turn up. The phone goes, yer know. An I think, this is it. No, I doh think he's anywhere, mate. I try not to think abaht it, honest. If I knew any-thing more, I'd tell yer.

Zubair finished his pint and they left. He was driving. Rob tried to tell him not to. Zubair ignored him. Said, Doh suppose yer want a lift, then?

Rob walked home in the rain, brooding, still something nagging away at him that Zubair knew more than he let on. Fair enough, maybe it was a family thing. There was something. The way Zubair said, He's too clever. *He is.* Present tense. They hadn't met the following week or for a couple of weeks after that. Then, the week before Christmas, Zubair texted to see if Rob wanted to go for a game of pool, something they hadn't done for years. Rob decided not to mention Adnan again unless Zubair brought it up.

**One-touch stuff from England.** Scholes was getting more space in midfield, put Beckham in. Beckham was running at them, went through, poked his chance wide, could've finished it.

That was a chance.

Golden.

Shoulda scored.

He ay fit, I doh care what anybody says.

It was strange the way momentum would change in a game at any level. The way that confidence or panic could spread with a kind of telepathy through groups of players. After winning that tackle, a big hole appeared in the middle of the park for a few minutes, their midfielder limping around, a big zero that Rob stepped up into.

Paul Hill misplaced a pass but Rob was onto it, decided to keep going with it, swerved around the limping midfielder, got his head down. It opened up suddenly and he thought about hitting it, took another couple of steps, veered away again from the defender who had come out to challenge, sidefooted it inside Zubair with Glenn saying, Yes, Rob, yes!

Glenn got to it a couple of yards inside the touchline, got his head up, floated a ball into the box for Rob. He'd continued his run. Rob watched it, the keeper flapping at it, waving it onto Rob's head and he rose and met it and put too much on it and the ball went a couple of inches over the bar. There were screams from the touchline, from the girls that swore at Zubair. Rob crouched in front of the middle of the goal, closed his eyes then looked up, saw the helicopter right above the park, saw the castle away on the hill, suddenly aware of the world outside the pitch.

As Rob turned to run back, Glenn put his arm out, ruffled his hair.

Great stuff, lads, great stuff, much better! Big Chris clapped his hands loudly from the other end of the pitch.

**She teased him about the work in New York,** said she thought he could do it all online. He'd gone that week, the first week of the new school year. Going back to Riverway had been awful; the gossip, avoiding Matt in the corridors and staff meetings, he didn't look great. She'd already moved a lot of clothes into Adnan's place and she'd half-hoped he'd ask her to come to New York. She'd have dropped everything, which shocked her, when she thought about how much she'd cared about school even a few weeks before.

His flight was due in on the Monday morning. She went to Heathrow to meet him. She phoned in sick, something she never did, from the airport, looking at the planes that he never got off.

She wandered around the airport shops, had a coffee, tried his phone repeatedly, told herself not to panic. Eventually she got through; work was taking longer than he thought, it would be a few days more, he was sorry. He loved her, reassured her. Still, it was a shock.

He phoned later. She was sorting out his kitchen cupboards, getting over the morning's disappointment; but what were a few days in the space of a lifetime? She would meet him from the plane on Thursday, Friday. She'd be more prepared. She'd been doing some thinking. She should put her notice in at Riverway. This was a new chapter.

He told her he was having second thoughts, that he couldn't do it, that he'd made a mistake. It had gone so quickly. It was a mistake. He was sorry.

There were bits she couldn't remember after that. She remembered dialling and redialling his numbers, screaming into his voicemail, pleading. She'd been so certain. This was something beyond her imagination. This was something beyond her. Out of the blue. That he could say this. It had been ten weeks, start to finish.

That afternoon, 11th September 2001, early morning American time, before the planes hit, she received a short email from an address she didn't know:

I can't do this. I am truly sorry. To avoid more pain I will not contact you again. I will not come to London. Forget about me.

**From the flats' walkway Rob could see down the hill across the ruined factory** and Juniper Close and across the plague of St George's flags his uncle kept moaning about. Flags as curtains, fluttering limply from bamboo poles on the allotments, roped between two units on the industrial estate. A flat on Stacey and Andre's walkway had a newspaper flag taped against the inside of a broken window, music pounding from inside. He rang the doorbell and looked at the castle, a flag flying there as well. He could hear the television playing inside, then there was the sound of bolts turning and he saw her shape through the frosted glass.

I've come to see how he's doin.

Her face didn't change, suspicious, defensive, but Stacey rattled the chain off, opened the door and walked through to the living room. Rob shut the door behind him.

Andre sat in the armchair watching *Neighbours* with the sound too loud. He was wearing a T-shirt and tracksuit bottoms, rolled up to below his knee, hairs sprouting on his legs, dark against his pale skin. He looked thinner than at school, as if weight had dropped off him in the couple of days since the attack; his face pinched, harder, older. That look Rob's old man sometimes had. And the scar, of course, a broken red line across his nose and cheek. You could see the padding of the dressing through his shirt.

Gemma played on the floor, things strewn around her, empty crisp bags, a cardboard box that the DVD player had come in, a plastic toy mobile phone, crayons and lipstick mixed together. She was drawing on the cardboard with some lipstick, big pink swirls. Rob stood still, not wanting to distract her after what his uncle had told him.

How am yer, mate?

Andre looked at Rob and shrugged, looked back at the television.

He ay sayin nuthin.

Iss all right, Andre, I ay come for a statement.

Rob picked his way through the debris to the settee.

No, I mean he really ay sayin nuthin. Yow ay said nuthin since we come back from the hospital, ay yer, mate?

What?

Andre shrugged again, looked at his mum, then Rob, then back to Harold Bishop.

Doh worry, Andre, I ay gonna try an mek yer talk.

Rob looked at Stacey standing in the doorway. Her face had softened a bit and she reached to take a pile of towels Rob had moved to sit down. The towels smelled chemically clean, like there'd been too much soap, like his mother made his sports stuff smell.

He ay said nuthin at all, she said and took the towels through to the kitchen.

Dyer like *Neighbours*, Andre? Rob asked.

Andre crinkled his nose slightly and shook his head.

What yer watch it fower then?

He grinned and shrugged again.

Yow ay sayin nuthin, am yer?

He shook his head more vigorously and looked pleased with himself; happy, even.

Thass all right. Just talk when yer like, son.

They watched the noisy television for a while. Gemma scrawled the lipstick across the cardboard box.

Yer doin yer writing, Gemma?

She looked at him and made a noise in the back of her throat, dribbled a little bit. There was a box of tissues on the low table between Rob and Andre's seat. Rob took one and went to wipe Gemma's face, but she squealed and turned away and went back to her scribbling. Andre motioned to Rob and took the tissue from him and leaned away from his chair to get to her. He ruffled her hair and kissed her head when he finished.

Apart from the big mirror over the gas fire the walls were bare, wallpaper that had been painted over with magnolia. The room seemed bright despite the three-quarter-drawn blinds. There were a few photos on and around the television: both of them as babies, Andre with Stacey on a ride at Alton Towers or somewhere like it. There were dried red flowers in a vase next to the fireplace and fresh ones – yellow freesias – on a table by the window. Rob wondered where they'd come from. There was clutter on the floor and washing draped on the chairbacks and a clothes-horse under the window. The room had been made to look bright, airy. For a moment it reminded Rob of the way he and Karen had tried to decorate the flat they'd bought – white walls, light wood furniture, plants and flowers. Everything weightless, blank, new. They'd got it from magazines. His eyes drifted to a row of Stacey's knickers, scrunched and small, splashes of colour like the flowers, drying on the clothes-horse.

The *Neighbours* theme blared out and the news started.

They watched British soldiers firing from an armoured vehicle filmed in night vision, streaks of phosphorus hanging in the greenish night, like the way old televisions used to show a ghost of the picture when you turned them off. Then there was a burning building. Andre changed channels to *Home and Away* when the pictures went back to the studio.

Rob got up and moved to the kitchen door to talk to Stacey. She'd laid out a couple of pasties next to the microwave in the small kitchen and was buttering some bread.

How is he really? he asked.

All right.

Has he really not spoke since they discharged him?

Not a word.

Well, I mean, that ay right, is it? Have yer tode the doctors?

It stops him havin to answer any more questions.

He ay in trouble, though, is he? Not for this.

That ay what it felt like.

He cor just say nuthin. Does he know them who did it? Is that what it is? He cor just say nuthin. How long can he keep that up? Is he scared, is that what it is? Iss understandable.

I doh know. Then, in a quieter voice, He's grateful yow was theer to help.

Ah, I was just at the shops.

I am an all.

Thass all right, yer know. He's a good lad.

The police come rahnd again earlier and banged on the door. I just left em, day answer it. They left after a bit.

They mighta found his bike.

Arr, course they have. The paper come rahnd an all, took a picture of him. I said no at first but, yer know.

What did they say?

Not much. Took a picture.

Did he say anything to them?

No, he's stubborn. Like his mother, I spose.

Her hand was shaking, he noticed, as she reached for a half-drunk cup of tea.

Look, if it was me, I'd give it a couple o days an if he still ay sayin nuthin, tek him back to the hospital, at least to the doctor's.

Yer cor goo to the doctor's for being quiet.

It might be shock or summat. Is he talking to yow?

Stacey smiled. She took a plastic Winnie-the-Pooh beaker from beside the sink and turned to walk past him. She looked up at him for a moment before he stepped out of the doorway, the last of the smile still flickering and her face suddenly alive.

He might have said a bit.

She slipped past him to give Gemma her drink. She kissed the little girl on top of her head like Andre had.

We'll have we tea in a bit, Andre. When Rob's gone.

Andre nodded, looking at the screen.

She came back out, pulled the door shut behind her.

Rob felt a bit deflated, more or less being asked to leave.

Yow shunt play games, yer know. Then a pause. If he's talking to yer.

I'm his mother. Anyway, I ay the one playin games.

Woss that meant to mean?

What yow really here for?

What dyer mean? I wanted to see how he was.

Comin rahnd tonight and textin me and that?

I've tode yer. I wanted to see how he was.

He's all right.

Obviously not, he said. Rob took a step towards her, unsure what to say, uncertain how to play things. They were standing close together.

Gemma shouted from the living room – a sudden yelp and then a long scream. Stacey pulled away from him suddenly, pushed him in the chest as she hurried to open the door.

The top had come off the beaker and there was Ribena all over the floor and the cardboard Gemma'd been playing with. Andre was already trying to mop it up with tissue. Stacey picked Gemma up, holding her with one arm, righting the beaker and picking up the cardboard with the other. Rob followed her and went to take the cardboard from her, but she shook her head and he had to step out of the way again.

Through the open door, he saw her put Gemma in her play-pen, and stroke her hair while she cried, before folding the dripping cardboard into the bin. She took a cloth from the kitchen, Gemma still crying loudly, and walked back through to Andre.

Rob's gorra goo now, Andre, she said, as they worked on mopping up the carpet. I've tode him how glad yer was he was theer to help yer. She got up, cloth in hand, nodding towards the door and at Rob.

All right, mate. I'll come an see yer soon when yome a bit more chatty. Yer look better than when I last saw yer, any road. Rob put his hand on Andre's good shoulder; Andre patted Rob and grinned. Stacey ushered him towards the door.

The door was open and he was halfway out of it before she put the flat of her hand without the cloth in against his chest, her face relaxed for a second. He touched her hair with his hand and she ushered him again out of the door.

And then he was sitting in the flats' car park, smoking and trying to relax, trying not to think about Glenn and what his reaction might be if Rob carried on like this. He'd gone round there for more than just to check on Andre, of course. After a few moments he threw the unfinished cigarette out of the window, deciding to drive home, pick up some cans and sit and watch Sky Sports with his dad.

**Sven was talking to Sheringham on the touchline.** The board went up for Heskey to come off. There was warm applause through the clubhouse as Sheringham came on. It felt slightly out of place, the kind of thing you'd hear in a different setting in response to a decent cover-drive or a violin solo. The lull saw a procession to the bar. Rob had lost track of whose round it was, thought he'd better buy Glenn a pint in return for his.

**She was reading a book of Greek stories to a small group of Year 7 kids** who'd assembled in her room when it hit her. It hadn't happened for ages. She'd go all the time when she first went back to Riverway. It hadn't happened here until now. She'd be doing well and then it would hit her again and she'd feel like the building was coming down around her and she'd struggle to get a grip of herself, have to grab the table edge to steady herself.

It was Icarus and his wings. She'd always secretly enjoyed his demise, the way he over-reached himself, enjoyed Daedalus's grief as revenge for building the Minotaur's labyrinth. She remembered feeling strange about the Minotaur as a girl; he was referred to as a half-breed in a book they'd got at school, locked away in his maze, frenzied, until Theseus, the blue-eyed boy, came along to get rid of him.

They'd talked about this in Crete, looking at the ruins that day at Knossos. Standing at what they decided was the entrance to the labyrinth, thinking about the bright, clear light outside, the darkness of the maze. She thought that was what had spurred him into telling her that stuff about Robert and Crete that night by the water.

When she turned the television on that evening and saw

the planes and the towers it was like the catastrophe had come from deep within her. The way they splintered and tumbled was like they were inside her, like she'd made it happen. There was part of her even then that knew there was a long way back from feeling like this, even if she wanted to get back.

She paused in the story, the children looking at her. Her throat felt tight. She looked down at the book, the picture of him falling and burning, back at the children's faces, and took a deep breath. She was back. She was OK. It was just that some days now she felt stretched, distorted, like she'd once been pulled too far out of shape.

**Tom got some boots like the Hungarians, Goliath ones like Stanley Matthews wore.** The older players joked with him about them, but out of earshot he knew they were asking who he thought he was. When he put them on he felt different, like he could move now, like he really could float across the mud. When they split, which they did regularly, and he had to go back to the old boots, it was like he was anchored to the ground.

Stan Cullis had him running. He had them all running. You were meant to run a hundred yards in ten and a half seconds. There were times for the other distances too. He could do the mile and three-mile runs easily; it was the shorter ones that were the problem. All Tom's speed was in his head. He ran though, had no choice, chest bursting, up and down the terraces, up and down the hills. It was how they did it. How they'd become the best team in England. After the Honved game Cullis said they were the best team in the world. Forward, always forward, running, pounding, unrelenting, with themselves and the ball. Square passes were banned. Balls inside were banned. Too many touches were banned. Forward, always forward, in waves of golden hordes.

In spring the pitches hardened. They weren't as good as the early season ones, but at least you could lift your feet from the mud. Tom got called into a practice game. Early on, the ball came into his feet, he could feel a player bearing down on him, it felt something like a stampede behind him, and then everything slowed and he took a touch out of his feet to show his opponent the ball and then rolled his foot over it, dragging the ball backwards, swivelling on his other foot as he did it. A pack of muscle shot past him, like a doomed bull. He got his head up, took another touch, hit it out to the wing for Deeley to chase. He'd put Billy Wright on his arse. Only Puskas could do that. Well played, son, Billy had said afterwards, clapped him on his back, I knew there was something in them boots. There was a running joke about how he'd laughed that the Hungarians hadn't got the right kit when they ran out at Wembley, before they'd beaten England 6-3. Tom thought he'd be in the first team soon enough but Cullis had him running, running, and the shout didn't come. They didn't need him yet. They had great players in front of him, Broadbent in his position, Deeley, Mullen, if they wanted to play him outside. He didn't mind. He had time on his side.

The next season he had a run in the reserves. He scored five in a Central League game against Stoke, just roamed all over the place. Give me the ball, give me the ball, he'd demand of players five, ten years older than him. There was a write-up in the paper: 'Five Star Catesby looks bound for glory'. His mother cut it out and put it up over the kitchen sink.

Nobody was ever sure where to play him; he'd wander all over the place and expect his team-mates to do the same, and it took the next season for him to settle in at inside-right. He started the season in the reserves, his head down, working away, but the doubts began to creep in.

This was the year the rumours started at Molineux about the great player they'd got in the reserves. Tommy Catesby, ex-England schoolboys and set to be the next Wolves great, said the *Express & Star*. There was a picture of him running next to Flowers and Shorthouse in training. One report referred to him as a will-o'-the-wisp. Charlie Buchan's *Football Monthly* called him 'skilful but lightweight'.

He wasn't lightweight, though, not in the way they meant. He knew what hard work was. It was just that he couldn't play in the way they wanted – he wanted to roam, take people on, pass it, all the time pass it, and move, and make shapes that would end in goals. He was stubborn and thought he knew best. It frustrated him when he made a run and nobody saw it, when he hit a pass into space and no one was there. There were teams playing like this now: the Hungarians, Real Madrid, Manchester United. The days of working at it like you were putting your shift in at the factory were dying.

Who does he think he is? came the whispers from the older pros. The challenges came in harder and harder.

He started to pick up a few knocks. He tried to play on a bad ankle through November 1957 and suddenly wasn't getting picked. His National Service was looming. He needed to be playing to get looked after, to get an easier ride.

The United plane crashed in the February, 1958. A fog hung over Cinderheath, down in the dip, like a cloud of ash. Duncan Edwards died after fifteen days. Tom sat on the back step in the cold looking at the banks of slush. He said a little prayer, apologizing for having been jealous of all the players at United. There was a rumour that Tom might go up to Old Trafford as one of the loan players to keep them going. They were taking players from all over. A few had gone up from Villa. Tom wanted to go, knew that it would be his chance, his chance on the back of the ruins – mangled steel, dead bodies, piles of ash and dirty snow. Nothing came of it. The season carried on, forward, forward, the Wolves were winning the league. He was back in the reserves, against Birmingham just before Easter, playing outside-right now. It was no good. He wasn't quick enough to go past the full-backs. He'd never been able to run fast, it was speed of thought he relied on, even in his carpet-slipper boots. That afternoon he kept drifting inside, had made a couple of goals. They were three-nil up, he was still getting shouted at! Twenty minutes left, he ghosted inside again, picked it up in the mud, got his head up, saw their left-half coming at him, flicked it past him to buy him some time, too many touches, always too many touches. That was when it happened.

He knew it was bad straight away. The left-half kept coming. Tom couldn't get his foot out of the mud, his body going one way, his right leg staying where it was. He felt something rip and tear inside his knee, felt it shatter like crystal. Straight away he knew it was the end.

They got him back in the dressing room and then to New Cross. He wasn't with it, knew it was bad though, knew it was the end. No pain, not really. Not when it happened. Nothing. The pain came afterwards. Everything had gone, his ligaments torn, kneecap shattered. The doctor talked about a couple of injuries he'd treated in the war.

We need to talk about ways of getting you walking again, Thomas; it's going to be a long process.

What about football?

The doctor had smiled and shook his head.

He lay looking at the tiled ceiling, then later through his bedroom window at the Cinderheath gantry, wondering what he was going to do now, a thought slowly forming in his head, through the gloom, that if it was hard work that they wanted, if that was all that mattered, that was what they were going to get.

**They met at Starbucks at Merry Hill.** She'd got an hour or so before she had to see her mum. He blushed when she got there, could feel it. She smiled at him, made him feel more relaxed, like things were going to be OK.

He'd enjoyed sitting there waiting for her. There was jazz playing. The coffee was strong. He'd been surprised she'd suggested a Starbucks. He'd imagined she'd have avoided it, not been a fan of giant American corporations. The thought must have crept across his face when she mentioned it.

Oh no, she said. Is that bad? I bet you think that's awful. You're quite political, aren't you? It's a guilty pleasure. I can't help liking it. We can meet somewhere else if you want.

No, no, that's great.

Quite political? He wondered how she'd got that impression in the few stuttering conversations they'd had since she arrived at Cinderheath. He'd mentioned his uncle, he supposed. Maybe she'd been asking other people about him at school. The thought filled him with a sudden excitement, although he doubted many of the teachers would've described him as quite political. He was actually a Labour Party member, if that counted, hanging on to his card at least until there was a leadership election and he could vote for Gordon Brown. He'd see after that. He wouldn't have described himself as political, wouldn't have known how to describe himself, not these days. It was all relative. He looked at the faces walking past, wondered how many of them would give the council elections a second thought. He was only bound up in it because of his family. Even in Cinderheath, with the whole pantomime that was going on, there'd be people unaware there was an election happening. Why should they be aware? Most people just wanted to get through the day. That was one of the things his Uncle Jim couldn't grasp. He needed it spelling out to him.

Rob liked the jazz, wanted to find out more about things like that, different types of music, other things too. How did you find out about jazz? He'd go to the library. He liked sitting here, the way you could be anywhere, America even, in an air-conditioned, artificially lit shopping mall drinking corporate coffee. He liked the sense of space, of blank space, the sense you could be who you wanted to be, just sitting here, listening to jazz. When he'd driven past the giant Beckham hoarding over the motorway it struck him that was one of the reasons he was so popular – people lived through him, projected their own hopes and fears on to how well he could kick a football.

He'd put all the reading work he'd done into a folder, made some notes in the margins.

God, you're really organized, she said when he sat down. He'd gone to the counter to get her a latte. I took a quick look in your folder, I hope you don't mind.

Of course not. He'd grinned, tried not to look too pleased with himself.

They talked about the reading scheme. Next year would be different. There'd be kids withdrawn from lessons to follow a reading recovery programme similar to the one he'd shown her. It was work she'd brought with her from her last school. They'd be in small groups, come out for three or four lessons a week. It was all about getting their reading age up to an appropriate level. He thought, as she explained it, how much he liked the way the school year followed the same pattern as the football season.

How about you? he asked. How are you settling in? What's it like coming back to Cinderheath after all this time?

Strange, she said. At first. I mean, the whole thing really. When we moved back here before, it was to live at my gran's. She had cancer. Then my grandad became ill, so we ended up here, what, for two years. You know this bit, class four and five. She smiled and he nodded. We'd never really lived anywhere very long in one place. My dad was moving around with work. They did settle, after that, my parents, my dad became a consultant when they opened Russell's Hall hospital. We moved to a house near Bridgnorth, by the river. That time at primary school, that class, made me want to become a teacher, I think, memories of it anyway. You remember when we all had to sit on the carpet at the end of the day to listen to *Narnia*?

Rob nodded again.

I loved that feeling. You'd have thought we'd have been too old for that sort of thing by then, but we loved it. I did anyway. The way that Miss Johnson could make us feel safe. I don't know. I tried to track her down, by the way, years later when I was doing teaching practice but I didn't have much luck. She'd moved pretty soon afterwards. I don't think there's any teachers left at the primary school who would know now. I might try again. I wanted to tell her, Jasmine shrugged, I don't know what I wanted to tell her, thanks I suppose. I was a bit half-hearted with my search, maybe, like she might not live up to what I remembered. Julia Johnson. She probably got married, changed her name. Anyway, here I am, back in Cinderheath. It feels strange. I think the job will be great. It's a bit of an adjustment being at my parents'. I hope that's not for too long. They're so lovely but, well, I didn't think I'd ever live with them again. I'll sort out my own place.

She stopped, took a drink of coffee. My God, that was a long and rambling answer, wasn't it? She smiled, was winding her hair in her left hand, looking at him.

How come you're at your mom and dad's?

She paused. He started to apologize.

No, no. I split up with my boyfriend, partner. I'm not sure what you're meant to say. We'd been together four, five years. There was stuff at his flat, at mine. It happened quite quickly. This job came up. You know I worked with Helena at Riverway? At my old school.

It was strange to hear the new Head, that everyone was so wary of, referred to as a normal person.

It's really hard, he said, more forcefully than he wanted to. That happened to me. I'm still there. At my mom and dad's, that is. I've been back there ages.

It had been nearly five years. He almost told her that, then stopped himself. It was ridiculous. Sleeping in a single bed at his parents' house. A man nearly thirty.

I used to live with Karen Woodhouse, he said. We had a flat together, down by the canal. We were together six, seven years. Girlfriend, partner. I doh know what yer say, either.

Jasmine didn't say anything. Perhaps she didn't remember Karen.

She left me for a bloke who sells fake tan. She runs a beautician's.

Handy for business then, I suppose.

They're doing very well.

It was the other way round with me. I left him. For someone else. It wasn't what I thought.

She bit her lip. He thought she was going to cry. He could tell she thought she'd said too much. They looked at the people going past outside.

The conversation went back to the reading scheme. She'd need people to deliver some of it, would he want to be interviewed?

What me?

Well, yes, as you've done so much work on it already. It'll be a lot of the kids you work with now. She'd misunderstood his response. You've got your sports stuff to do, I wouldn't want to take you away from that.

Don't you need qualifications?

Not really, she said, then asked him what he'd got.

Rob wasn't sure what he'd got. Not much. It hadn't seemed very important at the time. He'd got his coaching badges.

They're teaching assistant jobs, so it's the same as you're doing now.

He didn't say much. He knew that by not saying anything it would seem like he wasn't interested, but he couldn't think of what to say without making an idiot of himself. He really wanted to do it. He could tell her he'd thought about it tomorrow or next week. He'd love to do it.

He asked her about the years after Cinderheath. They jumped around different topics, each assuming the other knew more than they did. One minute she was talking about private school, which she'd hated, then university, which she'd loved, then teaching in Ghana and east London.

What do you mean when you say, At the Villa? she asked him.

Erm, Aston Villa, yer know, football club. I used to play for them. A bit.

Aston Villa? What, against Liverpool and Arsenal and teams like that?

Well, yeah. I wasn't in the first team. I was there when I was sixteen until I was eighteen, then I played for Wrexham. I played for Wolves for a bit.

As a proper footballer?

Well, as a professional, yeah. I mean, things didn't work out that well cos I'm not a footballer now but, yeah, I was.

That's amazing!

Well, not really.

No, really, that is amazing, Robert.

He liked the way she called him Robert.

It was amazing I believed I could mek me living at it.

No, it is amazing. I remember you were really good at football. Is that what you always wanted to do?

Yeah, I spose so. That an a few thousand other things but, yeah, yeah it was. Me dad was a footballer, yer know, played for the Wolves. He got injured.

He didn't know why he was saying this. She probably didn't even know who the Wolves were. *What do you mean when you say at the Villa?* That was great.

It's wonderful, though, to do what you always wanted. To achieve what you wanted to. No wonder you're such a hero to all those boys.

It didn't end well.

The start and the middle hadn't been too glorious either, he thought, but he didn't want to lay it on too thickly.

Some things don't. It doesn't stop them being wonderful at the time.

She was late for meeting her mother. There was so much to say.

I haven't told you about your dad, have I? he said, as she was pulling on her jacket.

What, my dad?

Yeah, he saved my dad's life. Operated on him after his heart attack. A triple bypass.

Oh my God, Robert, that's too much!

We're very grateful, he said earnestly.

They were both conscious she was late.

Oh my God, she said again, smiling, shaking her head.

Maybe we could do this again. It's nice finding out what happened to you. I mean we could, if you'd like to –

He realized he should try to finish his sentences. Especially as she was smiling and nodding, saying that would be great, she'd love to.

Later, on the escalator, heading out to the car park, looking up to see if he could see her with her mum, he thought about how they hadn't talked about Adnan. She'd mentioned a few names from school but not his. He remembered the fuss about the quiz that time. Adnan had been jealous he'd won. It was funny how things came back to you. It was twenty years ago. There was something else he thought of it now, that time they did the Diwali play. Adnan got picked to be the Demon King because he was the best actor, but that left Rob and Jasmine to be Rama and Sita. Adnan had been pissed off about that as well. Rob wished he'd asked her if she could remember it. She seemed to remember everything. There was all the time in the world to talk about Adnan, he thought.

A hero to all those boys, he muttered to himself, as he walked through the car parks. It was a new way of looking at himself.

**The voice in Jasmine's head, the voice she thought with, was her mother's.** Her mother's before that, probably. It used to worry her. If the voice in her head was her mother's, where was the room for her own voice? When she spoke, it was her own voice, gentler than the one in her head. Not that the one in her head wasn't caring, compassionate, more so in some ways. It was tougher, that was all, had more knowledge of the boundaries of things, of what was possible and what wasn't.

Her mum had trained to be a nurse, left for London. Her parents had been horrified, wanted her there. It was the sixties; she was independent. She'd met Jasmine's dad when he was a junior doctor at the Royal London. Jasmine used to go past it on the bus when she lived in Stepney, on the way to Matt's flat. Her parents got married at Marylebone Register Office, the same as Paul McCartney, her mother would add.

Jasmine understood now that it was only when they came back in those years, to nurse her grandparents in turn, that those old wounds were healed. She remembered there had been a picture of her parents' wedding day on the fireplace. Her grandparents hadn't gone to the wedding.

She'd liked it best in those years when she could help her mum. They'd bring her gran ice-cubes or crushed ice lolly to hold to her lips. A few times her gran talked about growing up. Not here, no; in Dudley, near the zoo, before there was a zoo. It had been crowded and dirty. They'd knocked those houses down. They all came to live here. She talked about it like it was a great sea crossing. Years later, when Jasmine mentioned it, her mum had said that was the only time she'd ever heard her talk about it.

It used to be about as easy as getting your dad to talk about his growing up.

His dad had died when he was a baby, she knew that. He said he'd decided to be a doctor when he learned about his dad. His mother died when he was at medical school. They'd lived in Karachi, with his sisters and cousins and his dad's uncle. Jasmine had family in Pakistan and the States she'd never seen. One of the things she'd planned in her brief summer with Adnan was visiting her cousins in Pennsylvania, didn't know why she'd never pushed to do it before. It was complicated. Her dad was never keen. After that they could go to Pakistan. One day.

He'd arrived in England in 1966, the week that England won the World Cup. He joked that he thought the celebrations were for his arrival. Only half-joked.

Never underestimate the size of a man's ego, he said to her.

**England had kept the ball for about five minutes.** The clubhouse had quietened. Scholes had it when Rob looked up from the bar, knocked it, got it back again. This looked all right. Scholes again. It was opening up for him. Rob glanced at his dad, nodding his head. Scholes again. Argentina nowhere, all over the show, thanks to England's movement. Scholes, Ferdinand, Sinclair, Cole, Sheringham, Scholes again. How many passes? Twenty-odd, thirty. A hundred? This was amazing. Sheringham floated free on the right-hand side of the box. The ball came in to him. Volley. He hit it.

Rob leapt away from the bar. Jim and Glenn jumped from their seats as well. Everyone's arms in the air.

Yeeeaaaaaa –

It flew just over.

– ooooohhhh!

There were screams throughout the clubhouse, probably the biggest shout of the afternoon, everyone together, nobody feeling on their own now. Tom thumped his hand down on the table.

Of all the strange things to happen, England suddenly almost conjured up one of the greatest goals of all time.

It hadn't even been that good a game, not really, too cagey, not enough space, so to have produced that was something else. The feeling buzzed back through Rob, that feeling of victory, that feeling of everything turning out OK; better than that, that no matter how unlikely, you might just get everything you ever wanted. What was that saying? It was the hope that killed you.

England would win the World Cup.

Rob put the pints down on the table.

Bloody hell, what's going on? Van Basten.

There was that volley Van Basten scored in the European Championship final. Sheringham struck it the same way. Except Van Basten's head had dipped in, of course.

His dad was smiling and shaking his head. You just never know what's gonna happen, son. Yer never know.

**He'd met Lee at the Lion not long after opening on Saturday.** It was really to keep him company. Lee had given up his ticket for the Wolves game at Norwich, said he was sick of it, but regretted it now. He'd been to every game that season. He'd agonized week-by-week as Wolves managed

to give up a ten-point lead at the top in the new year and
fade away to let West Brom catch them in the last weeks
of the season. He was fed up of losing, he'd said, sick of it,
claimed he was never going back. It was all Lee had got,
really, no girlfriend or anything, a job pulling boxes
around a warehouse on the Stourbridge ring road, no car
to spend his money on, no interest in anything else really,
all his money going on the Wolves.

What else yer gonna do? Rob said. Yow've got nowhere
else to goo, mate. Yome stuck with em.

Rob had laughed along with the Albion supporters as
the Wolves gave up their lead. Like a lot of decent players,
Rob didn't really support a team. Not in the same way as
the others. As a kid he supported the Wolves because his
dad had played for them. He signed schoolboy forms at
the Villa at thirteen, so then he supported them, or said he
did. After his spells at the clubs, Rob couldn't have cared
less about them. He felt like he'd seen behind the wizard's
curtain. His old man was the same. Maybe it was bitter-
ness. It was players, groups of players, that they followed.
Institutions would let you down, but there were certain
players, groups of players, types of player, you could trust.
It was the reverse of Lee's approach. He put his faith in
the Wolves and look what they did to him. It was players
you had to put your faith in, not shirts and flags.

That hadn't stopped him insisting to his Uncle Jim that
Cinderheath was their club. It hadn't stopped him putting
a flag on his car. It hadn't stopped him and his dad following Valencia on Sky and in the Champions League that year.
They'd done it with Ajax the year they won the European
Cup, the year Rob was at Wrexham. Distance, foreignness,
seemed to heighten their affections, or maybe they just had
better players, types of player. Rob thought that he could
feel himself turning into his old man.

The door was propped open; weak sunshine highlighted

swirls on the tiles where someone had mopped the floor. Every few minutes the pub Alsatian, Binda, padded to the open door, arched his back and stuck his nose into the street. Kevin the landlord would shout him back and he'd slink to the other end of the bar and his bowl of water. Kevin sat talking to a bloke in a leather jacket who Lee had nodded hello to when they walked in.

Rob breathed out a stream of smoke, looked through the open door across to Barrys' and almost as far as the car park and launderette. The only other drinker was an old man in a shirt and tie looking at the racing pages. Past Kevin and his mate, Rob could see the lounge in darkness on the other side of the pub, curtains drawn and the DJ's booth and stage dark shadows at the edge of the room, ghosts of weekend nights. They used to open the Lounge up for food on weekends, but all that had stopped.

Lately, the place had become a drinking den for Glenn and his new mates, more and more faces turning up with their England and Rangers badges, Stone Island jumpers and Burberry caps, a kind of uniform, with their *Say No to the Mosque* leaflets. Not that it was all outsiders. You couldn't claim that. Glenn was right there at the heart of it. His uncle told him Nancy and Wesley had got a BNP poster up. You couldn't even rely on your own family.

He'd tried to persuade Zubair to move their weekly drink to the Wetherspoon's. What yer scared of? I've defended most of em, helped get a lot of em off, Zubair had argued. They'm hardly stupid enough to glass their own brief.

Doh be so sure, mate, Rob had muttered but left it at that.

Lee got the drinks, gazed up at *Football Focus*, wishing he was on the coach to Norwich. Rob stretched his legs out towards the sun, the dog came and sniffed at his trainers. He felt good for having had an early night, let his thoughts drift to his conversation with Jasmine, started thinking about Stacey. It had been Christmas since he'd been with anyone. They'd had the school Christmas party at the clubhouse and he'd ended up on the same table as Elaine, one of the dinner ladies, who'd brought her sister along with her. He'd fallen into drinking tequila with Elaine's sister. She was younger than him, but married with a little boy. After she'd danced with the big group of dinner ladies and teaching assistants, Rob staying at the bar, washing the taste of the tequila away with a couple of pints and keeping his eye on her, they'd gone across to the park, ended up shagging on a bench by the side of the pitches, her on top with his coat around her shoulders and her dress pushed up around her middle.

All over Christmas he'd waited for a bang on the door from her husband, thought maybe she might text him wanting a bit more. When he got back to school Elaine made him a cup of tea in the library and said nothing and everything was back to normal. Somehow, he couldn't see Miss Quereishi wriggling on top of him on a bench over the park, steam coming off them in the cold air. Then he thought about how he didn't want to think of her like that, but was happy enough thinking it about Stacey, wondered what that said about him.

We had a Chinese last night. I had a couple in here early on and went rahnd Glenn's. We got the PlayStation on after they'd got the kids abed. If I'd known yer was in I'd a texted yer.

I doh think I'd a bin very welcome.

He's all right.

Honestly, shuttle runs and shooting practice over the park. Yer know what he said to me when I said I was already warmed up? Big game on Sunday, Rob. Couldn't be bigger. I thought, fuckin hell, Glenn, I might o played in bigger.

His indignation was pretend now and he was smiling

as he said this, trying to get over the embarrassment of storming off from training.

It was funny though, when yer fell in that shit.

Oh, Jesus. Rob shook his head.

I kept loffin after. We come in here for one. We've brought him to this, I said. From Villa Park to Cinderheath Park. I was winding Glenn up telling him yow'd had enough, that yer most probly wunt play on Sunday.

Was yer?

He wanted to phone yer actually, check yer was all right. I tode him not to bother, leave yer be.

Cheers, mate. I doh think I could o took another dose. Iss difficult wi this election stuff.

He means well.

No he doh.

He's done well with the team.

Fair enough.

This time tomorrow we'll be finished up, mate. Lee nodded at the clock behind the bar. We'll be back in here, celebrating.

Hopefully.

They woh beat us.

I was more thinking that we wor all dahn the police station, fighting, race riot, yer know.

We'd win the fight an all. Lee sipped his pint. There woh be no fighting. Wiv gorra have more discipline than that. They've got it comin to em, though.

Rob didn't say anything.

How's Stacey's lad? Lee asked.

All right. Out the hospital.

Yer see the paper?

No.

Said they cut him with tribal markings.

What?

Said they cut him with tribal markings.

Woss that supposed to mean?

I doh know. Iss what it said.

What, like in Africa?

I doh know. It said boy given tribal markings in knife mugging attack. Summat or that. An there was a picture.

Summat or that?

Arr.

They ay Africans.

Who ay? It just said that. He looked a right state.

He was in a right state. I doh think thass very helpful though, is it?

Teenager scarred for life, it said.

I suppose he ull be. It gets on my nerves, though, the way they put it in the paeper like that.

The paeper day cut him. There was a picture. Him an his mother.

I dare say there was, but tribal markings? Meks it sahnd like he's bin attacked by savages or summat.

They am savages, mate. Lee took a big drink from his bottle to keep up with Rob and got up to go to the bar, sensing the conversation was going nowhere, the money he'd got for his ticket burning a hole in his pocket. Yer want some crisps?

Goo on, then.

I went to that meeting last week, yer know.

Which meeting?

The St George's day meeting up Dudley. They had some blokes from London doing a speech and our man, Bailey.

Jesus, what was they on abaht?

St George's day and being English. Housing, mainly. Bailey talked abaht the mosque. It ay right. How we should stand up for weselves.

Many theer?

Packed. There was loads o police aht the front an all. There was a demonstration against the BNP by all the students an tha. It was interesting. I got invited to that April 23rd club do an all. Lee said this proudly. Rob had no idea what the April 23rd club was, could've made a guess, he supposed.

What did they say abaht housing?

All the houses gooin to Kosovans an everything. Not people from here.

How many Kosovans dahn yower road?

We had that family they had to shift aht.

They was Yemeni. Different continent. They ended up in a bed and breakfast.

Yow know more abaht it than me. Iss right, though. Our cousin's bin on the list for ages for a flat an her ay got one. Iss cos her's white.

Tell her to goo an see me uncle up the school on a Saturday morning, see what he can do. Iss actually cos the Tories sold all the council houses off.

Labour, Tory; they'm all the same, mate.

They ay.

Arr well. Yer know more abaht it than me.

Listen to what I'm telling yer then.

All I know is, things ay right. Nobody looks aht for we. Iss everything for them. Yome all right if yome a Muslim but if yome from here yow con look aht. Watch when they build that mosque. What abaht the school? Yow've said it yerself.

I day say vote BNP. Yow cor vote BNP, mate.

Why not?

It ay right.

I'll vote for who I like.

Have yer even voted before?

Once, arr. I voted for Blair when he won. Lot o good thass done, look.

Well, there's a lot o damage to repair. Yow cor vote for them.

Why not?

Rob struggled to find an argument that might win Lee over and felt his heart sinking.

Iss racist.

I am a racist.

Well, thass it then, ay it. Rob sat back in his seat.

It is really, arr.

The man in the leather coat had said his ta-ras to Kevin and got down off his stool. As he came past them he leaned suddenly towards the table and put his hand on Rob's shoulder.

I tell yer what I'd do if I had the chance, mate. If Rob had turned his head, their faces would've touched. Send em back to Pakistan an let the Indians nuke the lot on em. The world ud be a better place. I'm votin BNP, mate, fuck the lot on em. And yow.

With that he nodded at Lee then up to Kevin, still on his stool at the end of the bar, and strode outside.

Fuckin hell. Yer doh wanna get on the wrong side of him, Lee said.

Rob's heart was pounding, he'd felt his legs go watery. He gripped his glass, stretched and blinked, tried to look unruffled.

To be fair, yome on his right side, he muttered.

They watched the television for a while.

I bet they win today, Lee said out of nowhere. I might have changed their luck by selling me ticket. It might be me.

Rob went to the bar.

I doh wanna hear talk of politics in here, Rob, Kevin said quietly and pleasantly, easing himself off his stool. I doh want yer upsettin nobody.

Rob could feel his heart going again.

All right, Kev. No problem. Pint o Carling and a bottle o Bud please, mate.

**Something happened in the weeks and months after Tom's injury.** First he got to wobble across the yard on his crutches, light-headed, a bit further each day until he could make it onto Cinderheath Lane. He'd go and work the contraptions at New Cross hospital that they got patients using to help them walk properly, and he'd have to spend the next day in bed, exhausted. But as summer passed though, he was able to walk along the towpath with his stick. The season started, the nights getting darker, whispers began again, of how great a player Tommy Catesby was, how if it wasn't for his injury, he'd have been lighting the Wolves up this year, how he'd have been in the England team soon, especially after Munich, in the wake of Munich.

He let them whisper, half-believed it himself, had no control over it anyway. The other half of him knew the truth, of course. He didn't say anything, let them all think it. Sometimes kids would knock on the door to get him to sign an old programme or football annual.

That winter he limped up and down Cinderheath Lane, slowly getting stronger, could almost straighten his leg. By spring he could get up and down the slag-heaps, sweating, thinking of all the running at the Wolves. If they wanted hard work, it was what they were going to get. He managed a shuffling jog along the canal towpath. People who'd never seen him kick a ball looked on and said, There's Tommy Catesby who was at the Wolves, great player, would've played for England, and shook their heads like he'd become his own ghost. One morning in the spring he walked up to the works with his dad and brothers and they got him a job on the furnaces. If they wanted hard work.

**On the morning of the attacks he was already in Vermont.** He'd got as far as JFK the previous morning. He sat there as the plane was called. His name was called. Not his real name. He'd thought that he could do it if he kept his mind empty. If he thought of nothing, it was easier. If he thought of her all the other stuff flooded in. He thought if he could keep his mind empty he could go back. It was the whole thing or nothing at all. If he went back to her, it would mean one day going back to Cinderheath. He tried to imagine his parents' faces, his brothers', if one day he just walked back in. He imagined how he'd do it. He'd pictured it thousands of times since the day he left. These thoughts crept in despite himself. That somehow there would be a happy ending. He walked out of the airport, hired a car, drove out of his life for a second time.

He zigzagged across the country for months afterwards. There were times he'd catch himself thinking he'd caused the attacks; that somehow his own frustrations, anger, fear, had willed the planes into the towers, torn them down in a cloud of ash. It was as if all his old pent-up frustrations and aggression had come exploding into the world.

He'd drive in the day, check into a motel and sit watching the news channels. That was all anyone watched now. It surprised him that he didn't get more attention. The country was changed, burned, you could feel it wherever you went. Maybe he was just too light skinned, well dressed, softly spoken. A couple of times he thought people were watching him; once in Louisville, where he'd visited Muhammed Ali's birthplace, eyes burning into him, he thought he was being followed. He thought how ironic it would be, that his story might end in an orange jumpsuit in Guantanamo. Then one night, in Oklahoma somewhere, he watched pictures of Tipton, looked at houses very much like the one he'd grown up in, the American newsreader describing a small British town and three of its boys, *jihadis* apparently, arrested in Afghanistan. He felt a strange nostalgia as the reporter interviewed a man in a paper shop who said, They'm just normal Tipton lads.

He had been half-asleep, on the edge of a dream, when he heard the first news report; it felt like he'd imagined it into being. He swung his legs off the end of the bed and turned up the volume, stood up to watch the pictures.

There was a moment when he waited for them to say his younger brother's name, to flash his picture up on the screen. He would be seventeen now. When they showed the boys' faces, he didn't know them – but it was as if he did. He might have known them had he stayed. They were younger than him. They'd have been the younger brothers and cousins of someone at the taxi office, maybe. He flipped channels to see other reports. They were guilty already, it had been decided. The reporters wanted to know how these boys from the English Midlands could end up in Afghanistan behind al-Qaeda lines.

He laughed and looked around the room. How did you end up anywhere? he thought.

**Jim and Bill were putting up election posters on lampposts.** They should've been up weeks before, really, but there was only so much you could do with two of you. Jim hadn't intended being out this late, but Pauline said there was ten pounds missing from her purse and she thought Michael had taken it. He'd been answering back a lot lately and spending too long in the shower but that hadn't turned him into a thief. Pauline reckoned it had happened a couple of times but Jim thought it just as likely to be the new Saturday girl in the salon so they'd had an argument in lowered voices, eating bacon sandwiches in the conservatory. Then Jim started having it out with Michael, which was never very successful.

Michael, you didn't pick any money up yesterday, did yer?

Eh?

Yow ay picked any money up that was lying around have yer or maybe bin in yer mom's purse for any, have yer?

Bin dahn me mother's purse?

Well, yer know, yer might o needed it for summat.

Bin dahn me mother's purse like some sorta crackhead?

Michael was shaking his head, helping himself to some juice from the fridge.

Michael, love. I was just sayin to yer dad that I had thirty pounds in me purse an now I've onny got twenty. I wondered if you'd had to use it for summat.

What would I goo dahn yer purse for?

All right, if yer didn't take it, son, wim sorry. Iss just happened a coupla times lately an we want yer to say if yer need any extra money. We know yome gerrin older an maybe wanna goo out the house a bit more.

Accusin me o stealin. Michael was muttering.

Sorry, son, all right. Come an have yer bacon sandwich with us, eh? We can all sit together.

I'm gooin upstairs.

Come on, son, five minutes an we can have a chat.

I'm busy.

With that Michael had gone thumping up the stairs.

I cor say a word to him, Jim said to Pauline.

I'll try an have a word with him, while yome out.

That made Jim feel worse. You should be able to have a conversation with your own son, even if he was changing and a teenager now.

What dyer reckon he's busy doin up there? Jim asked, trying to make a joke.

Pauline smiled but he could see tears come in her eyes. He just couldn't speak to him.

He couldn't remember Rob being like it. Maybe he should talk to Kathleen, ask her what it was she used to do with him. Rob had his football, Jim supposed, when he wasn't at school he'd be out playing, if not for a side then up and down on the grass outside the flats or over the park, even if he was just on his own banging a football back and forth against the wall. They should get Michael into something, anything, karate with Mark Stanley, even the army cadets, something, instead of sitting in that bedroom looking at the computer screen or, even more worrying now, shuffling out the house to God-knows-where.

Jim was heavy and ungainly on the ladders. He'd meant to ask Rob if he could come and help him. There was meant to be a system through the constituency party for getting posters up but it had gone to pot – or Trevor had got so annoyed with him he'd taken him at his word, left him to his own devices.

Two men were walking on the pavement towards Jim while he stood on the stepladders waiting for Bill to pass him some more cable ties from the car boot. The bigger one, the one with the leather jacket, Jim had nodded hello to in the Lion on a Sunday. The bloke lurched towards the steps with an exaggerated stride. As he did it, Jim thought he was going to knock the ladders from underneath him and, despite himself, threw his arms around the lamppost. The man swaggered away from the steps.

Watch yerself, he said, and he and his mate looked up and grinned. He spat in the gutter and turned away mumbling. The only bit Jim caught was, Fuckin council.

In the past Jim would've been down and after him. In the past it might not have happened. In the past Jim would've been after him, big bloke or not, and would have had him up against the wall of the baker's. Say that again an yow'll have another bad eye to worry abaht. Or saying nothing, just straight in and at him, putting him on the floor with his nose or his teeth in his hand. You had to stick up for yourself.

Instead, Jim found himself clinging to the lamppost, his

feet not quite steady on the step, not able to say anything because his mouth had gone dry and his heart was pounding. The two blokes went down the road, laughing; the one in the leather jacket looked back, stuck his fingers up. Jim shook his head, finally righted himself. Bill turned back from messing with the cable ties in the car boot, oblivious, whistling a Robbie Williams tune.

All right? he asked Jim. Yer wanna break in a minute?

No, fine, mate, fine.

Some time later, towards the other end of Dudley Road, nearer the mosque on the rise of the hill, looking back towards the works and Juniper Close, Jim could make out figures moving from house to house. There were two or three of them criss-crossing the road and the green where the children were playing. He saw a door open and a man with a big bare belly standing talking to the one in the blue suit with blond hair. That was Bailey himself, out canvassing. Even from this distance, half a mile nearly, you could see they were laughing. The fat man clapped Bailey on the shoulder and then Bailey walked away, still smiling, towards the end of the street. You could see the whiteness of his shirt from here, and the sheen from whatever he'd got on his hair. There were two others with him, in shirts and ties with short hair but not as glowing as him. They looked like Jehovah's Witnesses. Then, as Jim watched, with his poster half-attached to the lamppost, they walked towards the dip, towards Pauline's salon, and Jim could see through the trees that the van Bailey bent down and got into was a council works van with the logo clear on the side.

Woss gooin on here?! Jim shouted and jumped off the steps. He nearly turned his ankle on the kerb. Quick. Get in the car!

Woss the matter now? Bill turned as Jim was already clattering the steps into the boot, half-fixed poster swinging from the post above them. You couldn't see back into the estate from pavement level.

Bailey, Jim said, fumbling with the keys. Canvassing up Juniper Close in a council van!

**There were cheers, people banging tables, when the board went up to bring Batistuta off.** It was almost a carnival now, almost enjoyable. Crespo was coming on. The ball came to Sheringham again, another volley. This time he nearly kicked it to Korea.

They wanna be a bit steadier here.

Calm it down, his Uncle Jim shouted at the screen.

Rob leaned back, enjoying it for a minute. England would win the World Cup. Everything was going to be OK.

Nicky Butt took the ball off Aimar.

Nicky Butt, bloody brilliant, Jim announced.

There'd been a spell where they were murdering them. Glenn went down the left this time, outside his man, got the beating of them all, stopped it a yard in from the corner flag, beat the same man again, put a cross in with his right foot this time.

If Rob had kept running he would've got on the end of it, should've kept running, they needed one from somewhere. It was Paul Hill who'd gone in there, got his head down and onto it, looping in the air, over the keeper, dropping in, until Zubair appeared inside the post – he'd been lagging and keeping them onside – and headed it off the line.

Their heads dropped a little bit, like it was never going in. You needed a bit of luck. Next minute Twiglet tried to lay it back from midfield to Rob, and was miles short, Tayub was onto it. He swerved round Rob, who was back-pedalling, but was never going to get anywhere near him. Carl Jones was across but Tayub was away from him, those red boots taunting them again, and he was through and that would be it, at two-nil, the league would be gone.

Carl Jones kept at him this time. Nibbled at his heels. Big Chris stood up. Tayub hit it off his shoulder, the ball came loose and Chris fell on top of it.

There was clapping again.

Chris was up quickly, bowled the ball out to Rob's feet.

**By the time they'd turned the car around, Jim guessed that the van might have gone.** There was part of him, suddenly, waiting at the pedestrian lights, that thought it might be best not to run across the van at all. Still, you had to stand up for what was right. Chauffeuring candidates around in council vans wasn't right. He'd never been one for conspiracy theories but thoughts had crept in lately, that there were darker forces at work.

He drove the back way, to the canal end of Juniper Close, the direction in which the van had been pointed. There were a couple of little lanes here that ran through brambles into the works site, never really sealed off properly. You heard of all sorts going on down here. A man was stood with a dog on a lead waiting for it to finish a shit against a fence post, looking at them as Jim peered up the alleyways that led onto the works site.

All this place is good for these days, Bill said drily. In his free hand the man was holding a Tesco carrier bag, ready for the dog to finish.

I ay shekkin his ond, Jim said quietly to Bill, and then wound the window down.

Yow ay sin a council van drive up and down here, mate? Man and dog seemed to think carefully for a moment and then the man shook his head.

A council van? Yer woh see them fuckers dahn here, our kid. They knock off at twelve on a Saturday, any road. If they bother at all.

This left them to drive the length of Juniper Close, which Jim was never thrilled about at the best of times. A group of boys were playing football on the green in between the houses. There was no one else around apart from three little girls sitting on the wall where he'd seen Bailey walking from house to house. The window still down, Jim leaned out.

Hello, girls. Did yer see a man in a suit get into a van just here?

The eldest of the girls, seven or eight, holding an electronic game in her hand that she'd been showing to the other two, looked at him vacantly.

Did a van drive down here just now, girls?

The girl took a step nearer the car. Out of the corner of his eye Jim became aware that the football had stopped. A boy walked towards him, he was wearing a Cinderheath Juniors training top.

Stop talking to me sister, yer fuckin nonce.

The boy put his arm across the girl and stood looking into the car. A crowd of ten or so kids from the green walked down towards him.

I doh wanna hear that sorta language. I'm looking for a council van. I think one just drove up here and I need to find it, mate.

What, am yer pretendin to be a copper now, yer fuckin paedo? Fuck off.

Oi, I've tode yer to watch yer language, son. I'm askin yer a simple question.

The crowd of kids had now gathered around the car.

Who dyer think yome fuckin talking to? The boy's face had twisted. Two minutes before he'd been playing a nice game of football that Jim hadn't wanted to interrupt. Now there were muscles bulging out of his neck.

I think I should be sayin that to yow, son. Jim felt the urge to get out of the car, grab this foul-mouthed little lad

223

by the ear and go banging on his front door. A woman came out of the gate behind the kids, she walked towards them with her arms folded.

Woss gooin on? She spoke to the boy, not to Jim.

This one here. Stopped his car and started talking to our Leanne. Now he's pretendin to be some sort of copper after a council van or summat.

The woman was young, in her twenties, pale. Her hair was tied back but it fell out in strands on to her blue T-shirt. Jim didn't know her although she looked familiar.

Sorry, love. He tried a friendly tone but the tension came through in his voice. I'm lookin for a council van that come up here abaht five minutes agoo. There was people come rahnd canvassing, banging on doors, for the BNP, I think. I'm Jim Bayliss, yer councillor, yer might've sin me on the leaflets that come through the door.

What yer askin them for?

Eh?

What yer askin them for? They ay sin nothing. They ay speakin to strangers.

I ay a stranger. They was out playing when the van come up here. I just wanted to know.

Less leave this, eh, Jim. Bill spoke quietly.

What dyer mean yow ay a stranger. Do I know yer? Her face had pulled into the same expression as the boy's. Do I know yer? Her eyes were bulging.

I doh know if yer do but I've served this area for twenty-three years an bloody lived here all me life. I'm bloody President o that club whose training top he's wearin. If yer wanna know who I know, the Woodhouses at 18 and 21, Billy Smith dahn the end theer I went to school with. I onny live up the road meself, for Christ's sake, I doh have to justify meself to yow.

He was going short of breath.

I'm a Woodhouse. I doh know yer. Her voice had softened

a bit with recognition. She'd put her arm around her little girl. We doh have nuthin to do with the council.

Look, I'm onny askin if anybody ud sin a council van. I sid the bloke get in it just here, abaht five minutes agoo.

Did yer see anything? Again, to the boy.

No.

They day see nuthin. We cor help yer.

They was just here. The man in the suit kicked the football back to em.

Jim, less leave it, mate. Bill was more urgent this time.

If yer sid so much what yer want their help fower, yer pervert? The boy's head was almost in through the car window.

All right. Jim sighed then his anger rose again. Is this yower son?

What if he is? Her voice wavered now, back towards the hostility of before.

Yow wanna have a word with him abaht his language.

Doh come dahn here telling we what to do. Fuck off.

She began walking closer to the car. He had no choice but to get it in reverse. He couldn't even try to turn it around because of the tribe of kids standing there, laughing.

They reversed and thumped into a speed bump, jolting all over the place; the kids laughed and the mother glared after them from the gate. He had half a mind to drive back up there. Thump on Tony Woodhouse's front door. She must've been his granddaughter or niece or someone, but there'd have been no way of getting out of the car through the kids and what if Tony told him to fuck off too? When they hit the second speed bump, the couple of kids who had followed them down the road stopped running but scowled after them. A young man, in his twenties, the woman's husband or boyfriend or whatever they called them these days, was standing on the path with her glaring down the road after the car. The bloke with the dog turned the corner as they drove away, bag of shit hanging from his loose hand. One last kid ran past him as they drove up the road, no more than seven or eight, and hurled a stone after them. Jim watched its arc in the rear-view mirror as it bounced and hit the back wing.

He drove on, his mouth clamped shut, gripping the wheel as tightly as he could to stop himself from shaking.

Iss allus bin rough up theer, mate, Bill said calmly. I wouldn't worry abaht it.

They were distracted slightly by the sight of a young Asian lad running towards Juniper Close, wearing camouflage and a Manchester United shirt, a bandage on his wrist and jogging bottoms tucked into his socks.

Jim tried to ungrit his teeth, managed to nod towards the boy.

Think he'll be all right?

Who?

That lad in the Man United top.

Course he will, arr. Yow all right?

I've bin better, Bill, to be honest, mate.

**Rob and Lee both went up for a corner.** Rob asked Mark, how long? Ten plus injuries. Thirty-five minutes had just disappeared, in need of a goal.

Rob stood on the edge of the box, Lee was in front of him.

Yow goo in first, mate, I'll come in the back of yer. Just wait, hold back.

The others started to crowd the area. Doh goo too early, Rob ordered. Doh goo too early. No one seemed to listen.

Glenn's corner barely left the ground. He looked tired, swore loudly after he'd hit it. Zubair was at the near post, hacked it clear. A better ball might have put Tayub away down the field but they were all tired and the clearance

226

was decent enough, just up in the air towards the touch-line. They didn't move out quickly enough. Rob stayed pushed up. Rhys Woodhouse got the ball under control for once, stuck it back in, another clearance went up in the air, Glenn ran into the box and went up for a header, another header by the penalty spot, another header, a clearance that dropped towards the edge of the D.

As it dropped Rob saw it, took a stride towards it, expected a challenge to come in, saw Glenn trying to duck out of the way as it came towards him. He wanted to take a touch but there was no space, no time, and instead he kept his eye on a patch of mud on the side of the ball as it dropped, and he was there, and striking through it, head down, laces, he thought, a decent strike on it, felt it as it dropped off the outside of his boot. Rob's head shot up, taking a step through it. It went straight at the keeper but then veered and dipped past his hands and dropped to-wards the corner and it was in. For a moment it was in. It made a sound as it hit the inside of the post on the half-volley, spun back into the middle of the six-yard box, rebounding the other side of the keeper's arms. All this was taking ages now, ages and no time at all. The ball landed in front of Lee, who hit it, toe-poked it, right into the middle of the net. There were shouts. He thought he heard Zubair shout, No. Glenn ran towards him with his arms out. Rob listened for the whistle and there it was, Mark Stanley pointing towards the centre-circle and it was in! The keeper sat down in the mud and Zubair was sat down in front of him. The ball had gone through a hole flapping in the net and rolled away down the bank. Rob turned away with a rush, after Lee, chasing Lee, who'd found a bit of pace, running back towards the half-way line, running away from them all.

And none of it mattered now. Who was playing, who they were playing for, none of it mattered, other than the fact that they'd scored, that they were winning the league. Rob's fists were clenched, pumping. He ran back past Mark Stanley towards their half, the rush fizzing away, chasing Lee, grabbing a handful of Lee's shirt. The figures on the sideline caught his eye, the bloke who'd spoken to him at half-time, Bailey, laughing and enjoying the goal. Rob pulled Lee's shirt and Lee scampered to a halt, arms raised, the others catching up. Glenn tried to jump on Rob's back as they pulled Lee to the ground. As he hurtled around Lee the figures came into view again, their arms raised in triumph. Mark Stanley blew hard on the whistle to stop the celebrations. Glenn's arm came round in front of his face and they fell in a nest of arms and legs on top of Lee. Rob could feel Lee's heart thumping against the cool muddy ground as he rolled across him.

**Collina blew for a high foot from Nicky Butt.** Rob tore half his little fingernail off as it was awarded, stuck his finger in his mouth as Argentina lined up the free-kick. Stacey was out collecting glasses. She put her arm on Rob's shoulder and leaned on him as she bent to the table. Rob saw Glenn glance across at them, look away, back at the screen.

**Rob had been waiting outside the Head's office for a while.** He should have been outside getting the tennis courts ready. The nets took a while to untangle but it was a nice job, laying out the nets and counting up the rackets, making a note for Jacko to order more tennis balls. There was the feel of summer around with the weather, the idea of a game of tennis. He planned to take a cup of tea out there and grab a few of the kids kicked out of lessons to help and maybe have a little game with them, but if he had to wait much longer, waiting for her to get off the phone, then he'd get caught up with the madness of swarms of kids coming out for lesson 4, running around with the rackets and wrapping themselves in the nets. He assumed she wanted to talk to him about the attack on Andre. The old Head would see him occasionally for a chat about things that were going on and whether he'd heard anything. It might've been about the reading scheme, though, about helping Jasmine next year.

He sat daydreaming about Jasmine. In the daydream they were playing tennis. Afterwards they went for a meal, sitting outside in the sunshine; after that they walked along holding hands.

Come in, Rob. Ms Dragovic popped her head around the door. He got up and followed her.

Sit down, please. She gestured.

She'd changed things around in here, turned the table more towards the window and got things up on the wall, some kids' artwork and a couple of African-looking fabric prints. Next to her in-tray and computer screen was a series of photos. A family group of her with her husband and two daughters. One of the young women on her own in university graduation gear; the other one dressed in outdoor stuff and wearing a helmet, standing in front of mountains somewhere like Australia or Canada. The room looked brighter, more cheerful for its makeover. He'd signed his schoolboy forms for the Villa in here, the old Head looking over his desk. He remembered how his mum was beaming. How his old man had looked like he'd rather not be there. The Head announced to everyone, He's a good lad, and nodded his head as if that sealed the deal. They were talking about Lilleshall, about England schoolboys, and Rob remembered his heart beating a bit faster as he listened but the letter or call never came.

The new Head sat on the edge of her desk, which felt too close, and it meant she was towering above him, even though she was short and wore astonishingly high heels with her smart business suits and perfect makeup. She looked the part, though, Rob had to say, fiftyish but with a hard, tight body that you could tell she'd be sorting out in the gym on her way home to her perfect family or with laps around the park listening to a self-help mantra on her headphones. He wouldn't have been surprised if she had a personal trainer; a couple of lads he'd played with at Stourbridge had gone into that, said it was all the rage with the older, wealthier, professional women and that sometimes there was a little bit of work on the side – but he reckoned they were making that up. He tried to push the thought from his head by thinking about the increasing size of his stomach and the way his body felt as if it was slowly turning to jelly. He was the one in need of a personal trainer.

You've made it look nice in here, he said for something to say.

Look, Rob, I'll get straight to the point. I was going to get Peter Jackson to speak to you but I thought I should see you myself. It's your shirt. I'm not sure it's appropriate for you to be wearing it given the nature of the school and the community we're in.

Rob pretended to look down to check what shirt he was wearing. It was the new, red England football shirt. He was wearing that over a pair of Umbro jogging bottoms, his shorts underneath, with the bottoms tucked into a pair of old Cinderheath first team football socks. That was what he wore to work. He had hundreds of football shirts, literally, in piles in the bottom of his wardrobe.

What dyer mean?

Well, a lot of people might not notice it at all, but given the nature of things that are going on, tensions in the community, the local election coming up, as you know, but wider concerns than that as well, I think that some members of our community might be offended. I wouldn't want you standing on patrol on the front gates wearing that, for example.

The message was really only dawning on him now.

Because it's an England shirt? he asked.

Well, yes. She was obviously uncomfortable saying this but it wasn't stopping her. Not just an England shirt but the connotations of it. I mean the message it gives.

I know what connotations means.

In that case you understand what I mean.

You don't want me to wear it.

Well, I'd like you to think about it, because of the message it might send out to people.

Dyer want me to goo home and change? he asked in a voice he'd intended to sound challenging but came out as a straightforward question.

No, no, not at all. That's not necessary. You're out in PE the rest of the day, after all, and you're not on the gate tonight, so that's fine.

Right, OK. I don't think it's offensive.

No, nor me personally, but, like I said, I think some people might, and we need to be sensitive about these things in our community.

She'd said our community about seventeen times. He knew for a fact she lived over in Edgbaston or Moseley, somewhere, somewhere not here.

OK. He said this meekly but couldn't look up, felt embarrassed. Are any other shirts banned?

No, your shirt's not banned. Not at all and I wouldn't want to give that impression. I'm just asking you to think about wearing something else. It's only overtly nationalistic ones that I'm worried about. I'd be happy to see you running around in a Villa shirt, for example. She was trying to joke with him now, authority imposed.

I think those days might be over, he said, realized she

didn't get the joke – why would she? – and said, I've got a few of them, actually. Then he said, What if I think there's nothing wrong with it?

Well, obviously I appreciate your opinion, Rob. We want to listen to the views of all staff here. Like I say, it's just that I've got some concerns. I think we need to think about these things sensitively. You could talk about it more in line management, of course, I've asked Daniel Bell to talk to Mr Jackson about your contract.

I haven't got a –

They were quiet for a moment.

I've got loads of football shirts, he said. Villa, everybody.

That's great. OK. Thank you, Rob, I thought you'd understand. I appreciate it. What've you got now?

I'm meant to be sorting the tennis stuff out, getting the courts ready. That's what they're teaching mainly, next few weeks.

Great. I have to see Mr Bell with some exam data.

She was still trying to be friendly. Shaking her head and smiling and arching her body as she got up to go back behind the desk, as if she'd like nothing better than to get out to the outdoor stores and roll around on top of the nets with him before they untangled them for the kids.

Rob took that as leave to go. In fact, as he got up, Daniel Bell, the new Deputy who she'd brought with her and Rob had never spoken to, knocked and popped his head around the door.

Bye, thanks, Rob said, kicking himself again for his own obsequiousness, his weakness.

As he left, he remembered that he hadn't even asked about the reading scheme, or mentioned Andre. He turned to go back and saw the Head through the half-open door blowing out her cheeks and nodding in his direction, thinking he'd gone, looking at her grinning Deputy. Rob had only ever seen that expression in school on teachers' faces, they must've been taught it at college or something. A kind of one-eyebrow-raised sneer that was followed by a roll of the eyes and then a smile as if something was incredibly ironic. They also used it when the kids he worked with turned up late to lessons wearing a tracksuit because no one had washed their uniform or when taking big gold jewellery off surly teenage girls found wandering the corridors.

He went to the staff toilets and sat in a cubicle for a while with his head in his hands and thought he might cry, repeating, I've got loads of football shirts, over and over, then jumped up and kicked a hole through the partition wall, smacked the cubicle door off one hinge with the flat of his hand.

**Sinclair kept going.** He'd got it again now, head down again, got a shot away, still all England.

Now time went slowly. Rob asked Mark again and he said four and a half. They'd got Zubair wide on the left, trying to launch it into the box. Kyle Woodhouse seemed to have ignored Rob's instruction to just fuckin stand on him. In fact, he seemed to have disappeared completely, which left Zubair trying that ball again, hitting it crossfield, trying to get it over Rob and behind the full-back. Now Rob was in control, though. He got up, flattened the lad with the beard in winning a header. Then another one. The next one Chrissie started to come for, was never going to make it, Rob got across, facing his own goal but managed to turn into it, got a bit of distance on the header.

As he turned to try to get them out again, he saw a figure standing up on the hill, clapping his clearance. His old man hadn't been to see him play for nearly twenty years.

**Mohammed came to see him the day Andre started speaking again.** Getting stabbed had raised Andre's status at the school no end. Girls fussed around him. The boys seemed suddenly to want him to hang around with them. He swaggered along the corridor with a new cockiness. He didn't turn up to the reading session Rob had agreed with him.

All right, Mo. Have yer got a lesson?

Mohammed waited around at the edge of the PE store. Maths.

Yer gonna go to it then, mate. Yow'll be late.

Mohammed stood there.

Come on, mate.

Yer know if there's a fight?

Yeah. Is there gonna be a fight?

Nah, not today, but yer know if there's a fight?

Yeah?

What if there's a fight and someone's there but the person fighting gets really beat up and there's someone just there but the person gets really beat up or even stabbed or summat, what happens if you was there? Would you be in trouble?

What you on about, mate? Has somebody been beaten up?

Mohammed shrugged.

Is this about what happened to Andre?

Who's Andre?

Yer know, the boy who's just come back to school. Someone did attack him with a knife.

Just say, say something happened that was like that. Say someone gets beat up but there was loads of people there. Do they get into trouble?

Depends if they get caught, I suppose.

Rob realized that wasn't the best thing to say, had another think. It just depends, mate. Depends on the circumstances. Yer know what's been said in assemblies. If you hang around trying to mek people fight one another that's just as bad as the ones fighting.

234

Say someone got beat up or stabbed and someone filmed it?

Filmed it?

Yeah, filmed it.

I really doh know, Mo. Is this something that's really happened?

Mohammed shrugged again.

Look, is this about something yow've seen?

No, I was just asking.

A voice called over from the fire-exit doors. Have you got a lesson to go to? The new Deputy, Mr Bell, shouted across towards them. Rob got the impression that he was talking to him as much as to Mohammed, pictured smacking him in the mouth. Mohammed could film that if he wanted to.

Yes, sir. Mohammed started to shuffle towards the doors. Rob got his head down, continued counting bent and broken tennis rackets.

**Argentina put together a series of one-twos around the edge of the England box.** Aimar got it again, put a shot over.

There was a story that Stan Cullis had come to Tom's house in his overcoat in the middle of the night to sign him for the Wolves. There were people who swore they'd seen the car edging down Cinderheath Lane. It was what Matt Busby had done with Duncan Edwards. No one was comparing them, really. Duncan Edwards was a one-off, a freak of nature, could do anything, everything. Norman Deeley from down Wednesbury was a better comparison. But the midnight visit, the drama of cups of tea in the front room in the early hours, just showed there was a ghost of Duncan Edwards before he died. Some people just rearrange the world in their wake without even noticing.

The story was when Cullis and the Wolves officials left

that morning, men were already on their way to the early shift up Cinderheath Lane, Tom's own dad stuffing his sandwiches and bottle of cold tea into his pocket, Tom heading slowly upstairs to bed for a couple of extra golden hours in bed, secure in his own destiny.

Jim asked him about it once.

Iss a load o rubbish, Tom said. I signed in the office like everybody else. I'd already bin there for years anyway, by then.

One night, after a few too many, Bill told him the story of how he'd seen Stan Cullis's hatless head in the back of the Wolves car as it drove up Cinderheath Lane, the morning they'd signed Tom Catesby.

**There was a turning off the road between Worcester and Stratford.** Then another turning, then another, into smaller and narrower roads. The last road had grass growing up the middle, fattening hedgerows, and hills on either side with tended fields. Two magpies sat watching on a fence-post, looking down at something in the hedge. A tractor spewed blue smoke halfway up a field. They drove on these roads for twenty minutes or so. Glenn watched through the minibus's back window, his arm across the seat backs, around Lee, so he could see where they were.

Anne hadn't wanted him to come. It was unusual for him to do anything without her and the kids, apart from go out to work and to football. And to election meetings, these days. He'd been flattered, though, by the invitation, but Lee had probably swung it. He wouldn't have come on his own and his eyes had lit up when Kenny had passed them the invites.

Kenny turned to pass a couple of cans back to Glenn and Lee, had to turn all the way around so he could see them with his good eye. Lee grabbed the drinks; said, Cheers. Glenn told himself to drink slowly, holding the wet can – they had two twenty-four packs sitting in a bag of ice leaking over the floor up the front. Something about Kenny didn't add up. They hadn't known him long; he was from Wolverhampton. He'd been in the army, been in Northern Ireland, talked in half-stories, like he always thought you knew more than you did. All those weeks discussing the election in the Lion, Glenn had just nodded his head, kept quiet, offered practical suggestions about where to get the vote out, local grievances, from the mosque down to Nancy and Wesley and the people in that row despairing about the kids drinking and fighting at the bus-stop. When he'd added his bit of local colour to conversations in the pub's back room, Bailey had nodded his head seriously and made a few notes. Kenny would just grin and stand up to get a round in. You had to concentrate though, break things down to specifics, as small as you could, win people over one at a time. Glenn realized vaguely that he'd picked that up from listening to Jim on Tuesday teatimes when he was a kid. Not that it had done them any good in the end. Sixty-odd votes. It had been so close. So close for nothing at all.

Something made Glenn think Bailey wouldn't be there today. If he was, he wouldn't be there for long. Something made him wary, not just Anne's instructions to be careful, to think of her and the kids. What he thought, he supposed, was that Kenny wasn't Bailey. There were layers. Or rather, there were things that overlapped. April 23rd Club, the invite said, Gentlemen's Luncheon, 4th May. He'd been flattered, of course he was. Kenny had given it to him as if it was a ticket to say he belonged. The thing was, though, he didn't need a ticket to tell him that. He knew he belonged, knew where he belonged. That was the whole point of this business. Lee, of course, had come back from the bar, eyes shining, like someone had given him the winning Lottery ticket.

He was getting the feeling they'd gone down the same road a couple of times, that they were the same magpies cocking their heads towards the back of the minibus, not flying away like the other birds, not bothered in the slightest, when they turned again. This time they stopped at a gatehouse of some sort, a gravel drive leading away from it through the trees. Kenny leaned forward to speak across the driver's shoulder to two men wearing black roll-necks and holding walkie-talkies. The men stepped back and waved them on.

The driveway rose for a few hundred yards and then fell away steeply. In the valley was a big house, yellow stone and eight chimneys in a black roof. There were outbuildings, probably stables and the like, and a big marquee pitched in the meadow that ran from the garden. A stream ran down from the far hill. They parked in the field on the other side of the marquee.

The place was busy already. Men milled around in little groups, some holding cans, some pints from the bar that had set up in the marquee; they shouted to people arriving who they recognized. A bloke wearing a regimental blazer shouted over to Kenny in a Belfast accent. Glenn looked at the groups, wondered whether you could tell the soldiers from the civilians, wondered whether it mattered when it came down to it.

There were speeches in the entrance hall of the main house before they ate. Their group was introduced as Cinderheath and got a round of applause and some cheering, despite the result. Glenn was feeling the drink already. There were toasts to St George and the Queen. There was a portrait of the Queen halfway up the stairs. It made Glenn think of the police station, that picture of the Queen looking down on him the time he got arrested. The only time he'd been in trouble, he got picked up with Dave Woodhouse for fighting some lads from the Wren's Nest outside the Saracen's in Dudley. After a few hours the police let them go. They walked down Castle Hill as it was getting light.

The bloke who had been talking to Kenny clapped Glenn on the shoulder.

Grand job over there, Cinderheath.

We day win though, did we?

Don't worry, son. Our day will come, as they say, eh? He laughed and thumped Glenn on the shoulder again, too hard. Glenn didn't see what was funny.

**Back and forth now, Rob rocking on his chair.** Cole had won a free-kick down the left, Beckham put it in, Sheringham got in front of his defender, flicked a back-header just over the bar. That would have finished it.

Rob brought it down on his chest when it ballooned up by the corner flag, got his foot through it, sent it up the line. Glenn almost kept it in. He was aware of his dad clapping again, his control, he assumed.

How long, Mark?

Mark made a big display of looking at his watch. One minute.

Glenn was shaking his fist. Come on, lads, this ull do it. Over the top if yer get it now. This ull do us. Discipline, keep it tight.

He ushered Lee further up the pitch.

**Rob had a break in the lesson between lunchtime and afternoon clubs.** Jasmine did her admin in this lesson. He'd taken to bringing her a cup of tea and sitting chatting for a while.

He was exaggerating his role in his uncle's election campaign. His input so far had been helping to put up a few posters and trying to win the Sunday League for the BNP. He talked to her about how things were going, stringing her

239

the usual line about the BNP coming in from outside to exploit the vulnerabilities of a place like Cinderheath, how really it was still coming to grips with the end of industrial life. I blame Thatcher, he said, which he did, but the truth was much more complicated than that. Jasmine was too polite to question it, but seemed interested, even said he should be proud of himself, being so bothered about it, as people generally wouldn't put themselves out.

I need to talk to you about something, she said.

He knew it was too good to be true. She was going to tell him she hadn't wanted to give the wrong impression. It was nice he brought her a cup of tea, but maybe not every day, and that drink they'd arranged to meet for, maybe that wasn't such a good idea.

Well, I need to show you something, she continued. Look at this.

She motioned him over to the computer, clicked on something with the mouse.

I'd got some Year 7 boys in here this morning and while I was getting their tests sorted out, they were playing a game on the computer. When I walked over to get them they'd got this up on the screen.

She clicked the media player open. You could hear the wind and children shouting. The screen showed the view of a block of flats, a St George's flag draped from a balcony, they looked like the ones near the shops. Mohammed's face appeared on the screen, holding his fist like a microphone and shouting something unintelligible. A couple of other kids from that year group waved their arms around in the background. It was the flats by the shops.

They were in the alley behind the shops. There were twenty or so of them, kids running around. It looked confused, the film was of a camouflaged sleeve and rubbish strewn on the floor as whoever was filming ran or jumped. There were huge shouts. The picture focused again. Andre.

He was half-sitting on his bike, pulling the bike towards him while two or three pairs of hands tried to pull it from him. There was blood on his face. The hands pulling the bike were all wearing camouflage jackets, you couldn't see their faces. Rob thought he could guess a couple of boys from the older years. A shape jumped in and kicked the bike, buckled it under Andre. The boy doing the kicking was little Rhys Woodhouse. Up until then, all the other boys shown had been Asian. Rob assumed they'd been Asian. The screen went blurred again. Then back to Andre, bleeding, still hanging on to his bike; an arm came over, someone with a knife, hit Andre's shoulder. Another white kid. The screen blurred again, then went blank. Rob went to say something. Then it started up again. Kids running. Mohammed's face with his fist up commentating again, then he ushered towards the camera, more muffled sound and blurred camouflage. Then Michael's face as they ran along, out of the alley behind the shops and out near the entrance to the park. Michael was grinning and laughing, then the screen went blank again.

It's saved on the school system, she said incredulously.

Rob blew his cheeks out.

Has anybody else seen it, yet?

Apart from all the kids, you mean? No.

We better go and see Ms Dragovic, I suppose. He sighed.

Oh, I'm sorry, Rob. She put her hand on his, the other up to her mouth. He wanted to stay sitting there, her hand on his.

**He was in the desert.** This thought hit him drunkenly as he leaned on the balcony at the front of the motel room looking across the scrubland and at the cold, hard stars. He took a drink from the bottle of Jim Beam that he'd rested on the balcony rail, the stars shooting as he jerked his head back to drink. He thought of the world turning through space. Roswell, New Mexico: dinosaurs and space-ships and a young Hispanic prostitute without much English lying on the bed in his room. He'd picked her up because she looked like Jasmine.

He could've just asked her to come with him. Could've told her he couldn't go home but that she could come with him. He could've tried something. Something other than running away, of course. That was what he did. Run away.

He threw his head back and the sky reeled. He used to be able to name all the stars. Not here, though, with so many. Time passed and you forgot and had to grope around in your memory to try to bring things back. A satellite blinked evenly above him, a satellite or an alien spaceship, and he giggled and shifted his view back to the highway in front of him and the desert beyond it. He stepped back and slung the bottle wildly across the road. It sailed in an arc, last drops of whiskey splattering the highway tarmac, and landed silently in the dust. Everything was quiet. He'd been seeing cowboys for the last few weeks. He thought of his dad, claiming to have learned English from Westerns. All the things he couldn't ask him. The stars blurred again with tears. He could go back, he thought, in a sudden wild surge of hope, could just go back. Then he turned and opened the door and disappeared into the room.

**Argentina again.** Campbell, looking bigger now, blocked a cross like a brick wall.

They heaved it one last time towards the box. Rob again, a few steps, pushing Lee out of the way as he got up, got his head firmly on it and away it went again. It dropped towards the halfway line. Out, out, out again, he said.

Mark Stanley let the ball bounce past him, put the whistle to his mouth and blew for time. They'd done it.

There were shouts of Yessss! from the huddle on the sidelines. The mosque players had their hands on their knees. Rob put his arms up. Felt suddenly self-conscious with everyone patting him on his back and went over to Lee.

Fuckin great game, Rob, Lee said. Over his shoulder Rob watched Glenn run across to Bailey and the others on the side, shaking hands and clapping each other on the back.

What abaht yow, mate. Eh? Rob had grabbed Lee round the neck. You ay scored since yow was in the Cubs, have yer? He ruffled Lee's hair, harder than he should have, still looking at the touchline. Lee looked delighted with himself, though. Fuckin brilliant, he kept saying, and shaking his head.

Three policemen strolled across the pitch with Mark Stanley. The plan was obviously to get everyone away with the minimum of hassle. Rob glanced across at the cars at the side of the pitch to see if anything was going to happen. Some of the players were shaking hands. Chrissie was going over to their players who hadn't walked off. Rob tried to shake Tayub's hand. He didn't really look at him. Rob walked across to Zubair, his hand out. They shook.

Hope yome pleased wi yerself, Zubair said and nodded towards the group that had pulled out a St George's flag to celebrate with.

Well played, mate, Rob said. I'm just glad it's over.

Zubair nodded. I'll give yer a ring, he said. Then, Less get out of here, over Rob's shoulder to Tayub.

Rob pulled his shirt off. He used to do it at the end of games when he moved down to semi-pro and still had a professional's body. Now he had a pot-belly beginning to emerge over the top of his shorts, pale and flabby skin, a promise of the middle age to come.

243

He jogged towards Glenn and Bailey and the bloke with the glass eye, who were doing a little dance with the flag. Kyle Woodhouse and Twiglet ran across to join them. Carl Jones had popped open a bottle of pomagne that he must've hidden in the kitbag. When he got to the flag-dancing Rob dropped the shirt on the floor in front of them and carried on towards the dressing rooms. The police were trying to usher them off the pitch. Rob just pulled a T-shirt on and grabbed his kitbag, turned and jogged back past the celebrating figures. More bottles of pomagne had emerged, Lee was spraying one around, flicked some towards Rob.

Yer comin in for the photo, Rob?

Lee nodded towards the group that was forming around the flag. There was someone from the paper. One of Bailey's mates had a camera with him as well.

Rob shook his head, didn't break stride, put his thumb up to Lee and winked, kept running, back past the goal and up the hill until he fell in step with his dad.

All right?

All right, Dad.

Yer played well, mate. Decent game. In the circumstances, like.

I'm glad iss over. Thass it for me, now, he said.

They'll want yer next season.

Rob shook his head.

Yow all right walkin, Dad? he asked.

Course I am. I ay finished just yet.


**Rob started leafleting down at the canal.** It meant calling by his old flat. Someone buzzed him in and the entrance hall still held a new smell of fresh wood, carpets and glue, like it had when he and Karen had lived there, fainter now but still there. He'd nearly given the block a miss. When he'd delivered general election leaflets this time last year, he'd felt like someone had put his chest in a vice and his eyes had filled with tears. He'd dumped the leaflets on the floor of the entrance hall and walked out, had a cigarette looking at the ducks on the canal to calm down. It wasn't even like he missed Karen any more. At first, he'd missed her so much it had felt like he was being suffocated. People said time healed; people said a lot of things.

Yow'll allus miss her, mate. I miss Jackie an I love yer Aunty Pauline, wouldn't have anything any different.

Jim knew a lot of things. Maybe he was right about these leaflets after all. He'd written different things for each language. The English ones said he had reservations about the mosque, the others said he thought it was a great idea. Jim guessed no one would read both. Rob wondered if anyone read them at all.

No tears on this visit. In fact, he went round to each of the flats, dropping a leaflet on each doormat. When he got to their number seven he stopped for a minute. There was a mat outside the front door that wasn't there before and a plant in a pot to the side, which he thought looked good. He breathed in and remembered the sound the door would make as it opened – like opening an air lock in a spaceship – and the flat's bare white walls and wooden floors. On the left on the way in he'd got a Villa shirt he'd played in, another one signed by Dwight Yorke and McGrath that he'd asked them for when he was released. They were sitting at the back of his wardrobe now, behind his piles of football shirts; perhaps he'd put one on for Ms Dragovic.

**They'd queued for tickets to the Saturday morning picture show.** Now they were queueing for ice-cream. Zubair was holding Camilla's hand while Katie messed in the bag she'd got hanging from the pushchair. Zubair couldn't believe the numbers of people. Dudley had gone ten years without a cinema at all, now it had a huge multi-screen that was always packed. It was good, he supposed, it must mean there was more money around. Right now, though, with children's voices echoing back off the plastic surfaces and niggling at the hangover in his temples, artificial light that reminded him of police station interview rooms and the prospect of an hour or so of blaring cartoons, he would've preferred to have been somewhere else.

They might not last long, he thought. It was the first time they'd tried Camilla at the cinema. His daughter moved her hand in his and it seemed to pump him more full of life. He felt suddenly guilty for wanting to have been doing something else. She was a beautiful little girl. He knew that he was bound to think so, but Katie told him that people came up to her in Tesco and said as much.

Camilla stood patiently in the queue holding his hand, watching serenely as other kids rampaged up and down around them. He wasn't sure how she had turned out so calm, given his and Katie's temperaments. Another of the miracles of parenthood, he supposed. She took after her gran maybe, Zubair's mother, who would move through her house steadily, slowly these days, but with an air that suggested whatever calamity might befall them – and calamity was never far away – she would wait it out. Things took their toll, though. She was looking tired lately, turned fifty now after all. She never mentioned Adnan but she'd touch the photo of his dad on the cupboard at the bottom of the stairs as she went up to bed. He'd seen her do it when he left late at night, as he watched through the little window at the side of the front door to check she was OK. Her life. As he got older he marvelled more and more at the adventure of her life, sent from a village up in the mountains that wasn't even there any more to come and join her husband here, of all the places in the world. He wondered when she realized she was never going back, and how hard that was. Women were more rooted than men, he thought. They'd wait things out. He didn't believe his dad took one backward glance, couldn't wait to leave.

The house would be too much for her on her own. If Tayub left. When Tayub left. She'd lost energy with her youngest son. When Zubair had gone round there the other day, there'd been a bass sound throbbing through the house, coming from his brother's room, the bigger room, the one he and Adnan had shared. If either of them had ever tried that, and they did, their dad would've been up the stairs, ripping wires from the walls, their mother at his heels. It had always been unclear to him whether she was chasing her husband because she agreed with him or whether she was protecting her boys. Both, he guessed now.

He'd thought it was hip-hop at first, the growl of the music that came from the earphones of boys who he spoke to about matters such as who exactly pulled the screwdriver first. It wasn't, though. As he climbed the stairs and his ears adjusted to the fuzzy sound of a stereo that Adnan had customized years ago he realized it was preaching. He'd heard him playing a Hamza Yusuf tape a few months before; this was different though, growling, angrier, talking about the infidel.

Zubair frowned. Tayub turned it off. He was going through some kind of crisis, travelling across Dudley to a more ramshackle, younger mosque, much less moderate than the one in Cinderheath or up in Dudley itself. He'd also spend an hour waxing his hair before he went out, was neglecting his college work, lifting weights in front of the mirror in the corner of the room where Adnan's computer had been. That day he'd wanted to show Zubair his new, bright red football boots.

They're boss, man, he'd said.

They'll see yer comin.

He'd enjoyed coming to pick Tayub up on Sunday mornings that season. The reason Zubair had carried on playing football had been to do this, to play in the same team with his brother. He'd try to give him advice light-heartedly in the car. He found himself suggesting that the solution to any problems Tayub might have was a few games of football and getting a girlfriend. Zubair thought they were the solutions to most young men's problems. Or rather, he knew they weren't, but they were as good a way as any to paper over the cracks. We never say the things we mean, he thought.

Tayub was a good player, quick, moved like Adnan, not like Zubair, who was built more like his dad, took after him more, or had become more like him: forward, always forward, work hard and you'll get on, try to stay on the surface of things. His dad had no time for the past. Not his own, anyway. He liked to watch old cowboy films and joke that this was how he used to practise his English. He liked other people's pasts, other people's stories.

Tayub was at the age now when he and Adnan had stopped really speaking. A bit older maybe. Zubair had been at university, getting on. Adnan had reduced himself until the only space he filled was the narrow one between the beds where he'd set up the computer. He knew he'd gone when he saw the computer was missing. He thought now, every day if he was honest with himself, which was rarely, that he could've done something more for Adnan, could've done something before it came to that, someone of all his talents reducing himself to a corner of the bed-room, the anonymity of the taxi driver's seat.

It was Zubair who was fidgeting, not Camilla, standing there in her jelly shoes and floral dress with a matching red flower hairclip. Katie folded the pushchair, they'd had to park miles away, he reached out to help.

Why don't you nip out and have a cigarette while you can, darling? she said, and kissed his cheek, folding the pushchair with one hand.

He'd been trying to give up, of course. She leaned into him as she kissed him and he put his arm around her. Katie went to the gym. He would have to do something. If he stopped playing football completely – Sunday mornings and Wednesday night five-a-side – he was going to be the size of a house. Smoking as well. Lately, when he had a cigarette, he heard his dad's rattling morning cough and then later, late on, the cough like he was drowning. His old man had been fifty-three when he died. If he went at that age Camilla would be twenty-four. He wanted to grow old, see his grandchildren. They planned on having more kids themselves. He was trying, cutting back, had taken to drinking wine lately instead of beer. The problem was he drank wine at the same pace as beer. That was why he had a hangover.

Zubair became aware of someone looking over as they shuffled along the queue. Glenn Brown was over there, wiping one of his kids' noses while they sat on a purple monster at the edge of the play area. They nodded hello to each other. Civil. Katie stiffened, glared, put her hand on his shoulder. This BNP stuff would all blow over. In some ways it was more honest. All this stuff would fade, dissipate like drifting smoke. Maybe he was like his mother, after all. You had to endure. That was all there was in the end.

Goo on, baby, while you've got the chance, if yer want one.

Zubair wondered if Katie encouraging his smoking was a new strategy. Reverse psychology. She was into things like that.

All right, then. He winked. I'll be quick.

Daddy will be back in a minute, sweetheart. He kissed Camilla's head.

He'd worried, lately, when reports came on TV, about who would be the first to bang on their door, to herd them into trucks or whatever, if things were different, if people decided they could get away with it. He watched the ash fall from his cigarette. A knock at the door in the middle of the night. He smiled at a woman, smoking as well, some kid's grandmother probably, sneaking in a crafty one before the cartoons. She was wearing a pink tracksuit and had her hair up in a spectacular beehive. The problem he had was that a cigarette was the only thing that could clear his mind, make him feel calm, keep him on the surface of things. There'd be no knocks on the door in the middle of the night here. Still, it made him uneasy; if he could think about it, imagine it, other people could. He looked up at the shape of Castle Hill. The football ground had been here, close to here; he couldn't work out where now, it was all built so differently. He'd walked up the road with Adnan and their dad to see the Wolves here before everything closed. Erasure. He looked at the cigarette smoke as it floated away. He'd read *The Castle* once. Kafka knew the way of the world. That was a reason to stay on the surface. He'd had to read *Metamorphosis* for his German A-Level and then read the rest of his stuff. He'd only picked German because he'd had that brief fascination with the Nazis. *Someone must have been telling lies about Josef K.* He came across it all the time in his line of work, of course. He smiled to himself. Smiled too, at what he'd say if Katie had been next to him, asked him what he was thinking about.

Kafka, our beautiful daughter, the way of the world.

You could never tell what people were thinking, imagining. He nodded at Glenn again on the way back in. He had some silver balloons tied to his wrist. One of his kids was screaming, not the one with the runny nose. He was probably thinking about floating far away.

**Butt slid towards Aimar.** Rob shouted, No. Everyone else was quiet. He won the ball. Great tackle. The others turned and grinned at him. Glenn was smiling at him warmly.

Wim all right, mate. Great tackle.

Great tackle that was, his Uncle Jim repeated. He's havin a bloody blinder, Nicky Butt.

**He was quickly around the rest of the route.** A dog tried to bite his hand off at the new houses, where the dairy used to be. He pushed one of the Punjabi leaflets through Glenn's door, just to wind him up. Further on, an old woman called him back to ask for a leaflet in larger print, said she'd voted Labour all her life and that his uncle had helped her when her hip went and they'd fitted a walk-in bath. Rob asked her if she wanted a lift on election day and wrote it down on the back of his instructions, felt he'd done a good deed.

He was soon outside the mosque, in and out of the cul-de-sacs around it. He was quick here because the houses fronted straight out on to the pavement. At the end of one road, where he had to double-back on himself, coming up against the embankment up to the main road and the traffic's roar, he watched a woman in a veil and long flowing dress walk along in front of him. There was a breeze and you could see the shape of her body through the dress, curvy and firm, and he daydreamed about her and thought about a funny story he'd heard of one of the Woodhouse boys planning to rob the petrol station disguised in a burkha. The woman went a different way to him at the end of Dudley Road and he turned his head to watch her briefly before returning to the leaflets. Immediately after that, a car moved slowly alongside him down the road.

He tried not to look, pulled the rucksack he was carrying the leaflets in from his back and stopped to pretend to look for something. The car was level with him. Still not looking he walked forward a few yards. The car edged alongside him. A horn sounded. It had stopped and was holding the traffic up. Rob looked now. The car was an old Vauxhall Cavalier that had been given tinted blue windows, flashing blue striplights around the trim and chrome wheel hubs and exhaust. He saw a long brown arm emerge from the driver's window to wave the cars behind it past. He was sure he heard someone swear, something *gora*, over the sound of the traffic. Three cars pulled out and around it. In the last of these, a grey-haired, middle-aged bloke with an unloosened tie shouted something at the car as he drove past. The brown waving hand turned into a finger.

Rob started to walk again. The car crawled alongside him. He wanted to run. At the canal bridge everything changed and the shops began. The kebab shop and A2Z taxis marked the start of a no man's land where people at least tolerated each other enough to shop on the same street. Halal butcher's and pork sandwich shop and all. But that was half a mile away and he wasn't going to out-run the car. He stopped leafleting and started walking, looked openly at the car now, blue lights flashing up and down the trim, like a police car by Dali. He could make out shapes behind the smoked glass.

At Mafeking Terrace, Zubair's old house, where his mum still lived, the last of the streets before the road went up-hill to the canal bridge, the car drove ahead slightly and pulled into the kerb. Rob considered trying to cross, but there were other cars parked tight against the pavement and a regular stream of traffic now. The passenger window came down as he drew level. A stream of smoke floated out and a sweet, damp smell of skunk. Two, three, four crumpled Coke cans hit the pavement just in front of him and he stepped over them, telling himself not to say any-thing, not to look. He did glance in, though. Saw the face of the passenger. Early twenties, maybe older, elaborately cut facial hair, an eyebrow piercing, collar of a Calvin Klein polo shirt sticking up. There were shapes in the back of the car and the hands of the driver resting on the steering wheel, spliff held nonchalantly in his fingers.

The driver revved up. Rob kept walking. He could feel the slope pull at his calves, decided he'd never make it up to the shops and, as they were on a main road after all, better here than a side street, clenched his right fist and almost, almost, turned to get one in, thought he might get a punch in through the open window.

The car revved again and did a wheelspin away from the kerb, there were clouds of exhaust fumes. The passenger turned and shouted something out of the window that Rob couldn't hear over the sound of the engine as the car drove up to the bridge. He could hear it turning around in front of the kebab shop after it dipped down the other side of the bridge and it got up speed coming back. Fifty, sixty even as it raced back in the other direction. Rob could still hear it roaring as he came down his side of the bridge, looking up at the castle and the space where the Cinderheath gantry had been and the new mosque's minaret would rise.

**On the Monday of election week, the paper predicted the British National Party would win the Cinderheath ward.**

I'll knock on a few doors for yer if yer want, Jim.

This was the longest sentence Tom had spoken to Jim for years. For once, for a moment at least, Jim was lost for words.

Will yer, mate? Am yer OK, can yer get up the road with em?

I'm all right. Gi me a list. I'll do the Juniper Close ones if yer want.

Jim had been telling the story about what had happened down at Juniper Close to anyone who would listen.

Am yer sure?

I wouldn't say if not.

That'd be great, mate. He tried a joke. I thought yer was thinking of voting for em.

There was a pause. Too long for it to be a joke. Tom nodded.

Sometimes yer just atta goo with what yer've got.

Thass a ringing endorsement, Jim said jovially, put his hand on Tom's shoulder.

**Aimar again.** God knows why Argentina hadn't started with him. He stood over a free-kick.

Is Beckham still on the pitch? someone asked. He was finished, exhausted, not fit. He'd done his bit.

Aimar whipped it in there. Pochettino got a touch, away from Seaman. Just over.

I doh know why Argentina doh start with Aimar all the time, his dad said quietly. Great minds, Rob thought.

He'd said why didn't they make it a bit later, they could get something to eat then as well. Jasmine paused. She said that would be great but that she didn't want him to get the wrong idea. She didn't want to give him the wrong impression. Doing this work together was great and it was nice to have a friend here at Cinderheath, but he knew she'd had a difficult time, that things were still difficult, complicated. She told him a bit about Matt, her ex. There was more to it than that, though. Maybe he still had a chance.

He stubbed the cigarette out hard in the ashtray, looked at the patterns of ash as if to decipher some meaning, lit another one.

**Jim got back early from work.** Pauline was still at the salon. Michael was God-knows-where. When Jim had read the paper's prediction, he'd hoped that it would stir people up a bit, make it clear what the danger was, that the BNP wasn't just a protest vote, that they might actually win. Then he realized that was why people were voting for them. Not as a protest: but because that was what they wanted, what they believed. He put a CD in, slumped down at the computer.

He clicked the link by mistake, musing over this business of whether it was just a protest vote, so was startled when the film began. He sat there, mesmerized, suddenly realizing what he was looking at. Andre's scared face, looking at the camera. What was this doing on the computer? They were on him like animals. That was one of the Woodhouse boys, he recognized him, suddenly intrigued, heartened even that this was a mixed crowd, not the usual racial stuff. He didn't know what to think. This was criminal evidence. On his computer. He didn't know how to turn it off when the screen went blank. Then it started up again. Michael's face. Laughing. Enjoying this. They could've killed him. The screen went blank again. Jim sat staring at the empty screen.

**Lopez got away from Mills but Mills came back at him.** That's what this game needed now, hard work. Corner.

How long left?

Woss that say?

Eighty-odd. I cor see it, iss a bit blurred.

Seaman caught the corner to big cheers.

**Jim asked Rob for Zubair's mobile number.**

I doh think he's that interested though, Uncle Jim.

What?

I mean, he'll vote for yer but I doh think he'll be interested in doing anything else. He's organized his mother's postal vote. He'll get his sisters and brother to vote.

Jim just nodded his head. Have yer got it, though? I need to speak to him abaht summat.

255

Tom looked pale when he got back in from Juniper Close. He was short of breath and had to lean against the kitchen table to catch it before walking through into the hall. He'd knocked on Tony Woodhouse's door. Tom had known him as a kid. People talked about that family being wild nowadays. They should've seen them then. When Rob and Karen were together he'd have a pint with Tony, her uncle, at family dos. When the door opened that morning, he could've sworn Tony had gone pale. It occurred to him afterwards that he might have got the wrong story about Tom's heart attack, thought he was dead. Tony told him to come in. That was more than he got from Wesley, even though he hadn't seen him for twenty years, who told him he wasn't interested, that he'd had enough of bastards like Jim pretending to represent people round there, it was too late.

Tony told him no one was that bothered about the election. Tom said if they weren't that bothered it wouldn't hurt them to go and vote for Jim, then. Tom didn't know what good it would do, his meddling or the vote itself.

Kathleen came down from upstairs. He held the flowers out to her.

Ooh, what am these?

Tom smiled. I got yer some flowers, love.

What for?

I doh need a reason, do I?

She fussed with them at the kitchen sink, cutting the stems.

I should get yer flowers more often, love, I know. I should do a lot of things.

He sat down to rest in the armchair. She turned from the sink and kissed his cheek, turned back to the flowers as a tear rolled down her own.

He'd intended to get some for a while, it was one of the things he'd promised himself after his heart attack and bypass. It was actually one of the things he'd promised to do if he lived. It didn't amount to much, he supposed, in the end.

On the morning of his heart attack, he hadn't felt great. He'd been going at the drink harder even than usual, he wasn't sure why. He'd given up explaining his own moods. He'd seen on telly once, the way crows would follow medieval armies at a distance, descend after a battle to eat the bodies. If he'd had to describe it to anyone, not that he ever would, or could, he would describe it like that. Mostly they'd be off at a distance, up high, but sometimes it was like you were there on the battlefield, still alive, awful things all around, and out of the corner of your eye you see them begin to caw and swoop.

Kath had gone round to her mother's; the nurse was coming to talk about a false leg. They all thought it was a waste of time, Evie included. Tom'd had a pain in his back and his arm felt tingly. He couldn't settle. He'd wandered down the shop earlier than usual, bought a paper and a few cans. The bag had felt heavy on the way back up the slope and he was sweating, felt tight-chested.

He made it to the front of the house, thought the worst had passed and was struggling to get the front-door key from his pocket when it hit him. No breath. He'd gone sideways off the path, was half in the roses, his face in the dirt. The pain came again, through his arm, his chest, his jaw. Pain like he was outside himself. In the ambulance he'd thought he'd smashed his jaw on the edge of the slabs, it was only afterwards he realized that was part of the attack. The pain came in huge waves. In between the waves he'd grabbed a rose bush stem. There was blood in his hand when Rob found him.

If Rob hadn't called home he probably would have died right there. It was the summer holidays. He was helping run the playscheme and had called home to get a pump for some footballs, hadn't got the right key for the stores.

In the moments of lucidity, wearing the oxygen mask in the ambulance, Tom thought about the roses. He should buy Kathleen some flowers. He *would* buy her some flowers. She hadn't deserved what he'd given. It wasn't the pain that was the worst in the end, it was when the pain went, and he was left with the feeling of how he'd wanted things to be different. How he'd wanted it all to be different. At the hospital he'd tried to tell her that, when she got there from her mother's, her worried face scaring him more than all the pain in the world; he'd tried to say it to Rob too. That he'd wanted it to be different, that he loved them.

What this was now, he wasn't sure, watching Kathleen cut the flowers, the sun coming through the window. He wanted to go to her, wanted to tell her now. The way that it would be different, if he could just do it over again.

**All Argentina.** They couldn't get the ball off them. Still no chances, though. Ferdinand put it out for a corner. It ended up with Zanetti, up and over the bar.

**On election day morning, Jim stepped out of the shower and wrapped himself in a towel.** This is where it started, he said to himself. This is where it began. The bathroom was steamy. He'd been in the shower a long time, and he leaned to open the window to let in some air, all the time imagining a speech he'd make if he got the chance, or rather, he would make in some parallel world, where he had some sway and always did the right thing. He imagined standing outside the chained-up gates of the Cinderheath works, quieting the crowd, nodding, as if a crowd of any sort might turn up to hear him speak. This is where it began for us, here, he would say, and the crowd would lean forward to hear.

This is what brought you in from the fields. This is what gave you the vote, sent you to school, put shoes on your feet, food in your belly, eh, this place here and others like them. This is what freed the slaves. What won the wars, made us rich. The idea of murmurs from the crowd. Yes, rich. Rich enough to forget, any road.

The steam was clearing in the bathroom. His face emerged in the mirror above the sink. It looked good with the little strip of lights they'd put in above it. He began to lather his face, picturing himself standing on an upturned crate or something, head above the crowd listening in front of him, the rusted gates and fence behind him, bleeding orange slowly into the ground around his feet.

Just because we've been forgotten doesn't mean we should forget ourselves.

I want you to think. I want you to think about a story you might've been told. A story you need to remember before it's too late. It could be anything, could be from anywhere. A story from parents or grandparents or passed down from before that. In the daydream he raised his arm in front of him as if waving something away.

The details weren't important but the gist of it was. They would know what he meant. A story of all being huddled up in bed together, brothers and sisters together, a blanket not quite big enough to cover you all and arms and legs out and exposed to the cold. A trip to the toilet in the middle of the night, out into the cold and dark, not knowing what's in the shadow, the mud and water all frozen as you crept your way across the yard. A younger baby brother or sister crying, wailing and then no sound at all. A knock on the door or a shout down the street. A collapse, an explosion, a burning.

Think. The razor felt good on his skin and he drew a clean line through his foamed cheek. It doesn't have to be here, even. Although here is where it might have ended up. A green field, a potato failure, nothing to eat. A dusty village in the heat, flies, babies crying.

I want you to think about this as a place of hope. He waves his arm again, this time more expansively, at the ruin behind him. This was a place of hope. Hard, hard work. Industry. Endeavour, eh? The ability to pull yourselves up. Together. To work together. He stumbled over the words in his head here, shaving the other half of his face and meeting his gaze in the mirror, humming softly. Not sure what he was saying. But the gist; the gist of it. To be proud of something. A wave now at the rusting gates behind him. Some lessons from this place of hope.

Jim turned the razor around, finished his neck and Adam's apple. He'd spent too long in the bathroom, he was late. It was too late. He was only too aware of that, deep down.

He took a fresh towel from the airing cupboard, dried himself quickly, reached for the aftershave.

It wasn't really a place of hope. It was a cenotaph. He imagined the silence around his words, maybe the wind in the trees, the creaking of a chain, the footsteps of a fox walking through the exposed ribs of factory buildings. You had to speak up to fill the silence. With words you could make anything happen. Put shoes on your feet, food in your belly. Win the wars. Raise the dead. You just had to have the right words.

He took his crisp white shirt from the hanger on the back of the door. Pauline had starched the collar and the arms. His shirt and tie were about the only things the same in the daydream and the reality. He thought of the words he really had to work with. A few badly photocopied sentences on how he'd worked on the Housing Committee and was a man who understood Cinderheath, a few others translated into Urdu and Punjabi that he didn't even understand.

The sun shone on him in the daydream. His blue suit and white shirt in front of the rusty works' gates, the castle, another ruin, further behind. The glint of an aeroplane in the blue sky and all that brought to mind now, a rain of blood and fire.

He opened the bathroom door and walked across the landing. There was music thumping from Michael's room, the voice over the top of it like someone shouting a warning. Pauline called up the stairs, Jim! Bill's here, love, yome late, come on.

I know, my angel, sorry. Be right with yer, Bill.

In the bedroom he pulled on his suit. He knotted the tie.

The right stories, the right words. To undo the rust. To heal all wounds. To raise the dead. A strange and unlikely task for a Thursday afternoon in the Black Country this late in the day.

He hurried down the stairs and picked up his car keys. Bill was at the door.

Yome all right, mate, doh rush, it ay too late at all.

Jim stopped daydreaming, pictured Michael's laughing face. He'd done a bit too much daydreaming, he told himself.

**The ticket had originally belonged to the Mexican FA.** It cost a fortune by the time it ended up with a tout in a Sapporo bar. His money was running low by now. He was thinking about selling the London flat. He'd got people renting it, had sorted agents out online and over the phone, but with their fees, and the amount the mortgage was, it wasn't giving him very much. Almost everything had been on credit. The bubble was bursting. He knew it should've been worrying him more than it was.

The ticket was too good a thing to pass up. The same as the whole trip itself. He'd got to California, looked at the Pacific, and instead of heading up to Palo Alto, like he'd thought he would, instead of starting to think about work and trying to stay somewhere longer than a night, he headed on to Los Angeles and the airport and a flight to Tokyo. If you head west for long enough, you end up coming back east. That sort of stuff used to fascinate him as a kid.

It was a great position, halfway up the stand almost level with the halfway line, close to the dignitaries. When he got there he was relieved he'd put a suit on, that he could perhaps pass for Mexican; this wasn't your normal touted seat. He thought he saw Franz Beckenbauer a few rows away, in the seats with armchairs. Occasionally, when he was in London, when Wenger was putting his first great Arsenal team together, he would get tickets through work, good ones like this, and go and watch Bergkamp. He would worry mildly that *Match of the Day* or Sky would solve the mystery of his disappearance by beaming his face into his brother's front room. He knew Zubair would be watching, his dad and Tayub these days too. Whenever he went to a game he thought of the climb up the bank that time Wolves played at Dudley Town.

This was where he'd always wanted to be, he supposed, in the expensive seats, at the top of the world. He'd had a couple of bottles of Asahi before the game. He couldn't work out if the beer killed his thoughts or fuelled them.

While the teams were warming up, Beckham stopped for a moment and looked up intently into the stand close to Adnan, as if searching for someone. For a second he was looking right at him. Adnan raised his hand and waved. Beckham turned, struck a ball with his right foot, cleanly, purely, it arced across the vivid green turf.

**Zubair wondered why he was suddenly so popular.** Rob had told him about Jasmine coming back, he was looking forward to seeing her. He had no idea what she wanted to see him for, certainly not why she'd made an appointment here at the office. It was probably to do with some kid at the school. He hoped she didn't ask him about Adnan.

With Jim it was probably something similar. Some kid in trouble. Some parents he'd told he'd get help for.

**Wayne Bridge came on for Michael Owen.**

Backs to the wall stuff now, eh?

Like the other week, Rob, Lee said.

Rob nodded and shrugged.

The news that the Gurdwara had put fourteen past Castle Villa and had won the league on goal difference filtered slowly through the Sunday afternoon. Jim had been tempted to wander down to the Lion himself where all of the Cinderheath Sunday players – minus Rob – and all the hangers-on were celebrating what they thought was their title. He thought he'd keep his distance, though.

No one believed it at first. Someone had a mate who played for Castle Villa, who told them how they'd only started with nine men and then had their keeper sent off after ten minutes, but they all thought it was a wind-up, kept on drinking and singing, Eng-er-land. The texting persisted though. It ended with Glenn phoning the league secretary who confirmed the result. He'd just come off the phone to the Castle Villa captain. Glenn smashed his phone, went in and told them the news. The drinking carried on.

Twiglet tried to fight Carl Jones. Bailey, who had been on his way out, sipping on an orange juice, told them they had to keep their discipline, that their time would come, was coming in a couple of weeks at the election after all.

**Jasmine said this was the hardest thing she'd ever done.**

I know what happened to your brother.

She told it him all from the start. How she could've come to tell him she'd found him. How she'd come to tell him she'd lost him again.

Zubair said nothing.

Will you be able to tell your parents?

My dad died the year after he went.

I'm sorry.

You'd better go, he said. She was crying and he almost went to her, but just sat there, shaking slightly.

When she left he opened his window like he always did at the end of the day, lit a cigarette and then another, thought about his dad and his brother. He had a bottle of whisky hidden in the filing cabinet drawer. He'd put it there to make him feel like Philip Marlowe, it matched the gold flaking lettering on the frosted glass, the seedy stories of stolen cars and hidden knives and even seedier defences he invented. A good imagination must've run in the family.

He sat with his feet up on the desk, sipping his whisky and smoking a cigarette, not sure when he'd throw the glass against the wall, turn the desk over, or if he'd just sit there all night, knowing that instead he should get back to his wife and daughter, probably call to see his mother. Tonight he'd intended to talk to Katie about the idea of a new house, about whether they could do something for his mother and Tayub. It would be a lot to ask. It could wait now.

He wondered whether he should tell his mother or not, staring vacantly at a report he was meant to be reading, not looking at the letters but at the white spaces around them, looking at ghosts, looking at silence.

**There was a conversation they'd had years ago.** Rob and Adnan must have been eleven years old, hanging from the school's rusting climbing-frame. It was not long after Jasmine had left. Zubair was picking his brother up after school. There'd been a fight or something. They were all miserable. Rob could remember the climbing-frame flaking away in his hand. He'd been smashed in the face in the game the week before, had been put in with the older boys, had black eyes and his nose was filled with dried blood. Rust and blood smelled the same.

Adnan had found something out about Hitler and the Jews and a conspiracy to rule the world. Some kind of hybrid, fifteenth-hand politics and religion that neither of them knew anything about. Adnan was talking him through the process of the Holocaust with some glee, the industrialization of death, a shaping of the world to your own desire. Blood and rust.

Rob wouldn't have thought anything about that conversation at the time, not for years afterwards. Adnan had always been going on about stuff he didn't understand. It was funny how things could assume such importance with hindsight. The photographs of the twisted metal at Ground Zero reminded him. They looked like the rusting climbing-frame they'd hang from when they were miserable, when there was nothing else to do.

Rob wanted to ask Zubair about that conversation but it felt like a closed world to him. It was twenty years ago, now, after all. Where to begin?

When they put that parade of bombers' faces on the television after September 11th, he found himself involuntarily scanning the faces to see if Adnan was there, fearful and yet somehow wanting to see it, wanting, what? A story to fill the absence, maybe. And now Camp X-Ray and the raids in Tipton, how it felt like a weight, like a pressure, things closing in, a subsidence.

The smell of rust, the smell of blood.

**Aimar was juggling the ball in the England area, couldn't turn, no space.** The defenders squeezed him out. It was coming. Glenn drummed his hands on the edge of the table, looked down at the beer-splashed floor.

I've come to mek amends. That was what he said to her. He'd practised it in his head as he walked up the flats' walkway. Thought it was the right thing to say in that situation, heavy, serious.

He'd talked it over with Anne a couple of times. She was really pleased, said it was the right thing.

He waited at the door, could see his sister's shape through the frosted glass.

I've come to mek amends.

She didn't say anything, just nodded, slid the chain off, opened the door, turned and walked down the hallway, checking that he'd followed.

**From mid-morning on, Rob and Tom drove back and forth between Juniper Close and the polling stations.** They were using the primary schools as usual, William Perry and Cinderheath.

Tom had a list that they worked to, from the walks he'd done in the previous week. In mid-afternoon, they worried that they were ferrying people who were voting BNP – Tom said it was what people used to do when only the Tories had cars. It was a risk they had to take, they supposed.

Back and forth. Back and forth.

How many dyer reckon we've done?

Sixty-four.

**Scholes won a tackle, got up, hit a pass, and gave it straight back to them.** England had eleven behind the ball now, defending off the edge of the six-yard box.

Too deep, Rob and his old man said together.

The whistle went. Somehow Ortega was offside. There were whistles all round the clubhouse now.

**At the count it was obvious straight away that it was close** and it was obvious that he was going to win. Jim felt strangely detached; he'd seen this for other people but his counts had always been a formality, a victory parade. He had a good feeling, though, looking at the piles, looking at the faces. Even Trevor managed a smile when he shook his

266

hand, hoping that the worries would lie elsewhere. There was something unreal about it all, like being braced for a storm but the clouds scudding by and nothing happening.

He nipped out for a cigarette at one point, saw on the news that they were talking about Barking, was delighted there was no mention of Cinderheath ward, of the new West Midland heartlands that they'd been talking about.

They'd got it to a hundred votes or so. They asked for a recount.

He strode around a bit. They'd never get that many. Bailey was over there in the corner in his little huddle tapping on mobile phones.

Even counting the smiley faces and ticks it was still only sixty-seven. They went through one more time. Sixty-four. They'd announced all the others. At one point they were all stood round looking at a voting paper that plainly said *My arse* but had somehow formed a cross in Bailey's box. This was how it ended, he thought, in the farce it deserved.

Bayliss, James, Labour, eleven hundred and seventy-nine votes; Bailey, Philip, British National Party, eleven hundred and fifteen votes.

There was cheering. Jim wasn't sure where it was coming from. He blew his cheeks out, felt exhausted. Someone from the *Express & Star* wanted to talk to him.

You still here? Jim said with false bravado, as Bailey and his crew bustled past, that bloke with the false eye at his shoulder.

We'll always be here, just remember that, always, Glenn turned to him and said.

**Samuel had it again on the left.** He got his head up, hit it one last time. Too long. It sailed over their heads. Collina blew up. That was it. All over. Players on their knees. Everyone up on their feet in the clubhouse, shaking hands, slapping backs, grinning with relief.

# FINAL SCORE

**The morning after the election** Jim sat on the edge of the bath, wondering why it felt like he'd lost.

His appointment with Zubair was at eleven. He'd have to take the film into school he supposed. Late on, with Pauline half-asleep, he'd asked her how bothered she was about becoming the mayor's wife.

She said she couldn't care less.

He said he was thinking of resigning his membership. He could stay as an Independent. Pack it in completely in three years' time. They could look at the Spain idea. Do it a bit earlier than they'd planned.

Pauline rolled over and muttered something.

**They sat in a semicircle in the Head's office.** The room was too small for them all, really. The Head was perched on the edge of her desk, not sitting behind it. The new Deputy, Daniel Bell, was standing. Jim felt uncomfortable, hemmed in, wanted to stand up. Michael sat to his left, then Mohammed and his dad, then Rhys Woodhouse with Karen, who seemed to have become the family spokesperson these days. Jim thought that at least it wasn't the girl who'd given him such a mouthful down Juniper Close. Rob sat opposite him, looking about as awkward as Jim felt, the chair too small for him.

They'd just watched the video of the attack. Jim had seen it four times now. The shock didn't really go away, even when he knew what was coming: Michael's laughing face.

There's no proof though, is there? Karen spoke up. She could have argued black was white, Jim knew that much.

Proof of what? Daniel Bell asked, with his arms folded.

Jim didn't like him but was trying to. He was too young for a start. Too young to be a Deputy Head. He couldn't have been teaching, what, more than ten years, even if he'd taught straight from college, which was never a great idea, from what Jim could see. He looked, unfortunately, not unlike Bailey, with his nice suit and carefully gelled hair, and there was something about him like that management consultant Jim had met occasionally going into the offices at the yard: knowing everything, knowing nothing.

He talks to the kids like they'm shit, Rob had told him. Mind you, he doh talk to the adults at all.

Proof that they cut him, Karen said. In fact, if he's nicking the bike, she motioned towards Rhys, an these two am doing the filming, how can they have had the knife?

We're not saying they did have the knife.

Yow am. Yome treating it like iss the same thing. Stealing a bike's different from stabbing somebody.

Of course it is. Daniel Bell nodded. No one's saying they're the same things.

Yow am. Yome showin the whole thing and talking about his injuries and yet Rhys has obviously taken his bike off him. It shows that on the film. I cor argue with that. These two, more fool them, have been messing abaht with a camera. But that's it. That's what they should be in trouble for. Thass what you should be sorting a punishment for.

Yes, exactly. No one's being accused of anything we can't prove.

Jesus Christ! Jim had heard enough. Less just hang on a minute.

He was startled for a moment, with the way everyone's heads snapped towards him. Mr Khan, whose head had been so low Jim had been looking at the top of his prayer hat, Karen's flashing dark eyes.

I thought we was meant to be having a conversation about right and wrong here.

The boys have obviously made some wrong decisions getting mixed up with this. Daniel Bell turned towards Jim with his palms outstretched, like he was trying to calm a fierce dog.

Wrong decisions! Wrong decisions! Iss more than a

bloody wrong decision doing what they've done. Iss just plain wrong. I doh care who pulled the knife out. I doh care who actually cut the lad. These three – I'm including me own son in this – was there and that's wrong. Full stop. I ay come here this afternoon to listen to talk about proof of this or that. They've done wrong. They need that made clear to them. No qualifications. Yow should know better.

He'd leaned between the Head and the young Deputy now, to glare at Karen. Her face tightened and she looked away towards the wall, defiant though. Michael squirmed in his chair. Rob too.

The Head spoke now.

I understand you're angry, Councillor Bayliss, but please don't raise your voice. We need to establish certain facts before we can bring any kind of closure to this matter.

He'd gone now. Really gone.

Closure! Raise me voice! It strikes me a bit more voice-raising might have stopped some of this sort of carry-on. If I can't rely on people here agreeing on what's right and wrong, we'll do it in our own family and I'll sort out a proper punishment and deal with the police or whoever. They need to take some responsibility. And so do you.

With this, pointing at everyone in turn, fiercely at Karen and Daniel Bell, more tentatively at Mr Khan and Rob, who both looked more than guilty.

Come on! he said to Michael.

Michael carried on his little dance of shame in his seat. What? he managed to mutter up at Jim.

I said come on! Jim grabbed Michael by the collar, hauled him from the chair and extended his arm towards the door. Michael was lighter than he thought, even with this new taller frame and first tufts of beard. Jim lifted him as easily as when he'd held him over the paddling pool, laughing, as a toddler. That suddenly didn't seem so long ago. It slowed Jim down a bit, this thought. When he'd first grabbed him he'd considered banging him against the door-frame on the way out in an attempt at knocking some sense, something, into him. Now he just wanted to get out of there, to run away from it all, all the ambivalence and prevarication and fudge. He marched Michael out through reception and across the car park, all the while fuming, craving some kind of clarity, some kind of agreement on right and wrong at least, Michael still muttering, What, what, what.

**Afterwards he sat in a bar and drank sake and beer.** He was drinking more and more now, later and later into the night, struggling to get up for check-out next morning. Where before he'd been careful, calculated, always had a plan, now he tried not to think too far into the next day. Maybe about travel plans or, at the moment, sorting out tickets for games but nothing much more than that. One of his cards was refused when he tried to pay for something to eat. It didn't matter, he had plenty of other cards, he'd giggled to the waiter. But it did matter. Things were running low. The drink was another way of disappearing, he supposed.

The TV in the bar showed highlights of the game, or rather it showed the penalty over and over again. There'd been a space shuttle launch and they were showing that on CNN on other screens, too. There'd been a time as a kid when he'd loved anything to do with space.

He thought about Robert, had thought of him often, these last few days in Japan, had thought how strange it would be to just bump into him, that maybe he was here for the World Cup. After he'd left, he tried to keep track of where Rob was playing. He hadn't allowed himself to check up on anything from home but if he read the football reports, which he always did, he'd look at team listings to see if he was still playing, where he was playing. He knew he was at Hereford for a while, then nowhere, nothing in the national papers anyway. Then he'd Googled him – seen his name crop up in two- or three-line reports in the *Sports Argus*, local teams. He hadn't gone very far.

When they were kids Rob had casually told Adnan he'd play in the World Cup one day, just another thing you think you'll do. Like the way that it wasn't so much that they thought they could become spacemen, more the idea that they already were, that they were living on a rock hurtling through space. That had been another of those ideas that had filled him with such energy when he'd been a kid. When the space shuttle blew up that time his brother had laughed, told him that NASA stood for need another seven astronauts, told him he should write to them to apply. The picture when it exploded: blue skies and then smoke and then nothing at all.

He got up to leave, to stagger back to his hotel room. And he paused as he was leaving, pressed his head to the cool of the glass door for a moment and briefly, in the glare of the lights in the street outside, he couldn't remember where he was, who he was, he had vanished just like he'd wanted. The screen showed the space shuttle in close-up now, now further away, the blue sky darkening as the spaceship got smaller and smaller, disappearing as it left the earth's pull.

**Karen.**

He almost didn't call after her. She was already at her new car, no sign of Rhys, although the Head had given strict instructions that they take the kids straight home. It was a big 4x4; he realized he didn't know the name or the make, didn't keep up any more. She turned with the driver's door half open.

All right, Rob. Her voice was softer than in the office.

How yer doin, all right? He nodded at the car as he said this, hadn't really meant to, smiled.

Yeah. You? How's yer family?

Well, me Uncle Jim's bin better but you know abaht that. Everyone else is all right, arr. Yours?

They'm all right. Always will be. Always the same.

Rob thought briefly of Alan, Kyle's dad, who'd been there the night of Yusuf Khan, who generally got the blame for the whole thing now, dead from an overdose after a spell in Winson Green. No, some of them were a long way from all right and ever being so.

He nodded his head back at the school building. That was a bit of a performance in there.

Yow've gorra fight yer corner, Rob. Doh less get into all that. Iss a fuss over nuthin. Kids am always fightin, doin things.

They coulda killed him.

They day, though, did they?

He felt that old anger welling up inside, wanted to kick her and kiss her, that thing Simeone said. Instead he tried to change tack.

That was a funny thing abaht the name business.

After Jim and Michael's departure, the Head and Deputy soldiered on with more chat. Mohammed started a rambling confession. He began with, Iss because wim all Woodies we did it at all.

What do you mean, all Woodies? Do you mean Woodhouse?

Nah, I mean, well, we'm all Woodies, Michael, Rhys, me, loads. Like a gang, yer know, called the Woodies. We write it up on the walls sometimes. He said this with a kind of sad pride.

We look after one another. That kid, Andre, whoever, he wudnt be a Woody. He's joined now anyway. If yer doh wanna become one, yer have to pay yer tax, but he wudnt pay that either, so we took his bike. Somebody else had got a knife. We was scared.

Rhys Woodhouse made a sighing sound and started to tell Mohammed to shut up.

Yeah, yer was, Rhys, we was all scared. Yow run off. We was pretending it was funny an that.

This gang, then, the Woodies. Can anyone join? Is anyone not allowed to join?

Anyone can join, if yome from round here.

Why do you need a gang, though, Mohammed? Who do you need protecting from? Daniel Bell asked. Mohammed looked at him in the way that the new Deputy looked at everyone else. Rob quite enjoyed that.

To look after one another. Thass what yome always gooin on abaht in yer assemblies an that, look after one another. To get things as well. Other kids, other areas, whites, Asians, blacks, whoever. If they come dahn we'll stick together.

The Woodies. I'll tell me Uncle Tony, it'll mek him smile, Karen said now.

Where's Rhys gone?

They'd been told to go home and stay there while the Head talked to some other witnesses. They'd be excluded from school for a while, let back in after a few weeks when things had died down.

Karen shrugged. I doh know. He did a runner when we got out the school. He's a nasty piece o work, to be honest. He's gooin the way of Alan an some o the others if yer ask me.

What dyer try and get him out o trouble for then?

Yow'll never understand, Rob, will yer?

They smiled in mutual incomprehension, like they used to at each other, a light in her eyes. All that mattered was staying out of trouble and grabbing what you could. It was the only thing anyone believed in, perhaps it always was.

Looking forward to the football? she asked.

He nodded. Course. How's Hardeep?

He could see some supplies on the back seat, boxes of fake tan and skin products.

He's all right. Wim opening a new place in Bromsgrove. Wim thinking o moving house again. We looked at a place in Blakedown the other day.

Thass good, he said. Thass good.

Yeah, yer gotta keep pressin on, cor stand still.

With that she was getting into the car. She looked at him through the open window before starting the engine.

Take care, love, eh.

Look after yerself, he said as she reversed and pulled the giant car around to the school gates. He could see a couple of kids looking at it admiringly as she waited for the traffic. He stood for a while in the empty parking spot, weighing up what to do, thought he might walk up the hill into Dudley to have a pint on his own.

**They sat finishing their drinks while people left the clubhouse.** Glenn was the first to jump up, had to get back home because Anne was picking the kids up from her mother's. The screen was showing the news with the sound off, people celebrating in bars and squares in London and Birmingham and Japan, then pictures of mountains somewhere, a man walking through a bright market, a blanket with a pile of AK-47s laid out on it.

Right, I'm off. Glenn clapped Lee on the shoulder, shook hands with Jim, who was leaning across the table speaking to Mark Stanley. Glenn turned and held his hand out to Rob.

I'll seeya, Rob.

Rob paused for a second. This was how things worked, he supposed. No mention of anything. If things died down they might go for the next twenty, thirty years, for ever, with never saying anything about the election, about the way things were. They would just bury everything, settle for silence, so that they could nod hello to each other, share a pint every now and then, moan about the Wolves. That was if things did settle down, of course. What was it Glenn had said to him? A change is gonna come. Rob thought he might ignore Glenn's hand, then reached out, shook it, looked at him.

See yer for the Nigeria game, then?

I doh know abaht that one cos o work. The second rahnd game ull be the Saturday woh it, probly. I'll be here for that.

Stacey sat down heavily in the chair Glenn had left, fanned herself with a beer-mat.

I'm glad that's over.

Well done, Stace, Jim said. Lovely job. He'd pulled his wallet out and from that he took a brown envelope and pushed it across the table. All right for Thursday, love? Great. If that second rahnd game is on the Saturday, I'll get yer some extra help on, we said we'd try and book that bouncy castle, do the face painting again, mek it a family day thing.

Am yow two talking to one another? Jim said. Glenn turned, thinking he was speaking to him. Stacey nodded.

Thass good news, love. Good news.

Rob nipped upstairs to the dressing rooms. It was quiet in here, and light. They'd painted the wooden walls since he'd last been in and had an end of season clear-out. There were usually odd bits of kit or clothing hanging on the pegs, training bibs, socks, single boots, bandages, crumpled newspaper, pieces of dried mud even after it had been swept out. The smell of linament still lingered with the smell of the paint. Rob went to his old hook automatically, the one in front of the mirror, sat for a while on the bench, looked at the mirror, then around the bare room, then out of the window. There was a plume of smoke again, away past the flats. It rose thickly into the air, past Great Bridge somewhere, and then drifted in the wind where it smudged slowly against the clouds and became nothing at all. The flags fluttered across the flats and allotments. There was a siren going somewhere. Rob thought his headache had finally gone. He thought about Beckham's penalty, thought that it was actually a terrible penalty, the way he hit it, giggled to himself and realized he'd had more to drink than he'd promised, then shook his head and wondered how Beckham had even been able to run up and take it, thought for a second he was going to cry.

Instead, he stood up and pulled off his England shirt, took his good shirt from the bag. He'd got his deodorant, aftershave, hair stuff, toothbrush and paste in there as well. He wasn't stupid. The best bit of planning was the little flask of coffee that he unscrewed now and poured scalding into the lid, that he'd prepared to sober himself up. He raised the cup to himself in the mirror in a toast. That same feeling like after the penalty went in welled up in his chest, that feeling of victory, that everything could be made good.

His phone began to ring. His Uncle Jim from downstairs, no doubt to tell him they were ready to make a move. He took his time, though, methodically finished his coffee, brushed his teeth, did his hair.

They were at the doors when he got down there. They'd left the tables and chairs as they were. There was beer all over the floor. Jim told him he was coming back afterwards, that he'd mop the floor and do the pipes, he'd sent Stacey home.

Jim locked up and did the alarm while Rob and his dad stood to one side in the car park.

Think they'll do it, Dad?

His dad paused, weighing things up, almost a smile.

They've got a better chance now than they did have this morning. I doh know, son. Yer never know woss gonna happen, really, do yer. They'll just atta keep at it. Why not, though, why not?

I think they can do it, Jim said, jangling the keys. I do. He started walking across the car park. Rob wanted to tell his uncle he was going too fast for his dad, but he seemed OK.

I've phoned yer mother. Everything's all right dahn there. We'll pop in, Tom, eh, say hello.

His old man nodded.

I tell yer what, though, Pauline onny wants me to goo up in the loft this afternoon. I said I've had half a dozen pints, how'm I gonna get up the ladder without breaking me neck. Her said her day care.

Rob left them when they got to the road. They turned to walk down to the shops and into the estate; Rob would walk down the hill to school. He waited though, watched them up the road, his uncle carrying too much weight, waddling at a pace, his hands waving as he talked to his dad, his old man, next to him, smaller, his limp really obvious from behind, nodding occasionally at the other man's monologue, the same position they'd adopted for the past forty years. Rob watched them all the way to the shop, imagined he could hear the greetings as they pulled the door open.

**There were thirty, maybe forty of them, in an upstairs room.** The wall flickered into life, the film starting, stopping, starting. The projector was like one of those Neil Twigg had nicked from the school and sold in the pub. The filming was jerky, like it was being done in secret. It was a street that looked familiar: a row of council houses, grey cladding, green doors, some decorated to show they'd been bought, tall trees. A car was pulled up at the side of the road, two black men inside. When the picture showed the open window on the driver's side and a close-up of the driver's face, there were boos, cat calls through the room, like when the baddie appears at the wrestling. Glenn realized some of them had seen this before. The face of the car's driver looked somehow familiar as well, a light-skinned black man in his late twenties, early thirties, a diamond earring.

Different shots of the same car, the same street. In one, a boy on a bike rode up slowly to the window, talked for a moment, took something from the driver and rode off quickly, zigzagging down the broad empty street. In another, two girls with dyed blond hair walked past, turned and laughed, called something towards the driver's window, doubled back to the car, smiling. Another shot of his face in close-up, sitting behind the wheel, shot through the open window as whoever was filming walked past, then darkness.

When the film started up again they were in something like an empty factory building, the light seemed filtered through dirty skylights. There was a pool of oil on the floor, a rusty chain hanging from the ceiling. The film flickered. The man from the car was sitting, tied in fact, with lengths of old seat-belt, into a punctured seat taken from a bus. There was a change in the room, men banging the arms of their seats, a low roar.

Two men wearing balaclavas came into shot. One carried a length of wood, the other a golf club. There was a conversation going on between the taller of the men wearing a balaclava, the one with the golf club, and the seated man. There was no sound on the film. It crackled every now and again. Glenn remembered watching the silent films they used to show on BBC2 when he was a kid. His grandad had loved them. He loved Harold Lloyd and Laurel and Hardy and war films and cowboys.

The taller man pulled something like a postbag from his belt, pulled it quickly over the seated man's head. One moment you could see his face, the next thing it had gone, there was this grey bag, the corners sticking up like monstrous ears. This was the worst bit, in lots of ways, the way this flickered on the screen now, a hooded man, rocking slightly, the men in balaclavas, the taller one practising his golf swing for the camera, the rusty chain swinging in the background. The roar came again. It was the waiting for it that was the worst.

Glenn looked around. Everyone in the room sat in the chairs in orderly rows but leaning out of them now, towards the wobbly screen on the wall. There were men standing at the back of the room, blocking the door. When the hitting started the room went berserk, everyone shouting and roaring. Glenn looked up, then away, up again, just at the edge of the screen, down at his shoes. There was shouting, roaring. He didn't think it lasted long.

The screen went black. The men in the room calmed. A last shot appeared. It was the same street, a different time of day, late, the shadows were different. The same car was there. In the gutter, just behind it, lay the shape of the driver. His body looked still; then, in more of a close-up, you could see him twitching. One last shot of the street, empty this time, then the screen went black again.

There was more cheering, people getting up, chance to get out of the room. Glenn looked for Lee but couldn't see him, was struck suddenly by the beauty of the room they were in. Someone had pushed the shutters open when the film ended. They were like the ones on Casey's doll's house. Light came in, lit the pale blue walls, he could see hills outside beyond the garden, the shadows of the men loomed on the walls. Glenn pushed through the crush at the door, hurried down the grand staircase. He could hear shouting and cheering coming from elsewhere. There was music playing, music from different rooms and from the marquee outside, merging.

He took the path down past the marquee. Through the garden, the rose bushes, where it was quieter and he thought he might get some air. He stopped, bent double for a moment with his hands on his knees, threw up. He heaved again, lost his balance on the edge of the path, put his hand out, grabbed a rose stem. Blood prickled the palm of his hand.

Someone walked past him, slapped him on the back.

Thass it, soldier. Get it up.

Footsteps staggered away from him down the path, stopped. He heard a long splatter of piss through the rose bushes.

Glenn threw up again and wiped his mouth, leaned over again with his hands on his knees, breathing a bit more easily.

They'd be going soon. He'd wait for them by the bus. He would go home to his wife and children.

**She was going to meet Matt.** They'd exchanged a couple of emails, talked on the phone. He seemed OK. She'd gone into school that morning to finish off a bit of work, was driving to London to spend a few days there, visiting a couple of people, meeting Matt for a drink. She wasn't sure whether that was a good thing or not. If it was fair. *Settling for half.* He said he missed her. She missed him as well. He said he'd been sorting things out. He'd been getting some counselling, sorting out his priorities, not hiding from things by putting school first. If she wanted to try again, maybe they could do things differently.

At school the kids from the half-term playscheme were watching the football. They'd fixed a projector screen up in the hall. She sat for a while with a few girls at a side table who were doing a jigsaw rather than watch the game.

She watched the boys in front of the screen, eight years old some of them, with their little England shirts on, drumming the tables, punching the air, leaping from their seats as the match went back and forth. She'd thought she might see Robert, remembered he'd said he'd got the day off to watch the match with his dad, which made her smile. She would have to tell him. She realized she wanted to tell him before Zubair did. More complications. She'd finally done the right thing with going to see him, though. The first right thing for a long time. She would tell Robert. She would talk to Matt, they would see how things went. She ended up not doing the work she'd intended, sat with the girls piecing a jigsaw together, watched the boys shout and whoop and slide across the floor when David Beckham scored.

**Jim pulled some mints from his pocket, handed them to Tom as they walked along.** It was an old joke from the days when they'd squeeze an extra pint or two in after a game.

I ay had chance to say to yer properly, mate, how much I appreciated yer help, with that bit o canvassing an that.

Yer doh atta say nothing. It was nothing.

No, I was glad of it. Yer know it wor nothing. I ay had chance to say what with all this business with Michael an all. Kath's tode yer abaht all that?

Tom nodded.

I dunno what to do with him, said I'd tek him for a game o pitch an putt tomorra, try an have a talk to him. What dyer reckon?

Sahnds as good an idea as any.

I day think things ud turn out like this.

Often things doh. Iss better to learn that, maybe.

They walked along sucking their mints.

Tell yer the truth, I'm thinking o packing it all in, Tom, the council and that. I've had me day, maybe. This is me last term for sure.

Tom didn't say anything until they were right by the shop.

Whatever yer think, mate. It ull be all right. Whatever happens, we'll all be all right. We'll all still be here.

He reached out and patted Jim's back as they walked in step. Jim did the same to him, neither of them looking at each other, just turning to walk up the salon steps, jangling the bell noisily as they went in through the door.

**She'd pulled out of the school gates to turn onto Dudley Road** and head for the motorway island when she saw Robert. She'd swung the wheel and turned the car in the direction he was walking before she'd really thought about it. She drove past him and sounded the horn and waved, pulled onto the taxi forecourt.

Do you want a lift?

I'm not going far, onny to the flats.

It doesn't matter, get in. I wanted to see you before I left.

She leaned across and opened the passenger door.

You off to London?

They'd talked about it the other day over coffee. She'd mentioned emailing Matt and he'd nodded, not said anything. She could tell he was maybe a bit hurt and glad he hadn't pushed her to talk about it.

Yeah, just going now, she said. I've just been into school. Everyone seems happy with the football.

Yeah, it was great.

Have you got a couple of minutes?

What do you mean? Now?

Yeah, I need to tell you something.

They drove along Cinderheath Lane. The day was suddenly busy again, people at the shops, kids on bikes, a van unloading at the butcher's. They slowed behind the bus outside William Perry Primary, their old school.

She'd got an email back from Miss Johnson, Julia

286

Johnson. She'd retired recently, was living in France, had been delighted to hear from her, was happy she was getting so much from teaching, as it had given her so much, she wrote. Jasmine had been judicious in what she'd written. Miss Johnson remembered a few other names from their class. Adnan's, of course.

She didn't take the turning for the flats, carried on along the main road, pulling out around a jeep parked half across the kerb and the road in front of the houses near the little shops. A woman and her son were unloading boxes, walking back and forth to the front door of a house with broken windows.

Kelvin, Rob said, pressing the flat of his hand to the window.

Who's that? asked Jasmine.

Oh, one of the boys you'll be working with soon. Rob grinned.

One of the many, Jasmine said.

Yeah, they've been away. I don't know where.

Rob pressed his hand up to the car window as Kelvin and his mother passed from view. She followed his gaze, realized Kelvin's mother was Janice Moses, who'd punched her all those years ago.

It's about Adnan, Robert, she said.

They pulled into the car parks by the new cinema; she realized she couldn't drive and talk. She told him everything, the whole thing, about Matt as well, more than she'd said to Zubair. A couple of times, he interrupted.

You've seen Zubair? You've told Zubair this?

Yes, she said. Yes. I had to really, didn't I?

Yes, he said. Of course.

His eyes were glassy, he looked as if he wasn't taking it all in; he'd probably been drinking during the football, probably needed a drink now.

It's a lot to take in, she said.

He nodded. They looked out of the window across the car park towards the cinema, busy now for half-term. They could've been anywhere, the flat car park and rect-angular, plastic-looking buildings.

I'm sorry, Robert, she said. For want of anything else to say. She thought she would cry again. There'd been enough tears by now.

What you sorry for? he said kindly. It sounded like his voice might break. They held each other for a little while, uncomfortably across the front seats of the car. Eventually she pulled away.

How about now? he said.

What do you mean?

How do you feel now?

She shrugged. Day at a time, I suppose. I'm much better than I was. I'll be OK.

He shook his head. She thought he might cry now, that the glassiness wasn't just the drink.

I always knew, he said. I always knew there'd be some story to it. He smiled instead, shook his head with incre-dulity, at the whole world it seemed. After a while he went to open the door and said, You better get going.

I'll drop you back.

No, I can walk back from here, he said. He leaned across and kissed her lightly on the cheek.

I hope everything goes OK in London, with Matt and everything.

Thanks, she said. I'll tell you about it next week.

**Rob stood in the empty parking space watching Jasmine drive away.** He was making a habit of this. He wished he hadn't had so much to drink, he couldn't feel anything. He couldn't feel anything yet. This was what Zubair had said he wanted to talk to him about. He wondered whether to phone him now, thought he'd wait, it could wait for now.

It was more of a walk than he thought. The place wasn't designed for pedestrians and it was a hike across the car parks and then down a side road with no pavement, worried for a moment that he was somehow lost. He couldn't think straight, couldn't think of anything. His mind was empty.

He'd be a bit late but that was OK, in the circumstances. He'd just act normally when he got to Stacey's. How else could he act? He'd told her about the Woodies gang. Then he'd told her that the money had come from school, that there'd been insurance taken out for this kind of thing, the value of the bike had been refunded. He could see she only half-believed him. It was the last of some money he'd put away in the Building Society when he was still being paid for football. He asked if there was there an afternoon someone could have Gemma; they could go and look at bikes at Merry Hill, see if they could choose one to surprise Andre. They could get something to eat afterwards, get a taxi back. She looked like she needed a break. He was surprised when she looked so pleased.

He finally emerged at the top of Cinderheath Lane, the top of the hill before it dropped into the dip. He could see the estate spread out, and the view opened across the old works and the shops, the church and the mosque, other estates much like this one, across canals and the motorway, fields, half-buildings and last factory chimneys. His head was full again now. He thought of his family down at the salon, probably finishing off some cream cakes and laughing about the penalty, worrying about Michael. He thought about Zubair in his office and whether he should ring him now. About Jasmine, Glenn, Lee, the kids at school, Adnan the ghost, Yusuf Khan, all of them, with the realization, both painful and comforting, that all things which go away might one day return.

# About the Author

ANTHONY CARTWRIGHT was born in Dudley in 1973. He completed an English and American Literature degree at the University of East Anglia in the mid-1990s. Having worked in factories, a meat packing plant, pubs, Old Spitalfields Market and for London Underground, he trained as an English teacher, working for nine years in East London, and now in Nottinghamshire. His debut novel, *The Afterglow*, won a Betty Trask Award in 2004.

# Acknowledgements

Many thanks to Alan Mahar, Luke Brown, Emma Hargrave – and all involved with Tindal Street Press – particularly for their encouragement and patience regarding this book. On the subject of encouragement and patience there are several people who have shown me this in the last few years – you know who you are – thank you. Much of *Heartland* was written in Brighton: thanks to Nic Johnston for making this possible. Thanks also to my parents, Keith and Linda, brother Chris, and, of course, my wife Isabel.